A SUITABLE MATCH

JAYNE DAVIS

Verbena
Books

Manuscript development: Elizabeth Bailey

Copyediting & proofreading: Sue Davison

Cover design: P Johnson

ACKNOWLEDGEMENTS

Thanks to my critique partners on Scribophile for comments and suggestions, particularly Kim, David N, Jim, Daphne and Alex.

Thanks also to Alpha readers Tina, Lynden, David F, Helen and Mary, and Beta readers Judy, Dawn, Trudy, Cilla, Susan, Wendy, Kristen, Marcia, Doris, Melanie and Leigh.

MAP

Some places in southern England mentioned in the text. Fictional locations are underlined.

PROLOGUE

arstone House, London, April 1780
Nicholas Carterton breathed a sigh of relief as he stepped into the hall and the butler closed the dining room door. What had his father been thinking of to suggest an alliance with the Earl of Marstone's family? Dinner had been tedious in the extreme, with Marstone sitting like a fat toad at the head of the table pontificating about the conduct of the war in the Americas. It hadn't been a conversation—Marstone had required only agreement. No amount of political influence was worth connecting their family with such a man, even if Nick's views had matched Marstone's.

Marstone's twin daughters had been too cowed to speak at all—so much so that he wasn't even sure which of the two young women his father had suggested as a potential bride. He'd claimed a prior arrangement as soon as the ladies left the room. At least the evening wouldn't be completely wasted—he could get back to his translation of Plutarch. Even checking household accounts would have been more entertaining.

He examined a portrait while he waited for someone to fetch his coat and hat. A previous earl, he guessed, in a long wig and lace collar

1

of the last century. The features bore some resemblance to Marstone, although this forebear was considerably slimmer.

"Psst!"

Nick spun around. A door opposite the portrait was ajar, and a hand poked through the gap, beckoning. A female hand.

"Hurry!" The word was no less commanding for being spoken in a whisper.

Intrigued, he obeyed. The parlour into which he stepped was cold and dim, lit only by a pair of candles on a table. He made out only a small figure, clad in a plain gown, moving further into the room. Once close to the light, he could see from her features she must be another Marstone daughter, much younger than the twins.

"Mr Carterton," she started in a loud whisper. "You *are* Mr Carterton, aren't you?"

"I am ind—"

"Shh." She waved a hand at him. "We must not be discovered here. Papa would—"

"Who are you?" As instructed, he whispered the words. He had as little wish as she for discovery, but he suspected their reasons were different. "Are you sure you shouldn't be in the schoolroom?"

"I'm sixteen in a week," she hissed. "I cannot help being short!"

Not so much younger, then. "My apologies, Lady…What is your name?"

"Isabella. I'm Lizzie's sister. You mustn't offer for her—she doesn't want to marry you."

"How flattering." He tried to keep the amusement from his voice—it was clear that she was serious. "She can always decline."

"No, she can't—you don't know our father. He would make her accept."

Amazing, the force she could put into a mere whisper.

"You haven't already offered, have you? Please say you haven't!"

"I have not," he admitted.

"And will you promise that you will not? Please, sir, you cannot want a wife who does not want you."

"I do not, but we hardly know each other yet."

2

"How could you?" she asked. "I expect Papa talked all through dinner."

"He did. And attempted give me orders, as you are doing."

"I'm doing it for Lizzie's benefit. And yours!" Her hand flew to her mouth—she must have realised how loudly she had spoken.

"Is he marrying off your other sister, too?" Nick whispered the question. It had been unfair of him to liken her to her father.

"He is making arrangements with Lord Drayton for Theresa."

Drayton? A drunkard who spent most of his days on a racecourse or at prize fights, and his evenings at cards or dice.

"Will is trying to stop him," the little spitfire went on.

"Who is Will?"

"Our brother, Lord Wingrave." Her chin lifted. "He'll stop you as well."

"Is that a threat, Lady Isabella?"

She glared at him, her eyes glittering in the candlelight, then she looked away, her shoulders slumping. "No, it is not a threat. I just thought that if you were a decent—"

"Lady Isabella, I will not offer for your sister." He should not tease her any longer.

"—man you would…" Her downturned mouth transformed to an uncertain smile. "Oh… thank you. I am—"

This time the interruption was a shaft of light from the opening doorway. Nick grabbed the candlestick, the flames flickering from his sudden movement.

"Under the table," he whispered, moving towards the door as he spoke, hoping his movement would conceal the rustle of her skirts.

"Sir, what are you doing in here?" The butler stepped through the doorway. "I thought I heard voices?"

"Merely looking around," Nick said, walking past him into the hall, blowing out the candles as he went. "I need my coat and hat, *if* you please." It was unfair to be brusque, but he didn't want the man investigating the parlour until Lady Isabella had had time to escape.

That glimpse of her ducking beneath the table would amuse him for some time.

CHAPTER 1

arstone Park, Hertfordshire, June 1782

Lady Isabella Stanlake, the youngest daughter of the Earl of Marstone, stared disconsolately at the fine drops misting the outside of her bedroom window. The park was too familiar, too controlled—like everything to do with her father. Low box hedges made intricate, neatly clipped patterns in the formal garden next to the house, with few flowers to show the changing seasons. The isolated trees in the parkland and the long curve of the drive were the only irregular features. Her father had made the gardens as tedious as he'd made her life.

Bella turned at a knock on the door, ready to welcome any distraction from her boredom.

"How is your mother, Molly?" she asked. "Did you enjoy your afternoon?"

The maid's plump face beamed. "She's much better, thank you, my lady. We had a nice talk. She's taking in sewing again now the curate got her them spectacles."

"That's good." She'd never spoken to any of Molly's family, and likely never would, but she'd learned more of life beyond Marstone Park from her maid than she would ever have done from her governess. And hearing Molly chatter on about her family, their hopes and fears, was almost as good as having a friend to talk to.

Almost.

"It's time to get ready for dinner, my lady. You're to put a decent gown on to dine with his lordship and Lady Cerney."

Bella sighed, meeting the maid's sympathetic gaze. "Let us choose a gown, then."

It didn't take long, for beyond the plain round gowns she wore daily she had few that still fitted her. The last social events she'd attended were dinners with their nearest neighbours, last year. She'd grown since then, but more outwards than upwards, sadly. At eighteen, she still only came up to the mark on the nursery wall that her sisters had reached at fifteen.

"This should do nicely, my lady," Molly said, holding up a robe à l'anglais in yellow and white stripes. "The stomacher's wide enough to fit without having to lace you too tight. Pity that blue gown's too small now—that went lovely with your eyes."

"Molly, is there any gossip in the servants' hall about why my aunt has come?" Bella hardly knew Aunt Aurelia. She'd seen none of her family since her twin sisters had been taken to London the previous year to have their seasons under the chaperonage of Aunt Honora. Now they were both married and hadn't been back to Marstone Park. And her brother—Will, Lord Wingrave—was not allowed on the estate.

"Not yet, my lady. I'll be sure to let you know if there is. But Langton says the butler was told a few days ago to send folks to London to open up Marstone House."

Bella felt a sudden spark of excitement—had Aunt Aurelia been summoned to supervise her season? After Lizzie and Theresa had made what her father regarded as unsuitable alliances, she had worried that she might not get a season at all. Papa was as likely to arrange a marriage for her with someone she'd never seen.

Molly broke off from pinning up Bella's hair. "I got this for you, my lady." She fished a slim packet from the front of her stays.

A letter! Bella took it eagerly, forgetting her speculation for the moment. "How long have you had this, Molly?"

The maid ignored the reproach in her voice. "Langton only just gave it to me, my lady. One of the grooms went over to Nether Minster on his day off yesterday." She met Bella's eyes in the mirror with a cheeky grin. "Didn't want you trying to read it while I was dressing you!"

Bella returned the smile, thankful that there were enough servants like Molly, Langton and the groom willing to help her.

The letter was from Lizzie, and was full of the usual domestic news—balls and assemblies on visits to York, dinners with neighbours when they were at home near Harrogate, her pleasure at being out and about now that she was recovered from the birth of little Edward.

Bella let her hands drop to her lap. Although she was happy for Lizzie, her sister's happiness only emphasised her own frustrated loneliness. Theresa didn't have any children yet, but Will had two daughters now. She hadn't seen either of her nieces or her nephew, or even Lady Wingrave, and wasn't likely to be allowed to until she married. Even then, if her husband was of her father's choosing, she might still be kept away from the rest of her family. Anyone Papa approved of was likely to disapprove of Will.

"There, my lady."

Molly had piled her hair high with a few ringlets hanging down the back. "Thank you, Molly. That looks very well."

"Dinner's in half an hour, my lady. But best to hide that soon in case someone comes for you early."

Bella folded the letter—Molly was right. She crossed to the bed and knelt on it, pulling up the curtain that fell from the top frame to behind the wooden headboard. The letter went next to all the others in a pocket she'd sewn at the base of the curtain. No-one would think to look there—she hoped.

"Molly, can Langton listen at the door?"

"I already suggested that, my lady."

· · ·

"Well, she's a little dab of a thing, isn't she?" Lady Cerney ran her gaze from the top of Bella's head to her feet.

Bella pressed her lips together as she made her curtsey. Most adults were taller than she was, but she didn't need reminding of the fact.

The gold silk of her aunt's gown was embroidered with large, intricate swirls of flowers in shades of red and pink. She wore her hair well powdered and dressed high, threaded with a string of rubies that matched the larger stones around her neck. Her eyes and mouth displayed the beginnings of wrinkles, despite the powder and paint on her face.

"Stand up, girl, and let me get a look at you."

Bella's glance slid to her father as Aunt Aurelia walked around her, resisting the impulse to raise her chin. Her aunt sounded far too much like her father, and she'd learned years ago that life was easier if she hid her resentment.

"She'll do," was her aunt's final verdict.

Do? For what?

The earl struggled to his feet. Bella hadn't seen her father for over a month, despite living in the same house, and he seemed to get rounder and redder in the face at each encounter. He hobbled across the room, leaning on a cane and breathing heavily.

"Dinner should be ready," was all he said as he left the room, not even glancing at Bella. Aunt Aurelia's expression turned to a scowl as they followed him.

Her aunt talked about her daughters as they ate. She was only a year or two younger than the earl, and her offspring were well into their thirties now, with children of their own. Bella hadn't met any of them and found it difficult to take an interest. Her father wasn't even pretending to converse, merely eating his way through the food piled high on his plate, impatiently tapping his glass whenever he emptied it.

Aunt Aurelia finally steered the conversation to Bella. "How is your education coming along, Isabella?"

Bella laid her fork down. 'Tediously' wouldn't be acceptable as an

8

answer. "You would have to ask Miss Fothergill about my progress, my lady."

"I will." Her aunt nodded. "What does your governess teach you?"

Nothing particularly interesting. "French, deportment, embroidery, painting, piano, harp, and singing."

"Not the art of conversation, clearly. What about dancing?"

"There is no-one with whom to practise, my lady."

"Hmm." Aunt Aurelia turned to the earl. "The task may not be as easy as you made out. I cannot introduce her properly if she cannot dance."

Introduce? Bella toyed with her food to hide her mounting interest. It sounded as though she might be allowed to go into society—at last, a chance to meet more people. But it was too soon to get excited; Aunt Aurelia might just be here to take her to someone her father had arranged for her to marry.

"Get a dancing master," the earl said, his face settling into a scowl. "You and I will continue this discussion in the blue parlour, Aurelia." He signalled to a footman, who hurried forward to move the chair as he stood. "Come along." He hobbled out, in spite of the fact that the two women still had food on their plates.

"Am I dismissed?" Bella's appetite had gone.

Aunt Aurelia's expression softened a little. "If you have finished eating, yes. I will speak to you tomorrow."

"Thank you, Aunt."

Bella returned to her room and rang the bell for Molly, her feelings in turmoil. Soon, she would get to see places and people beyond Marstone Park, but if her father chose someone like himself as her husband, she would be no better off. Worse, as there would be little hope for the future...

She must let her brother know about her father's plans—she would need Will's help if she wanted to have any say at all in her marriage. But there was a more urgent task.

"My lady?" Molly slipped into the room as Bella started to remove the pins holding her stomacher in place.

"Molly, find my disguise—I want to listen at the service door in the blue parlour, but I can't risk getting seen in the corridors in my normal clothes."

"Langton will be serving there, my lady," Molly said as she unearthed a bundle of dark clothing from the bottom of the clothes press and shook it out.

"Papa will send him out," Bella pointed out. "You'll need to show me the way, though—I've only listened at the library door before."

"Yes, my lady." Molly helped her off with her gown and into a drab grey garment such as all the female servants wore. "I'll come back and make it look like you've gone to bed with a headache," the maid said as she twisted Bella's hair into a simple knot and covered it with a voluminous cap. "I'll bring a tisane up and say you're not to be disturbed."

A servants' stair opened off the corridor. Bella followed Molly down it, taking a couple of turns through narrow, stone-flagged passageways before the maid slowed and held a finger to her lips. The corridor was dim, patches of darkness filling the gaps between the lamps, but a sliver of light ahead showed a door left ajar.

"That's it," Molly whispered. "If anyone opens it, keep going. The door to the breakfast room is just beyond, you might be able to get back to your room that way."

"Thank you."

Molly hurried off the way they'd come, and Bella crept towards the faint line of light. The sun had not yet set, but even on bright days the dark walls in the parlour made the place gloomy. Her father would not move from his chair once he was seated, so she only needed to worry about Aunt Aurelia spotting the open door.

All she heard at first was the chink of glassware.

"Yes, yes. Leave the decanter." That was her father's voice, his words muffled. "Give Lady Cerney her drink before you go."

"Very good, my lord."

Bella scuttled a few paces down the passage as footsteps came closer, in case her aunt saw her through the open door. Langton's tall figure blocked the light for a moment—he nodded in her direction before carefully pulling the door almost closed and walking off down the corridor.

She crept forward again—her aunt was speaking.

"—what is this about? You implied that Isabella is to be introduced into society, but that doesn't sound like you."

"I'm not well, Aurelia. I want her settled in a good marriage. Soon."

"Naturally. But why the sudden summons?"

"Damned girl's getting too friendly with the local curate."

Friendly? She'd only spoken to him twice after church, and merely about starting a school for the village children. The curate hoped she could persuade her father to fund it, but Bella knew better than to even ask.

"Nothing will come of that," Aunt Aurelia said. "Forbid her to speak to him, or get rid of the curate."

"I'd have to replace the man, and who's to say the girl won't want to befriend the new one? No, she's as likely to be as contrary as Wingrave. Better to sort it out by having her safely wed—she's old enough."

Sort it out? Bella scowled in the darkness. She knew her father did not love any of his children, but it still hurt to be reminded that she was regarded as little more than a problem to be solved.

"It's very late in the season—why don't you just arrange a marriage? There must be some suitable prospects willing to make an alliance with the Marstones."

"Pah. Most don't want to agree until they've seen the girl in company. Better to have them meet her in public. If they come here, she'll work out why they've come, and heaven knows what mischief she'll cause to put them off."

She would certainly do whatever it took to avoid a match arranged by her father.

"The girl seemed obedient enough to me," Aunt Aurelia said.

"Hmpf. So did the other two, until I arranged their marriages."

"You're not making this sound an attractive proposition, brother. Why should I put myself out to help?"

11

"Money, as I said."

"Ask Honora. She's in more need than me. Cerney isn't complaining."

Bella wished she could see her father's face; she was enjoying hearing someone argue with him.

"Not yet, but from all accounts you're heading that way rapidly."

"You've been spying on me? What are my finances to do with you?"

"Aurelia, your penchant for gambling is common knowledge."

Bella wouldn't put it past her father to have bribed her aunt's servants. All she heard in response from her aunt was a muffled tut.

"I'm not giving Honora the opportunity to bleed me dry again. She failed last year, allowing the girls to marry against my wishes. Understand this, Aurelia—"

"You were in Town last year. Why didn't you stop them?"

There was silence for a moment—Bella could imagine her father's scowl at being questioned.

"I want a *suitable* match for Isabella," the earl went on, ignoring Aunt Aurelia's question. "And by the end of the summer, at the latest. That means marriage to someone of rank. There's been enough dilution of our lineage, what with that damned brother of mine, then Wingrave."

"You picked Wingrave's wife."

From what Bella had read in letters from Theresa and Lizzie, and Will himself, her father had made a happy choice.

"Only to ensure he got an heir before he ended up dead in a duel. I wanted someone higher than the granddaughter of a viscount for him, but I needed to arrange things in a hurry."

"If you're so fixed on status, Marstone, why did you pick the daughter of such a woman for your heir's bride?"

"What do you mean, such a woman? Her mother was a baron's daughter."

"Ah, so you don't know." There was definitely triumph in Aunt Aurelia's voice. Bella put her ear as close to the gap as she dared. Too close and she risked pushing on the door and giving away her presence.

"Charters was married twice," Aunt Aurelia said. "His first wife was indeed a baron's daughter, and he had two girls by her. When she died, he married the daughter of a rich merchant—for her money, without a doubt. Your heir's wife is from that second marriage."

"What?"

Bella started at the roar from her father, then smiled. Did Will know? She thought he wouldn't mind.

"Oh, yes. You should check your plans more carefully." Her aunt's tone of smug satisfaction told Bella she wasn't the only one amused by her father's rage. "There was even a rumour that Charters wasn't the current Lady Wingrave's father. When Wingrave does produce an heir, the boy could well be the son of a bastard."

Bella heard a sucking in of breath and a thump. "I'll get the marriage annulled!" Another thump—her father must be banging his stick on the floor. "Deceit, that's what it was! Damn Charters."

"Good luck with that, dear brother. If Wingrave doesn't complain, the Church won't give you the time of day. An annulment would make bastards of Wingrave's children."

Bella resisted the urge to push the door open further. Putting her eye to the gap revealed only the fireplace and the back of her father's chair. She jumped at the sudden sound of splintering glass.

"Tut. Temper." Aunt Aurelia sounded like her old nanny; Bella had to cover her mouth to stop a giggle escaping. "Do not take on so, brother. You'll have an apoplexy."

A swish of skirts must be her aunt standing up. "If you still require my assistance, we can discuss the terms in the morning. I bid you goodnight."

Bella stepped away from the service door as her father muttered something. She felt a little less apprehensive at being put in Aunt Aurelia's charge after hearing that exchange, but the next few months could still decide her fate and she would have little control over it.

13

CHAPTER 2

rooke Street, London

Nick raised his head as the library door opened. Father shuffled into the room, and his annoyance at the interruption vanished. He put a weight on the papers he'd been studying and got up to hold the door.

"Don't fuss." Lord Carterton settled his thin frame into his usual chair with a sigh of relief, leaning his stick against the arm. "Don't mean to interrupt your morning for long, Nick," he said, when he had recovered his breath. "Not to beat about the bush, but I wanted to discuss your matrimonial prospects."

Oh—that talk again.

"You should be out at balls or soirées," his father said. "How are you going to find a wife if you spend all your time holed up in here with that?" He waved his hand at the papers and books on the desk.

"It's the middle of the morning, Father."

"I know, I know. But I'll lay money you'll still be at it this evening. Does it matter if the new text is really by Euripides? If it's a good play, is that not sufficient?"

They'd had this debate before, but Nick was quite happy to avoid the marriage lecture. "If the transcription is truly from a lost fragment of the play, collectors would pay a fortune for the original."

"Yes, well. If it's not Ancient Greek, it's that damned stuff about workhouses and paupers that keeps you hunched over that desk."

Or the analysis of intelligence information he did for Talbot, Nick thought. His father didn't know about that.

"It's not good for you, my boy. You should be out enjoying yourself."

"I do go out—I'll be meeting friends at Angelo's this afternoon." After his appointment with Talbot.

"A fencing salon isn't what I mean, and you know it."

"There are so many frivolous, chattering women out there, Father —they would drive me demented within a month. Why bring this up now? I'm only twenty-four—there's plenty of time."

"Come, Nick. You must have noticed that I'm not well. I'd like to see a grandchild before I go."

"You have five already, and you dote on them whenever my sisters bring them for a visit."

His father coughed. "Yes, well. It's not the same as having a grandson with my name. I've nothing against your cousin Cedric, but I'd like the title to go to one of my blood."

Nick sighed. It was a reasonable request, he had to admit.

"Pity about that Stanlake chit, Marstone's daughter. Don't see why you wouldn't offer for her."

"Father, you arranged that with Lord Marstone without asking either myself or Lady Elizabeth."

"I know." Lord Carterton flapped a hand. "I should have consulted you first, but I only asked you to consider the girl."

"You did. It is too late now, though—she's married."

"Missed your chance there, boy. You could have got to know her before offering."

"I did, last year, when she and her sister were brought out properly. We did not suit." He'd found her pleasant, but too willing to agree to everything he said and with few ideas or opinions of her own. He'd like to have some intelligent conversation with his spouse.

"What about her sister...Theresa, wasn't it?"

"She's wed too. See, Father, I have been keeping abreast of social events."

"It's no use having a list of women who *cannot* become your wife." Lord Carterton rolled his eyes heavenwards. "Isn't there another chit? Younger?"

"Yes." Lady Isabella would be seventeen or eighteen now. "But I have no wish for Marstone as a father-in-law, political connections or not." Now was probably not the time to point out that although Marstone's politics were similar to his father's views, his own ideas differed greatly.

He intended to play a full part in politics once he came into the title, although he hoped that day was still many years off. His work for Gilbert on the effects of the Poor Laws would be useful experience when he took his seat in the Lords. Until then, he was enjoying his work with Greek texts and on intelligence matters—very different topics, but both requiring analytical thinking. If he had to marry, he needed a calm woman who would not expect him to dance attendance on her all the time, and with wit enough become a political hostess in the future.

"Very well," he said. "I will go about more in society and make an effort to find someone who'll suit."

"Good, good." Lord Carterton set his glass down and picked up his stick. Nick stood and helped his father out of his chair, waiting for him to catch his breath before going to open the library door.

"Don't stay in here all day, Nick."

Nick watched as his father made his way slowly up the stairs, then returned to his desk. He tried to resume work on his Greek texts, but his concentration had gone. He couldn't help smiling as he recalled that evening at Marstone House, two years ago. Was Lady Isabella still as forceful, or had she matured into a placid young woman like her sisters? It didn't matter—neither temperament would suit him.

Talbot got to his feet as Nick was shown into his office. He was clad in his usual ornate garb, with heavy embroidery decorating his coat and waistcoat and a full wig. Although he must be at least twenty years younger than Nick's father, the spymaster's face looked gaunt with heavy shadows beneath his eyes. Nick was surprised to see Marstone's heir sitting across the desk from Talbot. Lord Wingrave's reputation before his marriage had been that of a reckless womaniser, although there had been no rumours in the last few years.

"Afternoon, Carterton. Pull up another chair. I believe you know Wingrave?"

"Indeed, yes. Haven't seen you around for some time."

"Good to see you again, Carterton." Wingrave smiled, without humour. "I prefer spending my time in Devonshire while my father's still alive."

"Tell Wingrave what you explained to me last week, would you, Carterton?" Talbot leaned back in his chair and closed his eyes, but Nick had no doubt that he was paying attention.

"In essence, Talbot has a new informant in Paris, but some of the information he provides is at odds with what we've already been told." Nick took his summary from his satchel and handed it over. Talbot had given him the information from both informants to compare with other intelligence.

Wingrave looked down the list. "The main discrepancies appear to be connected with the forthcoming peace negotiations."

"Yes—in terms of the likely French and Spanish demands."

"Which we will learn soon enough," Wingrave pointed out.

"The crux, Wingrave," Talbot said, "is that one, or both, of the informants is lying. Possibly feeding us false information."

Wingrave nodded. "And you need to know which. But I don't see what this has to do with me."

"You're in the business of dealing with spies," Talbot said.

Nick's brows rose—it wasn't Talbot's practice to divulge that kind of information to uninvolved parties like himself.

Wingrave tapped the papers. "Not these two."

"Which is why I have arranged your passage to Paris. I need

17

someone to determine which of them is misleading us, and why. An envoy unknown to them."

Wingrave shook his head. "No. I'm in Town because my father is about to send my sister here. The staff received orders to open up Marstone House several days ago, although none of the family has yet arrived. I'll do my damnedest to stop him marrying Bella off to someone unsuitable. I can't go to Paris now—you'll have to find someone else."

Nick waited for Talbot's attention to turn to him—could he plead his father's ill-health as an excuse? He was perfectly happy sticking to his analytical work, and wouldn't have the first idea how to deal with Talbot's problem.

"I need *you*, Wingrave. I cannot use my normal contacts, as one of them may be complicit."

Nick breathed a sigh of relief.

"I'm sure Carterton could ensure Lady Isabella comes to no harm at Marstone's hands," Talbot went on.

What?

"He did help you two years ago when Marstone was trying to marry off your other sisters."

Only by helping Wingrave to win a great deal of money from Lady Theresa's prospective husband.

"Carterton can talk to Lady Isabella more easily than you, I should imagine, Wingrave," Talbot said. "If your relations with your father are still as dire as they were, he'll do his best to keep you away from her." He leaned forward in his chair, elbows resting on his knees. "But this is all a distraction; you can discuss it with Carterton later. You will be added to the team conducting preliminary negotiations, and you will travel to Paris next week."

Wingrave opened his mouth, but Talbot carried on talking.

"That gives you long enough to get home to make your excuses to your wife in person, and return here in time to travel with them."

"Only just," Wingrave said, seeming to have accepted his fate.

"Prove yourself, Wingrave," Talbot said, more kindly. "You could make an even greater contribution to the government's information network than you do at present. However, I will need a specific achievement to convince others that you are capable, without letting the more loose-mouthed amongst our rulers know all the details of what you do in Devonshire."

It was masterly, Nick thought. That combination of praise and future preferment might well have worked on him, too.

"Why don't you send Carterton?" Wingrave asked. Talbot's brows drew together and Wingrave spread his hands. "My wife *will* ask why someone else could not be sent. You will get more use from me if I go with her agreement."

A quip about being under the cat's foot was on Nick's lips, but he bit it back.

"I need him here to continue to analyse any further information sent. And no, I don't want him doing it in Paris. Any documents we glean must be treated with a level of security that can only be ensured in London." Talbot waited, but Wingrave said no more.

"Call on me when you get back to Town, Wingrave," Talbot said. "I will have a detailed briefing for you then. Carterton, I will be in touch when I have more for you. You will excuse me, gentlemen, if I do not get up."

Nick exchanged a glance with Wingrave, and the two men left the room.

"We need to talk," Wingrave said as they left the building. "White's?"

"I live in Brook Street," Nick said. "It's not far, and it's a pleasant day for a walk."

"How long have you been working for Talbot?" Wingrave asked once they had handed over hats and coats to Hobson and settled themselves in the library with a tray of coffee.

"I don't work for him, as such. He occasionally gives me information to analyse or comment on, that's all." He slid a glance at his companion. "What is your involvement?"

Wingrave did not reply.

19

"No need to tell me if you'd rather not. Talbot would tell you not to, I'm sure."

Wingrave shrugged. "Talbot trusts you. I transport spies, mostly."

"Your place in Devonshire is on the coast, I understand."

"Yes. But we didn't... I didn't come here to talk about that."

"Your sister," Nick stated. "What does Marstone have planned for her?"

"I don't know—but he won't have any concern for her feelings in the matter, only his own advantage. I was only sent word that Bella and my Aunt Aurelia—Lady Cerney—are to come to Town, and my father is possibly to follow. They should be here within a day or so."

"Would Lady Isabella know what he's arranged?"

"I doubt it. I'll try to speak to her if she has arrived in Town by the time I return from Devonshire, but it's likely Talbot will rush me off to Paris. For now, I'm going home to see Connie before this damned mission. I need someone to ensure Bella isn't married off against her will."

"Couldn't Lady Wingrave come to London?" Anything to avoid Nick having responsibility for a girl only just out of the schoolroom. "Or your other sisters?"

"Connie's increasing. The twins... Even if they were in Town, they're not old enough, or forceful enough, to thwart our father."

"What about your friend Tregarth?"

"Travelling in Italy with his new wife."

Damn.

"His mama might be of assistance," Wingrave added. "Lady Tregarth was very helpful when I was preventing the twins being married off."

"There you are then," Nick said, relieved to have found someone else to take on the task.

"No. Even if she is in Town, it is unfair to ask her to take on sole responsibility."

"Can't you have a word with Lady Cerney?" The faint hope was rapidly dashed as Wingrave shook his head.

"She'll have been bribed or threatened to do as my father directs. No, Carterton, it has to be you, or I don't go."

Nick thought of pointing out Wingrave's patriotic duty, but that argument could be turned on him as well. And if Wingrave *did* cry off, Talbot might decide that Nick should go instead.

"Oh, very well."

"That's what I like," Wingrave muttered. "An enthusiastic collaborator."

"Ha."

"I'll send my man Archer to see you," Wingrave went on. "He has my complete trust, and knows some of Marstone's staff."

"Thank you."

"I'll bid you good day, then." They shook hands before Hobson showed Wingrave out.

It was flattering, he supposed, that Wingrave trusted him to do his best for Lady Isabella. In truth, it would be interesting to see what she looked like in daylight. He could only hope she no longer dragged strangers into darkened rooms.

And with any luck, Wingrave should only be away for a few weeks. What could happen in that time?

CHAPTER 3

*R*otherhithe, London

"Luis da Gama?"

Luis de Garcia watched a dead dog turning gently as it floated in the filthy waters of the Thames, its stiff legs jutting upwards.

"Senhor?" The voice was impatient now, and Luis turned to see a stocky man dressed in a long bottle-green coat, his hair neatly powdered and covered in a black bicorne.

"Yes?"

"I am Mendes. I have been sent to escort Senhor Luis Sousa da Gama. Are you he?"

"Yes." He must remember to answer to his new name. "My luggage." He pointed towards a single trunk near the end of the gangway. He was supposedly visiting friends, not about to enter the London season, so he hadn't brought much with him. As his trunk was hauled up to the roof of a waiting coach, Luis cast a last look at the *Nossa Senhora da Glória.* It was a lovely name for a dilapidated and dirty vessel, and he was glad to see the last of it.

"It will take an hour or more," Mendes said as they approached the coach. "There is much traffic."

Luis could see that—all manner of carts and drays crowded the road, men with hand barrows weaving their way between them. The vehicle lurched into motion and the masts and yards of the moored ships became hidden by buildings. He'd expected to arrive in more civilised surroundings, as befitted his rightful status, not to be treated little better than a piece of cargo.

The warehouses and small streets gave way to wider thorough-fares and more ostentatious buildings, and the carriage eventually drew to a halt outside one of a row of tall houses in white stone.

Mendes ascended the steps and opened the front door without knocking. A woman in a mob cap and dark blue dress awaited them in the tiled hallway, and curtsied as Luis entered.

"Senhor da Gama, your rooms are on this floor," Mendes said. "Mrs Hathersage will clean and provide basic meals, should you wish to eat here."

Mendes gazed at Luis, as if waiting for a response. Luis nodded.

"This way, if you please." Mendes ushered him into a parlour, furnished with a table near the window and several armchairs arranged around the fireplace. Bedposts and hangings were visible through a door at the far end of the room. The place was not what he was accustomed to at home.

"I will act as your valet," Mendes said, carrying the small trunk through into the bedroom. "This afternoon I will take you to have new clothing made. Be ready at two o'clock."

Luis grunted an acknowledgement, and Mendes left without unpacking his trunk for him. Luis scowled at the thought of taking orders from a servant, especially one who had the insolence to leave without a suitable bow.

"Brandy, Mrs Hathersage," he called, pleased to hear her polite acknowledgement. She, at least, knew her place.

It would have to do, he told himself. This trip was a means to an end—once he had his reward there would be no more insolence from his inferiors.

∾

Bella watched the gateposts of Marstone Park vanish as the coach rounded a corner and then sat back against the squabs in satisfaction. Excitement, even. An introduction into society under the tutelage of Aunt Aurelia was not ideal, but it was vastly better than continuing her exile at Marstone Park. It was even better that Papa was not coming with them, and Molly and Langton were—she would need allies.

The set look to her aunt's mouth hinted that her meeting with Papa this morning had been no less acrimonious than the one Bella had overheard last night.

"It's very good of you to escort me to London, Aunt Aurelia," she ventured.

"Oh, no. Not good of me at all. Marstone's paying me."

Bella met her aunt's eyes, her jaw dropping. She hadn't expected such frankness.

"Surprise you, does it, that your father should do such a thing?"

"No, it is what he did last year for Theresa and Lizzie. I was surprised that you told me."

"Yes, well, it's best to know where we stand. I'm being paid to ensure you make a good alliance, and I'll not put up with disobedience or lack of co-operation from you."

"Yes, Aunt."

"I hope you've no silly notions about making a love match."

"No, Aunt." A lie—probably the first of many.

"Come, girl, no need for such a glum face. You'll be better off wed than living with your father."

That depended on who she married. She could not count on being as lucky as her sisters. "Has my father chosen a husband for me?"

"He's trying to." Aunt Aurelia smiled—a small smile, but it was there. "I suspect that even the Marstone status and wealth is not enough, in some quarters, to make up for having my brother as a connection."

Bella let out a snort of laughter.

"Don't do that, girl. It's most unbecoming." The words were without heat, and for the first time Bella wondered what it had been like for her aunt, growing up with the earl as an older brother. Had he been just as dictatorial then?

"I'm sorry, Aunt."

"Understand me, Isabella; my aim is to get you a suitable husband. You will behave properly at all times, or I'll wash my hands of you. Then Marstone is likely to marry you off to the first man he can find."

"Yes, Aunt." She must remember that Aunt Aurelia was not an ally, despite their mutual detestation of the earl. "Will Papa be coming to Town?"

Aunt Aurelia's lips thinned. "At some point, yes. He worked himself into such a rage this morning that it made him ill."

It must be wrong, mustn't it, to be glad that her father was unwell?

"With any luck, it will be some time before he's fit to travel," her aunt went on. "The last thing I need is his interference in every decision. That's why I refused to have that pinch-faced governess of yours along." She examined Bella, her gaze travelling from her hair to her feet and back again. "Hmm. The first thing we must do is get you some decent clothing. Something that fits, and shows off your assets better than that gown."

Bella resisted the impulse to cross her hands over her chest.

"We will call on my mantua-maker first thing tomorrow morning. She should be able to find something you can wear to make morning calls, until the ones we order are ready. Perhaps a dinner or two, to introduce you to some useful people, but that could be difficult with no host."

"Will Lord Cerney be in Town?"

"No, he prefers to stay on his estates." Aunt Aurelia's pursed lips said she was not happy with this state of affairs.

"Will I have a ball? Aunt Honora organised one for Theresa and Lizzie."

"Honora had plenty of warning," Aunt Aurelia said. "Marstone's in a hurry—that is, no, not if I can avoid it. Besides, you told me you do not dance."

"I can learn," Bella said hopefully.

"Yes, and you will. But you'd be the centre of attention opening a ball. The whole thing is too much trouble, and too late in the season. People will already have engagements. There's nothing worse than empty space in a ballroom."

Bella sighed, although she didn't really mind. Molly had smuggled in a letter after her sisters' debut ball; Theresa had written about hundreds of people they'd never met before, too many names to remember, and their father's approved suitors mostly full of their own importance. It hadn't sounded enjoyable at all.

Bella watched the passing countryside as Aunt Aurelia opened a bag on the seat beside her and pulled out a notebook and pencil. "Lady Durridge," she murmured, scribbling. "Lady Yelland, Mrs Roper..."

She had been in London only once before, two years ago now, and then she had been confined to Marstone House. If nothing else, she would see more of the city.

～

Nick put his pen down as the butler knocked and entered the room.

"A Mr Archer to see you, sir. He said he is expected."

Nick carefully laid a ruler across the transcript to keep his place. Archer was a man of his own age, soberly dressed in a brown suit. Like Nick, he wore his own hair tied back. Nick had expected someone like a steward when Wingrave mentioned sending 'his man', but Archer's way of holding himself, and his weathered complexion, didn't suggest a man who spent his life with his nose in account books.

Archer took a letter from his pocket. "Lord Wingrave sent this, sir."

Nick broke the seal. Wingrave had sent a note to Lady Tregarth explaining the situation, Archer would be delivering a similar letter to Lady Isabella, and he should ask Archer for any help he required.

"Why does Wingrave send you with Lady Isabella's letter, instead of a footman?"

"Lord Marstone doesn't allow Lady Isabella to communicate with the rest of her family at all, sir. The servants are all instructed to enforce that, on pain of dismissal without a character."

Nick knew Marstone was a tyrant, but to forbid all contact seemed harsh indeed. "How do you propose to deliver the letter, then?"

Archer regarded him without speaking, his expression blank. If Nick had not had Wingrave's recommendation, the dull servant act would have been convincing.

"Archer, do you think Lord Wingrave would have delegated the care of his sister to someone he didn't trust?"

"No, sir." Archer smiled, and Nick got the impression that a new alliance had formed. "A few of the staff will smuggle letters to her— Molly Simons, her ladyship's maid, and Langton, one of the footmen. Lady Isabella arrived this afternoon, with her aunt. I should be able to get the letter to her by tomorrow, at the latest."

"The maid and footman are taking a great risk, are they not?"

"Yes, sir, but Lord Wingrave will ensure that no-one will suffer for helping his sister. Most of the staff, though, will report any attempts at communication."

"I see."

What, exactly, was Wingrave expecting him to do? More, he suspected, than merely wait for a call for help. Marstone probably wouldn't inform his daughter of a match until it was too late to do anything about it—not without causing scandal.

He would have to see her himself. Not only that, but he would need to keep an eye on her admirers and find out about them. Ask her opinion of them, too. Wingrave hadn't asked him to prevent her marrying, only to prevent her being married against her wishes. The prospect of being able to devote time to his analytical work was diminishing by the day.

"Archer, can you find out Lady Isabella's engagements?" Morning calls were tedious, and he would know few of the women that Lady Cerney was likely to visit, but he could ask Lady Tregarth to accompany him.

"I'll do my best, sir. I'm staying at the Dog and Partridge, on Davies

Street, if you need to contact me. A note left behind the bar will reach me, or they may know where I am if the matter is urgent."

Nick raised his brows.

"It's best to be prepared, sir."

He couldn't argue with that.

"If that is all, sir?"

"Yes, for now. Thank you, Archer."

The door closed behind his visitor and Nick returned his attention to the Greek transcript. Comparison with Euripides' other works had persuaded him that this was no lost text but a clever forgery. All that remained was to note his reasoning. Then he could look at Jarndyce's new information about the workhouses near St Giles. All this to do, as well as looking out for Wingrave's sister.

With a sigh, he mended his pen and drew a sheet of writing paper towards him.

~

Luis surveyed himself in the mirror, and smiled in the way that was so successful with women. The powdered wig and snowy neckcloth framed his face nicely. His top boots shone, his buckskin breeches clung smoothly to his thighs, and the embroidery on the silk waistcoat set off the dark green of his coat. This was his favourite suit, but the ones they had ordered this afternoon should make him look just as good, and would be the latest in English fashion, too.

"Some of the garments I ordered will arrive tomorrow or the next day," Mendes said, brushing traces of powder from Luis's shoulders. "But this will be sufficient for your immediate use. Don Felipe will see you in half an hour."

Luis remembered seeing his mother's cousin a couple of times in his childhood, but had forgotten about him until he began to receive letters from him last December.

"Did you hear me?" Mendes asked, his impatience verging on insolence.

Luis bit his lip—he'd already lost one argument with the man, when he'd told him to use more deference in his address. Mendes had merely stated that he was masquerading as a valet, and he would not behave like a servant unless in company.

"I heard. Where?"

"Upstairs."

Luis had been surprised to find he was the only resident of the house, apart from Mrs Hathersage and several maids. Many of the rooms above stairs were locked—the ones that were open had furniture shrouded in white sheets, save for the back parlour to which he had been summoned. Don Felipe sat in a high-backed chair, looking much older than Luis remembered—thinner and with more lines around his eyes.

"I am pleased to meet you again, Don Felipe."

Luis' smile was not returned. "You will refer to me, if you must do so at all, as Senhor da Garcia. We are Portuguese here, not Spanish, and you must play your part at all times."

"Very well." He did his best not to snap.

Don Felipe walked around him, his assessing gaze travelling from Luis' new wig to his boots. Finally he nodded. "You'll do. Sit."

Trying to control his mounting irritation, Luis took the seat indicated.

"A horse will be available should you need to ride—Hyde Park is the fashionable place to be seen. One of your first tasks will be to familiarise yourself with the area."

Luis nodded without speaking.

Don Felipe looked down his nose. "You will not endear yourself to English society with such a churlish response. You are posing as a gentleman—"

"I *am* a gentleman. Or I will be, when you—"

"When you have accomplished your mission, yes." Don Felipe's voice remained cold. "As your manners will not miraculously improve when you are given your rightful place, it would be wise to start now, by treating me with due respect. We have not invested so much in you that we cannot send you back if we choose."

Luis opened his mouth to reply, but closed it again. If he was to achieve his goal, he would have to endure men like Don Felipe. It would not do to antagonise the man now.

"Good. I should not need to remind you that your success relies on you being accepted into society here, particularly by certain women."

Luis knew that already.

"My associate will point out the women you are to… befriend, to the extent that you are admitted to their homes. We may require you to obtain, or read, various documents, or it may be necessary for you to invite confidences from your targets."

"Invite…?" He was to ask them to disclose secrets? Voices in the hallway stopped him questioning Don Felipe further, and Mrs Hathersage opened the door.

"Lady Brigham, Senhor."

The two men rose and bowed as Lady Brigham entered. She was expensively gowned in rich brocade, but lines around her eyes and mouth revealed her advancing years.

Lady Brigham said nothing, but inspected Luis much as Don Felipe had earlier. Luis did his best not to squirm or scowl under her scrutiny.

"Hmm. He has the looks for it, certainly, Senhor."

Luis pressed his lips together against a retort.

"Lady Brigham will introduce you into society as the son of an old family friend," Don Felipe said. "Pray greet her as if you have just been formally introduced."

A test, he supposed. He advanced, bending over the hand she held out. "My lady, it is a great pleasure to meet you."

"Hmm." Lady Brigham tilted her head to one side. "You would be more convincing, young man, if you met my eyes while you smiled." She turned to Don Felipe. "Do not hold me responsible if your plan fails. This… this *boy* will have little success with most women of my acquaintance."

"Your targets will be older than you, da Gama," Don Felipe said. "One by ten years or so."

Lady Brigham must be thirty years older, or more.

"You need to seduce them whether or not you are attracted to them. Be aware of that."

"Send him to me at midday tomorrow," Lady Brigham added. Nodding at Don Felipe, she swept out of the room.

Wanting to protest that he was not a child to be discussed in that way, Luis managed to hold his tongue.

"This explains your acquaintance with Lady Brigham," Don Felipe said, holding out a folded paper. "Learn your background, and do not forget who you are pretending to be."

CHAPTER 4

*B*ella took a deep breath as she felt the mantua-maker's eyes running from her head to her feet. This seemed little different from her father inspecting her appearance.

"A whole new wardrobe, you said, my lady?" Madame Donnard directed her question to Aunt Aurelia. Bella seethed—yet another person who talked about her as if she were not there.

"As I said in my note," Aunt Aurelia replied. "A day dress is the most urgent—do you have one partly completed?"

The mantua-maker turned towards two women waiting by the door. In contrast to Madame's elegant silver-grey gown, both their dresses were a drab brown. "Dawkins, bring the gown for Mrs Charlbury. She is of a similar size, and has not come for her final fittings even though it has been ready for weeks." The plumper of the two women disappeared. "Fletcher, take Lady Isabella for measuring."

Fletcher was thin, her face almost gaunt. "If you will come this way, Lady Isabella?"

Bella and Molly followed her into a room with long mirrors on the walls. Molly shut the door behind them.

"I need to measure you with only your chemise and stays on, my lady," Fletcher said.

Bella sighed, and stood with her arms out as Molly and Fletcher between them unpinned and unlaced. Then Fletcher brought out a long strip of paper and moved around Bella, marking on it more different widths and lengths than Bella thought possible. As Fletcher was taking the final measurements, Dawkins returned with a gown draped over her arms. It was of orange fabric, embroidered with huge swirling patterns of green leaves entwining red and yellow flowers.

Fletcher looked at the gown as Dawkins held it up, then at Bella. "Is that the only one we have?"

"The only one far enough along to be ready for tomorrow."

"What's wrong with it?" Bella asked, hoping that these two weren't also going to treat her as a mere object to be discussed.

"It will make—" Fletcher broke off as Dawkins jabbed an elbow in her ribs.

"Madame will advise you on patterns and styles, my lady," Dawkins said. "Please, would you try this on so we can see how well it fits?"

Bella stepped into the petticoat and stood patiently while she was pinned and laced, and the two seamstresses pulled on tapes to drape the overskirt à la polonaise. Then she twisted in front of the mirror. The petticoat was a little long, but higher heels or re-hemming would fix that. However, the large fabric bows on the stomacher made her bosom appear too big, and the neckline gave the impression that she had very wide shoulders. And with those puffy skirts and the bright patterns...

"I look as broad as I am high," she said. Wide was fashionable, but surely not so wide that she looked even shorter than she was.

"You look lovely, my lady." Molly's comment was loyal but not convincing.

Fletcher and Dawkins said nothing. Bella could see from their faces that they agreed with her, but were unwilling to say so.

"Miss Fletcher, can anything be done to make me seem less... wide? *I* can suggest a change to Madame, if I know what to say."

Fletcher said nothing for a moment, then gave a nod. "Removing the bows and having a darker petticoat might help, and some matching dark trimming on the front of the bodice. That would draw attention to the centre of your body, and not the width. The neckline, too, could..." She broke off, shaking her head. "There is no time to remake the bodice."

"We'd better go back before Madame comes to find out what we're talking about," Dawkins said, low voiced. "My lady, if you will follow me, please?"

Back in the salon, Bella stood while Aunt Aurelia and Madame scrutinised her. "It will have to do, I suppose," was her aunt's verdict. "Is this the best you can manage, Madame Donnard?"

"It is all I have that can be ready for tomorrow, my lady."

"Aunt, could we not delay morning calls for a few days? This makes me look short and fat."

Madame Donnard shook her head. "Oh, no, it—"

"It does," Aunt Aurelia interrupted. "You are right, Isabella. We should try somewhere else."

"What did Dawkins and Fletcher say to you, my lady?" Madame Donnard asked, with a downward curve to her lips that Bella disliked.

She raised her brows, in what she hoped was a supercilious expression. "Are you implying, Madame, that I cannot see for myself that this polonaise style does not suit me?" She didn't wait for an answer. "Would a darker coloured petticoat make a difference, Madame?"

"That's a good notion, Bella," her aunt said. Bella felt inordinately pleased at this small sign of approval, even though the idea was not her own.

"My lady, it is not necessary—and it will take time and cost more."

"A simple yes or no would suffice, Madame," Aunt Aurelia said. "A new petticoat is surely not too difficult? I like the garments you design for me, but if you truly think that this suits my niece's short stature, I cannot rely on your judgement for the rest of her wardrobe." She stood up. "Go and change, Isabella. I will wait for you in the carriage. Lady Yelland swears by Francine's for her—"

"I'm sure we can come to some arrangement, my lady," Madame said hastily. "Fletcher, find some suitable fabrics."

When they finally settled on a dark green for a replacement petti-coat, Bella's respect for Fletcher grew. She had been right to ask the seamstress' opinion, rather than relying on Madame Donnard.

Madame turned to Aunt Aurelia. "Fletcher should have it finished by late afternoon, my lady. I'll send her to your home to do the final fitting, if that is convenient?"

"Very well," Aunt Aurelia said. "Now, to start with we will need more day dresses, and one ball gown, at least. What styles do you recommend?"

Madame walked over to a cabinet full of dolls dressed in myriad styles and colours. She extracted several and set them on the table. Her aunt picked up each one in turn, setting aside several with knots of ribbon down the bodice, and large embroidered patterns. All similar to the gowns Bella had seen her aunt wearing.

That would not do—she needed gowns suited to her own figure. Fletcher would be a better advisor. "Aunt, I need hats and shoes and stockings before I am seen in public—will there be time to buy those today?"

"I hope so, Isabella, but we do need to order more gowns."

"Tomorrow will do for that, will it not? Madame's women will be busy enough today with the alterations for this gown. Could we borrow some of these dolls and some fabric samples, and think about them at home?"

"That would certainly give us more time for our other shopping." Aunt Aurelia turned to the mantua-maker. "I trust there will be no difficulty with that arrangement? I will return the samples with our order tomorrow."

"Yes, my lady." Madame did not look particularly pleased.

"Now, while Lady Isabella changes, you may suggest some fabrics that would suit this style, for me." She held out one of the beribboned dolls.

Bella was exhausted by the time they returned home. She was happy to be getting a new wardrobe, but a long walk would have been less fatiguing than the interminable discussions about styles and colours, ribbons and lace. Footmen had been sent back to Marstone House several times with hats, parcels of gloves and stockings, fichus, and shoes, with more items ordered for delivery the following day.

They weren't all for her, either; Aunt Aurelia had remarked how she was enjoying spending Marstone's money while she could. It was a shame, Bella thought, that her aunt was only being paid to arrange her marriage. She would enjoy her first season under her aunt's chaperonage if Aunt Aurelia could be relied on not to foist the first eligible suitor on to her.

"We will have tea, Isabella, then we must choose some designs from those fashion dolls."

"Can we do it after dinner, Aunt? We have made so many choices today."

Aunt Aurelia nodded. "By all means. Take them to your room if you like—you can look at them when you've had a rest. I'll get your tea sent up."

Bella took the box of dolls and fabric samples to her room and spread them out on her bed. Molly soon arrived with the tea tray, and handed Bella a sealed letter. "Langton just give me this, my lady."

Will's handwriting! Bella lost all interest in the dolls, taking the letter over to the window while Molly poured the tea.

Dear Bella
I have learned that you are being brought to Town, but unfortunately
I must be absent on business that I cannot avoid.

Her heart sank. Only Will's interference had enabled her sisters to marry the men of their choice. And she'd hoped that being in society might allow her to see Will again, even if that could only be in public.

However, I have asked Mr Carterton to act in my stead.

Carterton…? Oh, the man Papa had wanted Lizzie to marry two

years ago. The man she'd dragged into a darkened room! She couldn't help smiling at the memory.

I have left Archer in Town—you may remember him as a former groom at Marstone Park. Your maid knows him, and you may put complete trust in him, as you can in Carterton. I have also written to Lady Tregarth, who will help you if she can.
Your loving brother
Will

Unlike the letters of news from Will or her sisters, she would not want, or need, to read this one again. She crossed to the fire and consigned it to the flames, stirring with a poker until it was nothing but fine ash.

"Molly, the letter said that you know Archer."

"Yes, my lady. I spoke to him last night. He asked me to tell him where you would be each day, if possible. So Mr Carterton can meet you."

"It seems you and Archer know more about this than I do."

"Sorry, my lady. Archer said as how Lord Wingrave was writing to you to explain."

"Never mind." It wasn't fair to be annoyed with Molly—the maid was helping her. "Now, come and look at these dolls with me." Entering society would be sufficiently daunting without having to wear gowns that made her look like a chubby child.

"How is it that you know more than Madame about styles that flatter other women?" Bella asked later that afternoon, as Fletcher stood back to assess the new petticoat. She still looked too wide, but the changes did reduce the unfortunate effect.

"I was a lady's personal maid for a time, my lady. My mistress had a good eye for colour and shape." She dropped to her knees and started pinning the hem.

"Do you have time to advise me before you go?"

The seamstress cast a glance at the clock. "I'm expected back, my lady."

That was a shame. "Madame will be angry if you delay, I suppose."

"It's a pity my lady was busy when you arrived, Miss Fletcher," Molly said, before the woman could reply. "You had to wait half an hour to do the fitting."

Fletcher sat back on her heels. "I... I could say that."

"I'll make it worth your while," Bella said. The seamstress nodded, and carried on pinning.

"There, it's done," she said at last. "Let me help you take it off—"

"Never mind that," Bella said. "Molly can help me. I want you to pick the dolls and fabrics that will suit me, please."

"Madame does not like anyone other than herself advising—"

"I will not tell her, I promise."

Fletcher met her eyes and then moved over to the table. By the time Bella had finished redressing, the seamstress had sorted the dolls and fabrics into groups.

"Which do you think I should choose, Fletcher?" Bella asked.

"You must decide for yourself, my lady. But these..." She lifted one pile of fabric samples. "These, I think, will suit you." She pointed to the next pile. "These would suit you as well, but they are costly. My last mistress used to say that very expensive fabrics like some of these were flaunting wealth, and a sure way to attract men in need of a fortune."

Aunt Aurelia would mention her dowry often enough, no doubt—but there was no need to advertise it further. "And these?" The final pile.

"The patterns are too large to suit you, my lady."

That made sense. "What about the dolls?"

"You can wear gowns of either style," Fletcher said, picking up a doll wearing the draped back of a gown à la française, "but the skirts must not be as wide as this shows." Bella listened carefully as Fletcher explained how the cut of the bodice and the neckline could subtly enhance her shape, and how ornamentation could distract or attract attention.

"Thank you," Bella said, her head spinning. "I think I can remember enough of that to discuss a few gowns with my aunt." She emptied her coin purse and pressed a couple of shillings into Fletcher's hand. "Molly will show you out."

Fletcher glanced at the coins in her hand, her eyes widening. "Thank you, my lady." She followed Molly out of the room.

Bella looked at the dolls they had chosen with satisfaction. She would ask her aunt if Madame Donnard could send Fletcher here to do the final fittings for her new gowns—she might be able to glean more valuable advice. She would have more confidence in society if she knew her clothing and hair suited her, and this was something she *could* control.

CHAPTER 5

*B*ella looked at the people in Mrs Roper's parlour in dismay. She'd had difficulty remembering the names of everyone she'd been introduced to on their first call today, and now here were dozens more.

"Smile, Isabella!" Aunt Aurelia whispered. "That long face will not attract anyone. Ah, Mrs Roper, how lovely to see you again."

"Lady Cerney, welcome." Mrs Roper's smile was friendly as she pulled forward a girl of Bella's own age. "May I introduce my daughter, Jemima?"

"My niece, Lady Isabella Stanlake."

Bella made her curtsey, returning Jemima's curious gaze. She was slender, and her emerald gown brought out hints of green in her hazel eyes. Bella smoothed a palm over her own dress, wishing she were clad in something as becoming.

"I haven't seen you in Town for some time, my lady," Mrs Roper said. "Jemima, why don't you introduce Lady Isabella to some of your friends?"

Jemima sighed as Aunt Aurelia moved away with Mrs Roper.

"You need not introduce me to more than a few people, if it is onerous." Bella tried to keep the hurt from her voice.

"Oh, no!" Jemima's hand flew up to cover her mouth. "I didn't mean that at all." She leaned her head closer to Bella's. "Mama will persist in thinking that everyone my age must be my friend, and there are some I would prefer not to know. Come, I will introduce you to a few people."

Bella listened to a young man with a round, serious face making unexceptionable remarks about the décor of the room, but could think of little to say except to agree with him. A decorative man in a laced pink coat and mint-green breeches lisped a greeting before turning back to the elderly lady with whom he was conversing. Then Jemima stopped beside two women who appeared to be a little older than Bella.

"Lady Isabella, may I introduce Miss Celia Quinn?" Miss Quinn had a flawless oval face and golden hair dressed high, and a smile that failed to reach her eyes.

"Delighted, I'm sure," Miss Quinn said, and turned to her dark-haired companion. "This is Miss Diana Yelland."

"Lady Isabella, how nice to meet you. Who is your father?" Miss Yelland's words were friendly, but the tone was not. Bella was uneasily aware that Miss Quinn was inspecting her gown while Miss Yelland spoke.

"The Earl of Marstone."

Miss Yelland's brows rose.

"I'll introduce you to some other people," Jemima said, taking Bella's arm before Miss Yelland could say anything else. "You see?" she whispered, once they were out of earshot of the two women. "Mama thinks they are my *friends*."

"Why does Miss Yelland dislike me? She doesn't even know me." Surely her appearance was not so off-putting?

"Because you are of higher rank, most likely. Her father is a mere viscount, and Miss Quinn's father only a baronet."

Bella grimaced, and Jemima's hand tightened briefly on Bella's arm. "Not everyone is like those two," she said. "Oh, Mama wants me. Will you be all right?"

"Of course."

Bella took a cup of chocolate to an empty chair. She didn't want it, but holding the cup and saucer would make her lack of acquaintance less obvious. A group of women were talking behind her, and she recognised the icy tones of Miss Yelland amongst them. Some of their comments carried with distressing clarity, and removed any desire in her to turn to see who was speaking.

"...not been in society... must be something wrong with..."

"...a little thing, and that gown!"

"...large dowry, and an earl's daughter will always..."

Bella's face flushed. She'd hoped she might make some friends—girls she could talk to and who could share the experience of their first season with her.

"...and her hair!"

"...trying too hard to appear taller, but..."

Bella's grip tightened on the saucer. Tamworth, her aunt's maid, had shown Molly how to dress her hair—pulled up, padded, and powdered. It was fashionable enough: her aunt and several other ladies were wearing a similar style. And Tamworth had indeed said it would disguise her lack of height. For all the spite in the overheard words, Bella thought they held an element of truth. Her coiffure made her resemble a shorter replica of her aunt, as well as being uncomfortable and an unaccustomed weight that she felt would topple if she moved her head too fast.

"Lady Brigham and Senhor Luis Alfonso Sousa da Gama." The butler's voice cut across the chatter, and all eyes turned to the door. Lady Brigham appeared to be of a similar age to Aunt Aurelia, and was just as expensively dressed. Senhor da Gama didn't look much older than Bella. Tall, with broad shoulders, he was dressed in a deep red that suited his olive complexion and dark eyes. He regarded the company warily as Mrs Roper hurried to greet the new arrivals.

Senhor? Was that a Spanish title?

They were too far away for Bella to overhear, but the bows and curtseys suggested that introductions were being made, and then the two ladies conducted the newcomer around the room. The giggling, smiling, and fluttering of fans indicated that Senhor da Gama was as

new to society as Bella, but was being received far more enthusias-
tically.

"I am happy to make your acquaintance, my lady." Senhor da Gama
bowed over her hand when they reached her corner of the parlour.
Sadly, Lady Brigham led him away before he could say more. Aunt
Aurelia bustled over.

"Come, Isabella, it is time we moved on. You need to meet more
people."

"Yes, Aunt." Senhor da Gama was the most intriguing person she'd
met so far, but she was unlikely to get the chance to talk to him in the
present company.

"I didn't know Lady Brigham had the money to dress like that,"
Aunt Aurelia muttered as they descended the front steps. "Where is
that coach?"

"We will try Lady Pamington next," Lady Tregarth said as Nick closed
the door on her sedan chair. "Tenby, to Portman Square, if you please."

The chairmen set off, with Nick walking beside them in the warm
sunshine. This part of his task was pleasant enough, but he fervently
hoped that they would strike lucky soon. They were working their
way down a list of names that Lady Isabella's maid had passed on as
possible destinations, but so far there had been no sign of their
quarry. Instead, he had endured numerous exchanges—he could not
call them conversations—with giggling misses and put up with several
unsubtle enquires about his father's title and estates. The only young
woman who hadn't inspired him with an instant desire to be elsewhere was Mrs Roper's daughter, who he had met on their first visit
today—but even she had only talked about the weather. It did not
bode well for his quest to find a suitable spouse.

"That looks like Marstone's coach," Lady Tregarth said as they
turned into Portman Square, and Nick's spirits lifted. "Now if the
footman knows which house they are in…"

A bored coachman sat on the box and an equally bored footman leant on the closed door. The latter stood as Lady Tregarth's chairmen set her down, and Nick saw a flash of recognition.

"Lady Tregarth desires to know where Lady Cerney is visiting," he said. Best not to bring Lady Isabella into this.

"They went into number seventeen, Mr Carterton," the footman said. "I don't know whose house it is."

"Thank you." Nick didn't recognise the footman, but the man clearly knew him, even though it was two years since he had been in Marstone House. "You have a good memory. What is your name?"

"Langton, sir. Part of my job, sir."

The trusted one. Langton's gaze met his own, returning Nick's appraisal. He was tempted to ask what Langton knew, and if Archer had spoken to him, but the coachman was within earshot and probably curious by now.

"This is Lady Pamington's house," Lady Tregarth said, as Nick escorted her into number seventeen.

Their hostess hurried towards them as they were announced, and greeted them with an arch glance at Nick. "So good to see you in my salon, Mr Carterton. Can I hope that you will be taking a full part in society this season?"

"Yes, indeed." Having answered a similar question several times during their earlier calls, Nick perjured himself again without hesitation. His promise to his father didn't involve attending every rout, ball, and picnic.

"Now, who should I introduce—?"

"Good heavens, is that Marstone's daughter?" Lady Tregarth interrupted, to Nick's relief. He followed her gaze, not recognising any of the young women on a sofa at the far side of the room. Two talked to each other, their heads close, while the third, who was wearing a heavily embroidered orange gown, stared out of a window with a blank expression.

"She needs rescuing from more than Marstone," Lady Tregarth said quietly as they crossed the room. "Where's the aunt?"

The girl in the orange gown looked up as Lady Tregarth stopped in front of her. She did seem vaguely familiar, once he looked past the powdered hair, and she had Wingrave's blue eyes. With her quiet demeanour and unattractive gown, Nick didn't think he'd have to fend off too many unsuitable swains.

"I wonder if you remember me, my dear?" Lady Tregarth said with a friendly smile. "You must have been quite young the last time I saw you. I'm Lady Tregarth, the mother of Wingrave's friend Harry."

Lady Isabella stood up, her eyes barely level with his shoulder. A tentative smile curved her lips as she greeted Lady Tregarth.

"I would like to introduce Mr Carterton. He is a friend of your brother."

Nick bowed over her hand, trying to reconcile this quiet creature with the girl he had last seen diving for the cover of a table. "I am happy to meet you, Lady Isabella."

"And I you, sir." Her smile grew more confident as she looked into his face. "I believe you were acquainted with my sister, Lady Elizabeth, before her marriage?"

"I was, yes."

The twinkle in her eye indicated that she did recall their previous encounter—it seemed Marstone hadn't managed to knock all the spirit out of the little minx. The animation in her face drew attention from her unfortunate gown—she could be as attractive as any of the young women he'd met today if she were better dressed. He might not have such an easy task after all.

"Mr Carterton, I must introduce these young ladies to you."

Nick sighed as Lady Pamington joined them. No chance to find out what Lady Isabella might have said next.

Politeness required him to make inconsequential conversation with the two young women who had been ignoring Lady Isabella. By the time Nick had extricated himself from their clutches—both were much more interested in him once Lady Pamington let drop that he was the heir to a barony—a blond youth he didn't recognise had drawn up a chair and was making stilted conversation with Lady Isabella. There would be little chance to talk to her now.

· · ·

45

"The poor girl has little confidence," Lady Tregarth said when they were finally back in her parlour. "Hardly surprising, with that gown and hairstyle. And no conversation, either. That's down to Marstone keeping her immured in the countryside. If he'd even allowed her to visit her sisters after their marriages, she'd have had more to say."

He could see how it must be difficult for her, and he was surprised that she'd managed to retain some of her spark over the past two years.

"I don't know Lady Cerney well," Lady Tregarth went on. "I think she is not as fanatical about social standing as Marstone, but we cannot rely on her goodwill towards Isabella. Marstone is paying the piper, and she is like to dance to his tune if there is a conflict between Isabella's interests and Marstone's."

"Point taken, my lady." Although he'd promised Wingrave only that he'd do his best to stop her being married against her wishes, the easiest way of doing that might be to find a suitor she did like. It seemed he would be taking a fuller part in this season than he'd anticipated.

"We have a box at the Drury Lane Theatre. Would you care to join us one evening? *School for Scandal* is being put on again. I will invite Isabella, and you may find an opportunity to talk with her then."

"I would be delighted, thank you."

"Well, Isabella, you didn't have much to say for yourself at any of our calls today," Aunt Aurelia said as they sat in the back parlour overlooking the garden.

"I didn't know what to talk about." Thankfully, her aunt appeared exasperated rather than angry.

"You needn't *start* conversations, but you can say more to continue them."

Bella's chin rose. "They talked of people I have not met, Aunt. Or about fashions. You don't suppose my father allowed magazines and fashion plates in the house?"

Aunt Aurelia scowled, but then shook her head. "You have a point, child. Marstone is pig-headed and arrogant, but I hadn't realised he is also stupid."

Bella's mouth fell open, then she laughed. To her surprise, Aunt Aurelia smiled.

"I'm taking his money—that doesn't mean I have to like him, or even respect him. But I need to find you a husband."

Bella's amusement died again.

"Oh, don't look so glum, girl. There are plenty of suitable men out there. If you co-operate, we should be able to find one you can tolerate before Marstone loses patience and makes arrangements with someone you find repellent. You only need to give the man an heir and a spare, then you can please yourself."

Please myself?

"Fetch the newspaper from the bureau, Isabella. There must be something we can do to supply you with more conversation."

Aunt Aurelia took the paper and turned the pages.

"Aunt, it's not only conversation. I heard people talking about me." She repeated some of the hurtful comments, and her aunt put the paper aside.

"Hmm. Perhaps that amount of powder in your hair doesn't suit you. Tamworth uses a lot on me to disguise the grey. Oh, yes," she added, as Bella's brows rose at this unexpected confidence, "there's no use hiding such things between ourselves. You were right about that gown, too." She picked up the paper again. "The Royal Academy Exhibition... Lady Tregarth said we could use her box at the theatre... Yes, that will do to start with."

Bella nodded, although she had little idea what her aunt had been talking about.

"Now, Isabella, to whom did you speak today?"

"I can't remember all their names. But there were Lady Jesson and Miss Yelland—"

"Which *men*, Isabella! Do concentrate."

"Mr Trent."

"That popinjay? No, I don't think he'd do. No title, and Marstone won't want such a pretty boy in the family."

"Lord Barnton."

"Hmm. Eligible, certainly."

"Senhor da Gama."

Aunt Aurelia shook her head. "I know nothing about him. I'll have to ask Lady Brigham. Marstone may not favour a foreigner, either."

That was a pity. "Mr Carterton," Bella went on.

"Carterton—wasn't he one of the ones who got away two years ago?"

Bella giggled. "He decided that he and Lizzie would not suit, if that's what you mean." A twitch of his lips when they'd been introduced indicated that he still recalled what she had done. She couldn't regret it, but she was glad he didn't seem to hold it against her. He had kind eyes and a pleasant smile—she wasn't sure how he might help her, but it was reassuring to have someone beside her aunt she could turn to if necessary.

"That was it, yes. Hmm—if Marstone chose him once, he may not object this time. I thought my brother was after higher rank though—Carterton is only heir to a barony, from recollection. Who else?"

"Lord Narwood." Bella had been introduced to him on their last call. He was older, much older than Will, with a full, powdered wig but without the paunch that men of his age seemed to develop. He'd been polite enough, and talked the usual commonplaces, but his manner had been cold.

"Hmm. A viscount, I think. That's another possibility. Fetch me the Debrett's, child."

CHAPTER 6

*L*uis gazed around the exhibition hall in Somerset House as he walked in with Lady Brigham. The room was huge, with high walls leaning in towards the top. Paintings of various shapes and sizes filled the walls, with hardly any space between them, all lit by the wide windows above. People thronged the floor, some wandering around or standing gazing at the paintings, others seated on long benches.

"Over there," Lady Brigham said. "The woman in the dark blue gown."

The lady indicated appeared less than ten years older than Luis himself, and was wearing only the lightest film of powder on her smooth cheeks and in her dark curls. Her gown, although lacking the elaborate trim and ornate brocade that Lady Brigham wore, was stylish and elegant.

"That is Lady Milton, one of the people you are to... befriend."

Luis took a keener interest. "Will you introduce us?"

"No. Even if I knew her personally, I do not want to be remembered as the person who introduced you if you make a mull of this enterprise." Lady Brigham paused, as if waiting for him to protest, but he said nothing. "You will escort me to Lady Henderson's ball this

49

evening, and on more calls tomorrow. After that, you should be able to get your own invitations. I will leave you now—you will find the paintings here give you some topics for conversation."

He glanced at the catalogue as Lady Brigham left and then stuffed it into a pocket. The crowd was thinnest near a collection of portraits —all beautifully painted, as good as any in his father's mansion. Brighter, too, as many of the ones at home had darkened with age. The paintings above them looked more interesting. As he looked up, a woman in front of him stepped back, one heel landing on his toes.

"Oof!"

The woman spun around and he recognised the shy girl in the wide gown he had met the previous day.

"Oh, I'm so sorry, sir." She looked horrified, one hand flying up to cover her mouth. "I was standing back to admire the pictures at the top."

He smiled down at her—the pain in his foot was already wearing off. "That is quite all right, my lady. Pray do not distress yourself." He made a bow. "My apologies, but I have met so many people since I arrived in London that…" That he'd forgotten her name, although it did not seem polite to say so. He waved a hand, giving her his best smile again.

"Lady Isabella Stanlake," she said, a breathless quality to her voice. "And you are Senhor da Gama… I'm afraid I have forgotten the rest. Is that a Spanish title?"

"Portuguese," he corrected her. "My full name is Luis Alfonso Sousa da Gama."

"Goodness!" Her hand covered her mouth again.

He chuckled—it was a relief to talk to someone he did not need to impress, and about whom he would not be quizzed later. "Yes, I have many names, but it is the way of the Portuguese. Tell me, which of these paintings do you admire the most?" At least here they had a ready source of conversation, and he would not have to struggle for compliments.

"I… I've only just arrived." She hesitated, and bit her lip—a nice, plump little lip. "I admire the skill in the portraits, but I can see people around me all the time. I am more interested in the other subjects."

"Ah, the battles, perhaps?" He pointed upwards, to where lines of ships in full sail fired guns at each other. He pulled the catalogue out of his pocket and riffled through it. "Admiral Rodney defeating the Spanish off Cape St Vincent," he said, locating the description. It was only a small engagement these English were celebrating.

"I'm glad you're not Spanish," Lady Isabella said.

What?

He frowned, then let out a breath of relief. She'd said he *wasn't* Spanish.

"I… I'm sorry," Lady Isabella stammered, taking a step back. "I only meant that it would seem so odd, if you were Spanish, to be admiring a painting showing a Spanish defeat. Wouldn't it?"

"Ah, of course. My apologies, Lady Isabella, I mistook your meaning." He resumed his smile as he looked up—he must remember not to let his expression betray his thoughts. "It is a good painting, I think, although I have not been on many ships, and certainly not in a battle. Shall we look at some more pleasant subjects?"

He held his elbow out and she laid her hand on it, a delicate blush rising to her cheeks.

"Now, here are some landscapes." He consulted the catalogue again. "Hah—that is the peak in Tenerife—a Spanish island." His lips quirked as he caught her eye. "Although your country is still officially at war with Spain, I think we may admire Spanish scenery?"

"Indeed we may, sir." She gazed at the painting, then back at him. "Have you been in London long?"

"A week or so, only," he said smoothly, having been asked that question numerous times over the last few days. "I do not recall meeting you before yesterday, my lady."

"I have only recently arrived myself. This is my first chance to go about London. It will give me something to converse about."

The innocent confidence was charming, and her reason for being at the exhibition matched his own. "It will certainly make a change from you English talking about the weather. Now, how do you like this scene?"

The painting depicted craggy mountains and foaming water. "That looks so wild and... majestic." She was examining it with care, unlike many of the people around them, who appeared to be conversing with each other and ignoring the art. "Where is it?"

"In the north of England," he said, consulting the list.

"Really?"

He laughed. "I have seen paintings like this of my own country. The real scenery is magnificent, yes, but not *quite* as dramatic as the artist depicts."

"I would like to see those places for myself," Lady Isabella said. "The countryside in Hertfordshire is pretty enough, but I've never been far from my father's estate.

"I'm sure you will one day, Lady Isabella." He patted her hand where it lay on his arm—he would have to leave her soon and talk to others here, but he could enjoy a few more minutes of her admiring glances.

There were more people at the exhibition than Nick had anticipated, given that the paintings had been on display for some weeks. Talking to Lady Isabella might be difficult amongst this many people, but he should try. He pretended to examine the pictures while he walked around the hall, hoping to avoid unwanted conversations.

He spied Lady Cerney first, talking with a group of women of similar age, none of them appearing to pay any attention to the art on the walls. He wandered on until he recognised the orange gown that Lady Isabella had been wearing the day before. She stood with her back to him, gazing upwards with one hand on the arm of a gentleman in a burgundy coat. As Nick made his way towards them she said something to her companion, her face displaying the same lively animation he'd caught a glimpse of yesterday.

"Good afternoon, Lady Isabella."

Her eyes widened, and she gave a polite smile. "Mr Carterton, good afternoon. May I introduce Senhor da Gama." She turned to her companion, her cheeks dimpling as her smile widened. "I'm sorry, but I have forgotten most of what came in the middle."

The senhor made his bow. "Senhor Luis da Gama, at your service, sir. I am but recently arrived in your country."

Nick returned the compliment. "I hope you are enjoying your visit to England," he added.

"Very much." Da Gama's eyes slid towards Lady Isabella. "Especially with such charming company."

To Nick, the words felt... oily. That was the only word for it. Lady Isabella clearly did not think the same, for she dropped her eyes and a delicate blush spread over her cheeks.

"But I have monopolised you for long enough, my lady," da Gama went on. "I hope to meet you again."

"I'm sure you shall, sir."

Da Gama bent over Lady Isabella's hand before making a bow to Nick and walking away. Lady Isabella watched him go, quickly schooling her expression from wistful to careful politeness as she turned to him. "Are you, too, enjoying the paintings, Mr Carterton?"

He glanced around—there were too many people within earshot. "I have only just arrived, Lady Isabella. May I accompany you for a while?"

She inclined her head and rested one hand on his arm. "I am tasked by my aunt to find something to say about ten items," she said, "so that I can make conversation next time I am in company." She met his gaze, a twinkle vanishing as her lips formed a pout. "I probably should not have said that."

"Such honesty is refreshing," he said, meaning it, and torn between amusement and sympathy. "Have you chosen your ten paintings?"

"Not yet."

"Well, let us proceed." He tried to recall the reviews he had read. "You will want to talk about the interesting new artist who did this," he said, leading her over to a painting of a young child holding out a begging bowl. "He is said to be self-taught, but has an astounding mastery of texture in his painting."

Lady Isabella moved closer, inspecting the canvas closely. "Opie," she said, as if committing the name to memory. "Texture." The enjoyment he'd seen in her face when she talked with da Gama had vanished. "The child looks very clean and plump for a beggar. I suppose the artist fed the boy properly before using him as a model."

Nick chuckled. "It is more likely that the lad is a relative, rather than a real beggar. It might be best to admire the brush-work. Polite society does not like being confronted with discussions about the poor."

Her brows drew together for a moment before she moved on to the next canvas. "And what should I say about this one? How well the painter has captured her expression, perhaps?"

"That would be unexceptionable."

She nodded, repeating the painter's name under her breath. Nick found himself unaccountably irritated at her air of concentration, which was quite different from the animation he had seen when she was talking to the Portuguese. Had da Gama's conversation been particularly amusing, or was the man just a practised flatterer?

"What is this one?" Lady Isabella asked, moving on to another portrait.

"Ah, there you are, Isabella." Lady Cerney appeared next to her niece before Nick could reply. "And Mr Carterton. Lady Tregarth mentioned you as an old friend of the family yesterday."

"Lady Cerney, I would like to invite Lady Isabella for a drive in the park tomorrow. Would four o'clock be suitable?"

"Why yes, thank you, we would be delighted."

We?

"But you should accompany *us*, Mr Carterton," Lady Cerney continued. "Marstone's calèche is most comfortable. Shall we collect you?"

"I... No need, my lady. I will attend you at Marstone House."

"Until tomorrow, then, at four." Lady Cerney inclined her head. "Isabella, come with me. You must have something to say about the painting over there; everyone is talking about it."

Nick frowned as Lady Cerney almost dragged her charge away,

Lady Isabella casting an apologetic glance over her shoulder. How had he allowed himself to be dragooned into escorting both of them, and in Lady Cerney's carriage, too? That would put her in charge of the expedition, and probably remove any chance to have a private word with Lady Isabella.

Well, there was no help for it now.

Late that afternoon, Bella watched in her bedroom mirror as Fletcher pinned the hem of her new pastel blue walking dress. The skirts were much narrower than the ones on the orange gown; dark blue ruffles along the edges of the overskirt set off the paler colour of the fabric.

She had enjoyed looking at the pictures with Senhor da Gama—he'd been entertaining and seemed to enjoy her company. It was a pity that Mr Carterton had interrupted them. He had been easy to talk to, as well, but not nearly as amusing as Senhor da Gama. Or as good looking, but not many were when compared to Senhor da Gama's broad shoulders and lovely eyes. She suppressed a giggle as she remembered the expression on Mr Carterton's face when Aunt Aurelia had changed the arrangements for their drive.

"There, my lady," Fletcher said, standing back to inspect her handiwork. "It won't take me long to finish this."

"That looks lovely," Molly said.

Fletcher nodded. "My last mistress said that being dressed well was like wearing armour. It helped her to ignore spiteful comments."

Bella wanted to ask who Fletcher had worked for, but she didn't think the seamstress would tell her.

"I can sew the last bit, Miss Fletcher, if you like," Molly offered. "There's the ivory ball gown to be done, too."

Fletcher looked to Bella. "I'm sorry, my lady, but I can't finish that one as well this evening, even if I start now."

"Don't worry, Fletcher, I'm not expecting you to." Bella wasn't sure her aunt would approve of what she was about to say, but she'd made up her mind to ask. "You said you were a lady's maid once—does that mean you know about hair styles?"

"Yes, my lady."

"If Madame is not expecting you to go back to her salon this evening, I would like you to show Molly how to arrange my hair in a way that suits me."

"She is not expecting me, my lady, but I have—"

"I will pay you for your time," Bella assured her.

Fletcher sighed. "It's not that, my lady. I have to... that is, Billy..."

A husband? Would he not be glad of the extra money? "I can have someone take a message, if you wish?" Bella offered.

The seamstress hesitated a moment longer. "Thank you."

"Do you want to write—?" Bella broke off as Fletcher shook her head. Perhaps she could not read. "Shall I send a footman? Fletcher, do not worry if you cannot stay. I will not hold it against you."

"I'll fetch Langton, my lady," Molly said. "He can be trusted not to talk, Miss Fletcher."

"Thank you, Molly. Now, while we wait, Fletcher, will you go through these hats with me?" She was determined to look, and feel, her best the next time she was in company.

Would she meet Senhor da Gama again? She might see if there was a book in the library about Portugal.

CHAPTER 7

The next afternoon Mr Carterton handed Bella and Aunt Aurelia into the calèche and politely took his place on the rear-facing seat. He showed no sign of impatience, even though her aunt's last-minute change of mind about her hat had kept him waiting for a quarter of an hour. Aunt Aurelia kept up a gentle flow of remarks as they drove the short distance to Hyde Park, requiring little in the way of response from her or Mr Carterton. Once through the gate, the buildings gave way to a grassy sward dotted with trees. Used to walking in the grounds of Marstone Park, Bella found it crowded; the gravelled drive was a press of vehicles and riders, and people on foot spread across the grass and walked along narrower paths. It was nice to see greenery and trees, though, and breathe fresher air.

"Oh, there is Lord Barnton," Aunt Aurelia exclaimed, but the carriage she indicated was moving in the opposite direction and Lord Barnton merely inclined his head as they passed. Bella wasn't sorry— in spite of her aunt's approval of his eligibility, she hadn't found his conversation very interesting.

"What a pity," her aunt said. "Still, it is always too busy to stop this close to the gates, and the point is to be seen, after all."

Bella had thought the point was to meet people. A fleeting grimace on Mr Carterton's face made her wonder if he thought the same.

"I understand Marstone tried to arrange a match between you and one of the twins," Aunt Aurelia said to their escort. "There can be no objection, then, if you wish to take a turn about the grass with Lady Isabella."

Bella bit her lip and looked away. That sounded more like a command than a granting of permission, as if her aunt was promoting a match between them. It could be worse, she supposed—he was certainly more interesting to talk to than Lord Barnton.

"Thank you, my lady," Mr Carterton said. "Lady Isabella, would you care to take a stroll?"

"I would be pleased to." What else could she say? The carriage came to a halt, and Mr Carterton helped her down.

"I will meet you near the gate in half an hour," Aunt Aurelia said. "Drive on, Jones."

"I… My aunt…" Bella felt she should apologise, but couldn't think of the right words.

"I am happy to obey," Mr Carterton said, smiling. He held out one arm, and she rested a hand on it as they set off. "I was hoping to have a word with you in private anyway. Did you receive Wingrave's note?" he asked.

"Yes, thank you. Where has he gone?"

"A matter of business, I understand."

He knew more, she was sure, but she didn't feel she could press him further. "What did he mean by acting in his place?" She could ask him that, at least.

"Only to ensure that neither your father nor your aunt forces you into a marriage you do not want."

Will had helped the twins meet eligible men, but his wife had been with him then. What could Mr Carterton do on his own?

"Think of me as a brother if it helps, Lady Isabella."

Lady Isabella looked up at him with a smile and a shake of her head.

She barely came to his shoulder, but he must not make the mistake of thinking of her as a child. She was a woman grown, even if not grown very tall. The dark blue redingote set off her figure well—a vast improvement on her previous gown. Her dark hair was arranged in a mass of unpowdered curls that framed her face and set off her clear complexion, topped by a broad-brimmed hat with ribbons and plumes that verged on the ostentatious.

"Thank you."

How did one talk to a younger sister? His sisters were both several years older than him, so that was outside his experience. As a friend, he supposed, but one that needed protecting. "How is your aunt treating you?"

"Well, thank you. That might be partly because my father is not yet in Town, but we rub along together well enough considering she is only here for Papa's money."

"They told you that?"

"Oh, not Papa. He rarely speaks to me. No, Aunt Aurelia admitted it, but I already—" Her mouth clamped shut.

"You already knew? Servants' gossip, I suppose."

She hesitated, then merely nodded. His lips twitched as he wondered if she'd been listening at doors.

"Oh, there is Mrs Roper," she exclaimed, pointing to a group of women ahead. "I enjoyed talking to Jemima. May we stop and talk to them?"

"By all means." They changed direction to intercept the group. Nick recalled Mrs Roper and her daughter from the calls he'd made with Lady Tregarth, and he also recognised the two young women with them. He felt a sudden grip on his arm; Lady Isabella's eyes were on the same two young women.

"Do you know them?"

"They were rude about me," she said, her voice low. Her chest rose and she stood straighter. "But I am *much* better gowned today."

"That's the spirit."

She chuckled at that, and put her chin up as she made her curtsey to Mrs Roper. Jemima smiled a greeting.

"You are looking… better today, Lady Isabella," Miss Quinn said, although her expression did not match her words.

Lady Isabella did not reply immediately, and Nick wondered if she was going to ignore the comment. Then she turned her head a little, tilting it back so she appeared to be looking down her nose.

"I'm *so* pleased you approve, Miss… er…"

Jemima took Lady Isabella's arm. "Miss Quinn."

"Ah, yes. Thank you for reminding me. I was going to ask you, Jemima, if you wish to…"

Her words faded as the two young women drew ahead. He managed not to smile at the chagrin in Miss Quinn's face as she and her friend walked off in the opposite direction—that had been a masterly putdown.

"I have not seen you in company much this season, Mr Carterton," Mrs Roper said, a twinkle in her eye.

"I have been busy, to my regret." The truth and a lie in one sentence.

"I am holding a rout next week," Mrs Roper went on. "Not a large affair. May I hope you will attend if I send a card?"

About to politely decline, Nick reconsidered. Jemima Roper seemed a pleasant young woman, and it might be worth getting to know her better. "Thank you. I will come if I am free." Perhaps he would also call before then.

"I will send Lady Cerney an invitation too."

Nick bowed as Mrs Roper attracted the attention of her daughter, and the party went on its way. "Miss Roper is a friendly young lady," he said as Lady Isabella rejoined him.

"Yes. We are to go shopping together one day, and she may come to my dancing—" She broke off and put a hand to her mouth.

"Dancing lessons?" Marstone hadn't had her taught to dance?

"I had no-one to learn with," she said.

"Lady Cerney could invite some young people to join you, perhaps?" He wasn't going to volunteer himself—he was far too busy.

"Such as Miss Quinn and Miss Yelland?" The quirk of her lips as she looked up at him was both a challenge and rather endearing.

"A good point," he admitted.

"We are to go to the theatre tomorrow evening," she went on. "Lady Tregarth has invited us."

"She invited me as well."

"Oh, good, I will see you there, then." She smiled, but then her expression changed, some of the fun vanishing. Following her gaze, he thought she must be looking at an open carriage nearby. A finely dressed lady was talking to a man standing beside it; the lady reached a hand down and the man bent over it, then watched as the carriage drew away.

Senhor da Gama, the Portuguese who had been with Lady Isabella at the exhibition.

"Shall we rejoin Lady Cerney?" he suggested.

She smiled as her attention returned to him.

He should find out about da Gama's background—the man had seemed very friendly with Lady Isabella at the exhibition. If he was to take his task seriously, he should find out what he could about her potential suitors. Limiting his attention to only those men suggested by Marstone would not be in the spirit of his arrangement with Wingrave.

Would he have *any* time to follow his own interests?

Aunt Aurelia had arranged for more fittings at Marstone House later that afternoon. While she was waiting for Fletcher to arrive, Bella looked through the travel guide to the Iberian Peninsula she had found in the library. The cities of Portugal and Spain sounded fascinating places—would she ever have the chance to go to any of them?

"This is Nokes, my lady." Molly ushered a strange woman into the room.

"Why have you come instead of Fletcher?" Bella asked, as Nokes and Molly helped her to don a half-sewn evening gown in lemon and cream stripes.

"Fletcher doesn't work for Madame Donnard any more, my lady,"

Nokes said, letting out a sound of protest as Bella twisted round to face her.

"She said nothing about leaving when she was here yesterday," Bella said. "What has happened?"

"If you please, my lady, would you stand still while I finish pinning these seams?"

Bella sighed, but did as she was asked. It wasn't fair to make the seamstress' working day even longer.

"So why *did* Fletcher leave?" Bella asked again.

Bella felt the woman's hands still as she replied. "Madame said she'd been stealing." The pinning resumed. "Madame said Fletcher should be grateful that she hadn't called the constable."

Bella resisted the impulse to turn again, to see if Nokes was lying to her. But why would she lie?

"Fletcher didn't seem the type of person who'd steal," Bella said. She'd been thinking out loud, but Nokes answered.

"It didn't seem right to us, either, my lady. Sarah was good at her job, and kind when she could be."

"Will she get another position?"

"I dunno, my lady," Nokes replied, mumbling through a mouthful of pins. "It'll be difficult without a reference."

It sounded strange to Bella—could it just be coincidence that Fletcher had been accused of stealing after she'd been at Marstone House for fittings?

"What was she supposed to have taken?" If it was items from this house, Bella could refute that accusation.

"Money, my lady. Madame said Fletcher kept money meant for her."

The coins Bella had given Fletcher for helping with her hair? She opened her mouth to explain but thought better of it. Telling Nokes would make no difference.

"Where does she live, do you know?" She twisted her head around again when the seamstress did not answer. "I mean her no harm, I assure you."

"I don't know, my lady," the seamstress said, her tone doubtful. "She kept herself to herself, mostly."

Bella waited, but no more information was forthcoming. When the gown was adjusted to Nokes' satisfaction, Molly helped her remove it, working carefully to avoid dislodging any of the pins.

"I'll take this gown to be sewn up tomorrow, my lady," Nokes said, folding it. "If you will put the ball gown on now, it needs only a few adjustments."

This would look good, Bella thought, running a hand over the ivory silk with a delicate pattern in pink. She wished she'd had the forethought to place the mirror better, but Fletcher was still on her mind.

"What about Dawkins?" she asked. "Would she know where Fletcher lives?"

"I don't know, my lady. They seemed friendly enough when they were at work. You would have to ask her."

Bella said nothing more while the woman finished her work, and gave her a shilling as she left.

"It looks lovely on you, my lady," Molly said, starting the process of removing the ball gown.

"It does," Bella agreed. "Molly, what can I do about Fletcher? If I hadn't asked her to do extra, she would still have her job."

"It wasn't your fault, my lady. Fletcher didn't have to stay."

"I could explain to Madame Donnard."

"Wouldn't help, my lady," Molly said. "Folks like her won't admit to being wrong. I'll bet she gets that shilling off Nokes tomorrow, as well."

That wasn't fair, not at all.

"You can't do nothing about it, my lady, not if you don't know where she lives."

"But we do! Molly, ask Langton if he can remember where he took the message the other night." A message to Billy. If Billy wasn't Fletcher's husband, he might know where to find her.

"I can ask, my lady. But I doubt it'll be a place you should go. You'd be robbed, like as not. Or worse."

"I'll take precautions," Bella said. Langton would have to go with her to show the way, and she should also take Molly for propriety's sake. It would be safer still if she had someone else with her. Mr Carterton, perhaps, or even Senhor da Gama.

Luis tried his best to keep his eyes on his partner's face as the final dance drew to a close. Lady Sudbury was certainly well-endowed and, judging by the low cut of her bodice, not shy about displaying her assets. He had to bite his lip and look above her head as he imagined partnering her for one of the more energetic country dances.

"Is something wrong, Senhor da Gama?" Lady Sudbury asked, and he looked into her eyes, a muddy shade of green. She was not pretty in the way the little Stanlake girl was, but what her features lacked in form they made up in vivacity and a definite look of invitation. This target would not be too difficult to seduce—his main difficulty might be fighting his way past others wanting to sample what she appeared to be offering.

"I was merely overcome by your plenteous charms, Lady Sudbury," he said. He wondered if he was overdoing the compliment, but she giggled.

"How nice of you to say so, but do call me Amalie." Her gaze dropped to his mouth, and her lips parted slightly.

He stepped back as the final chords sounded, and made his bow.

"It has been my pleasure dancing with you, my lady," he said. "I hope we meet again." He inclined his head and then turned and walked away, ignoring her moue of disappointment. Whatever Don Felipe wanted with the woman should be easier if she did not think she'd made an immediate conquest of him.

He pushed through the people waiting for their carriages and walked down the street, breathing deeply. The air outside had the stink of coal smoke, but it was cooler—welcome after the stuffy air inside the ballroom.

As he turned out of Portman Square a closed carriage pulled up beside him, and Don Felipe spoke. "I will take you home, da Gama."

"No, thank you." It was not far to his lodgings, and he'd arranged for Mrs Hathersage to have a bottle of decent claret awaiting him. The need to keep his wits about him in company was becoming tedious.

"Get in."

Luis did so, suppressing his irritation at the peremptory tone and wondering why Don Felipe's manner had changed from the amicable tone in his letters. As the coach set off again. Don Felipe was a dark shape on the opposite seat, his face lit only briefly as the carriage passed link boys carrying flambeaux.

"I danced with Lady Sudbury this evening," Luis started, assuming Don Felipe wanted a report on his progress. "And talked to Lady Milton this morning." On yet another round of tedious calls.

"I know about Lady Milton," Don Felipe said. "She was also at the exhibition yesterday, but you made no attempt to be introduced to her there. Instead, you wasted your time talking to that child in the orange dress."

Child? Lady Isabella was young, certainly—but equally certainly not a child, not with her figure.

"What does that matter? And how do you know who I talked to?" He just wanted to get back to his lodgings and have a drink.

"You are being watched, of course."

"Of course? Why 'of course'?" Luis took a deep breath, and managed to get his next words out in a more controlled tone. "Can you not trust—?"

"I need to *know* that I can trust you—and to do that, I need to have you watched." Don Felipe's voice held ice and contempt in equal measure.

"I am the son of Don Pedro de—"

"Here, you are the second son of a minor Portuguese noble. Do not forget it."

"There's no-one here," Luis protested. "I would not say that in public."

"Do not even think it, or you will let the truth out inadvertently. Now, that girl, who is she?"

"Lady Isabella Stanlake," Luis said, scowling into the darkness. "I know I have to concentrate on the women you tell me to, but will it not appear suspicious if they are the only ones? What is special about them anyway?"

"You will be told when you have befriended them properly." Don Felipe banged with his stick on the roof of the coach, and it began to slow. "You do have a point," Don Felipe added. "But make sure you spend *more* time with the essential ones."

Luis descended into a wide street lined with large houses. Where was he? He turned back to protest, but the coach was already pulling away.

Muttering curses under his breath, he started to walk, hoping he would recognise somewhere he knew without having to ask for directions. Then he wondered how many bottles of claret Mrs Hathersage had in her cellar.

CHAPTER 8

*B*ella gazed in awe at the interior of the theatre, and the number of people packed into it. The Tregarths' box on the second tier was spacious enough, as Bella and her aunt were the only guests yet present.

"Do sit at the front, Isabella," Lady Tregarth said. "You won't see much from that chair at the back."

"The idea is to be seen," Aunt Aurelia added. "And your new gown becomes you well."

Bella sighed as she took the seat indicated, wondering if her aunt ever had any other reason for doing things.

"*I* come to enjoy the play," Sir John said. Bella glanced up, and smiled as she caught a wink. She hadn't met Sir John before, but he seemed as friendly as his wife. He pulled an enamelled tube out of his pocket, and handed it to Bella. "You might enjoy using this until the performance starts."

It had glass at each end—a spyglass? Bella looked through it, but all was a blur.

"Pull the end out until you can see clearly," Sir John added.

Bella gasped as the people in the box opposite jumped into sharp focus. She lowered the tube—it seemed rather rude to spy on people like that.

"It's intended to get a better view of the actors," Sir John explained with a chuckle. "But many people use it as you were."

Looking more carefully, Bella could see several other spyglasses in use, most by young men training them at the crowd on the main floor of the theatre. She raised the glass again, sweeping it along the boxes opposite.

"I don't know why we came so early," Aunt Aurelia complained. "I've seen *School for Scandal* before, several times."

"Isabella hasn't," Lady Tregarth said. "Do stop complaining, Aurelia. Leave, if you wish. We will take Isabella home afterwards."

Bella bit her lips as her aunt settled back in her chair and waved her fan. Continuing her scan, she spied Lord Barnton in a box with a much older woman—his mother, perhaps. There were others she recognised, although she could not recall their names. She thought she saw Senhor da Gama in the upper tier, his dark red coat blending into the shadowed background, but a voice rang out from the stage and she turned her attention to the play. The chatter from the audience quietened a little, but she had to strain to hear the actor's words. Then a partition was moved, revealing two women drinking chocolate in a dressing room, and she became lost in the story.

Nick entered the box as quietly as he could. He'd intended to arrive before the performance started, but his meeting with Talbot had taken longer than expected. Lady Tregarth and Sir John nodded in greeting, but Lady Isabella and her aunt didn't notice his entrance. Lady Cerney was busy inspecting the occupants of the other boxes; Lady Isabella was leaning forward in her chair, absorbed in the happenings on the stage, where Sir Peter Teazel was complaining about the behaviour of the women in his family.

Knowing the plot well, he took a chair towards the back of the box, scanning the audience opposite. Gilbert was here—that was good, he could have a word in the interval about the analysis he was doing for him. The Ropers were in their box on the tier below—he'd had to turn down their invitation to join them when he called on Miss Roper this afternoon, as he was already promised to the Tregarths. That Portuguese was in a box on the upper tier.

As da Gama was newly arrived in England, no-one he knew had heard of him. Nick had resorted to asking Talbot this afternoon after he'd finished looking through new information Wingrave had sent back. The spymaster hadn't heard of him either, but had promised to make enquires. He'd also said that Wingrave's investigation might take some time, so it seemed Nick would be looking out for Lady Isabella for a few more weeks yet.

Lady Isabella sat back and turned towards Sir John when the curtain came down at the end of Act One. She seemed surprised to see Nick, but greeted him with a happy smile.

"Ah, Carterton," Lady Cerney said. "Have my seat. I'm going to speak to Lady Pamington." She rose as she spoke. Nick caught Lady Tregarth's amusement as he sat down—Lady Cerney's attempt at pairing him off with Lady Isabella was rather blatant.

"How are you enjoying the play, Lady Isabella?"

"Oh, very much. It isn't easy to follow, sometimes, with the audience making so much noise. Is it always like this?"

"Usually, I'm afraid."

She gave a little pout, then smiled again. "I can always ask you or the Tregarths if I lose the plot." She lifted a spyglass resting in her lap. "Before the play started, I was looking at the other people—it seems it is permissible to spy on others here."

"Impolite, perhaps, but many people do it."

Her smile dimmed, but although she dropped the glass back in her lap she still turned towards the boxes opposite. He tried to see who she was looking at.

Da Gama again—and the Portuguese appeared to be returning her gaze.

"No-one seems to know anything about Senhor da Gama," he said, keeping his voice low so that only Lady Isabella could hear. "You had better not have too much to do with him until I can check his background."

She stiffened as he spoke. "I enjoyed a conversation with him at the Royal Academy, Mr Carterton. That is all."

"Your brother would—"

"Will is not here. My aunt asked Lady Brigham about Senhor da Gama, and she vouches for him. Is that not—?" She broke off, and when she spoke again it was in more measured tones. "I am in my aunt's charge, Mr Carterton. But thank you for your concern."

He let out a breath. All he'd done was to offer sensible advice, and she'd ripped up at him. Her final words were conciliatory, but the icy delivery was not.

"You're welcome, Lady Isabella. If you will excuse me?" He might as well speak to Gilbert now, and hope she'd calm down without his presence. He could ask Lady Tregarth later what she knew of Lady Brigham; a recommendation was only as good as the reputation of the person making it.

Bella clenched her hands in her lap, but made an effort not to scowl—hundreds of people could see her, if they chose to look. She needed help to find Fletcher, and she'd thought to ask Mr Carterton. But if he was warning her against something as innocuous as merely talking to a man, he was bound to tell her she should not go. No, she would have to find someone else.

She turned her gaze to the boxes opposite. Senhor da Gama had returned her smile earlier, she was sure. Who was that with him? She raised the spyglass; the occupants of the box were talking to each other, so they would not notice her inspection. Lady Brigham was there, together with a younger woman. Lady Brigham looked bored, but the younger woman smiled up at Senhor da Gama and fluttered her fan. It was the woman she had seen him with in the park yesterday. Bella shut the spyglass with a snap. As she had told Mr Carterton, she and Senhor da Gama had only enjoyed a brief conversation. Just because he was the most amusing and attractive man she had met so far, it did not mean he thought the same about her.

Lady Tregarth sat down beside her with a rustle of skirts. "The next act will start soon, my dear. And I suspect you will have some visitors at the next interval. Your new gown has given you more confidence."

Bella gave her a grateful smile. "I am enjoying myself, my lady. This is all so new." She would be foolish not to make the most of it while her father was still at Marstone Park. Who knew what would happen when he recovered enough to come to London?

Lady Tregarth's prediction proved correct. When the next interval came, Lord Barnton made his bows to Lady Tregarth and Aunt Aurelia, and asked Bella if she would care to take a turn in the corridor with him.

"She will be pleased to, my lord," her aunt said, before Bella could answer.

Bella followed Lord Barnton out of the box, irritated by having the decision made for her. Lord Barnton was pleasant to look at, however, even if his conversation was rather tedious, and the clear admiration in his glance was welcome. Mr Carterton had not returned to the box after the last interval, but his permission was certainly not required.

"Is the play entertaining you, my lady?" Lord Barnton asked as she took his arm and they joined the other people promenading up and down the wide corridor.

"Indeed it is, my lord. I am wondering how close a reflection it is of society."

His brows drew together. "Undoubtedly it is too close for comfort. Gossip can cause all manner of harm."

Surprised by the force in his words, Bella wondered if he had suffered from gossip himself. "Yet I have found that gossip appears to be the main topic of conversation," she said. His frown deepened—a change of subject would be a good idea. "Did you view the paintings at the Royal Academy exhibition?"

"Indeed. There was much to be admired. I found the depictions of naval encounters particularly interesting..."

There may be more to the man than she'd thought.

"...intricate brushwork needed to show details of the rigging and foam on..."

Was he an artist?

"...watercolours cannot compete with the brilliancy of a work in oils..."

Oh well, he wouldn't be interested in her artistic skills, then. Bella had always thought that a conversation involved both parties talking and listening. She was beginning to feel as if she were still in the schoolroom.

"Have you visited the north of England?" she asked, when he paused for breath. "There was a painting of mountains there, but I am told it makes the mountains look more dramatic than they are in reality."

"Lady Isabella, there are conventions to be followed when depicting landscapes. The classical school, you know, always—"

"Lady Isabella, how fortunate!" Senhor da Gama spoke from behind them. Bella turned, releasing Lord Barnton's arm. Any interruption would have been welcome, but she was particularly pleased to see him.

"May I join you?" he asked. He didn't wait for a reply, but moved to stand next to Bella.

"I say, sir," Lord Barnton spluttered. "I am—"

"You should not keep such a treasure to yourself," Senhor da Gama interrupted. "But my apologies, we have not been introduced." He cast a quick glance at Bella, laughter in his eyes, before bowing with a flourish. "Senhor Luis Alfonso Sousa da Gama, at your service, sir."

Relieved that he hadn't asked her to make the introductions—and remember that string of names—Bella tried to hide her smile. Senhor da Gama had not sounded so pompous when they'd talked before.

"Lord Barnton," her escort said. "Heir to Viscount Chevington."

"Ah, how nice for you," Senhor da Gama said. "I, myself, am merely a younger son of the Visconde de Santa Ines."

"Your servant, sir." Lord Barnton glared at Senhor da Gama, his posture stiff, but the Portuguese only smiled pleasantly in return.

Lord Barnton finally turned to Bella and bowed over her hand. "It has been a pleasure, Lady Isabella. I hope to see you again soon."

"Thank you, my lord." She turned to look at Senhor da Gama as Lord Barnton stalked off.

"I hope you do not mind the interruption, Lady Isabella," he said, his voice deepening a little as he looked into her eyes.

"No, not at all." Bella's heart began to beat faster.

"I am here with friends of my family, but I could not resist the chance to pay my respects to you."

Could the younger lady be his aunt? Bella smiled up at him.

"I think that one does not like me," Senhor da Gama said, glancing at the retreating form of Lord Barnton. "Did you listen carefully to his lecture?"

Bella giggled, his answering smile making her heart race. "My attention might have wandered," she admitted. As she spoke, the bell for the third act rang—she had to ask now. "Senhor da Gama, may I ask you to do me a service?"

He bowed. "It would be my pleasure, my lady."

"You don't know what I am going to ask yet," Bella said.

"Ah, well. If it is an impossible task, then I am very good at thinking of excuses."

He had lovely smiling eyes.

"But tell me what you need, Lady Isabella."

"I need someone to escort me to… to a part of London of which my aunt would not approve. I will have a maid and a footman, but someone more…" Her voice tailed off. Stronger? With more authority? "It is nothing improper."

"How could it be? I will happily escort you, my lady. What time shall I call?"

He must not come to Marstone House—that would destroy her plan. Bella tried to recall the names of the streets near Grosvenor Square.

"Could you meet me tomorrow at two o'clock on the corner of Green Street and Park Street?"

He raised a brow, but nodded. "I will be there. Farewell, minha dama." He lifted her hand and pressed his lips to the back of it.

Bella felt her cheeks heat, and pressed her hands to her face as she watched him walk away. No matter if she was blushing—the lighting in the box was dim.

Nick hurried up the stairs, not wanting to interrupt his hosts' enjoyment of the play with another late arrival. He was jostled by a man hurrying in the opposite direction.

"I beg your pardon."

The apology drifted to his ears and he stopped, turning abruptly. All he saw was the back of a burgundy coat and matching breeches. But the words had been accented, and the Portuguese had been wearing that colour.

Damn it. He'd bet money that Lady Isabella had talked with the man, in spite of his warning. How was he supposed to help her if she would not do as he advised?

"She took a turn on the corridor with Lord Barnton," Lady Tregarth whispered, in answer to his question. "No-one else called on her."

He hadn't seen Barnton on his way back to the box, so she could have spoken to da Gama. His concern might be unfounded in any case. Although the Portuguese seemed to have a way with women, that did not mean he would behave improperly towards Lady Isabella.

He turned his attention to the stage, irritated that he now had to keep an eye on da Gama as well as everything else.

CHAPTER 9

*L*uis leaned against a wall at the end of Green Street, tapping his stick against one boot. If this business took too long, he'd be late for his meeting with Lady Sudbury.

He pulled his watch out for the third time—he'd been here for twenty minutes now. Not only had the novelty of listening to the cries of milkmaids, flower-girls, and other hawkers worn off, but a fine drizzle was beginning to mist the air.

His eyes on the street, he didn't notice Lady Isabella approaching until she stood beside him. She was clad in a drab brown redingote, her hair stuffed into a plain cap beneath an even plainer bonnet. She looked little better than the frowning maid standing behind her.

He transferred his stick to his left hand, and made his bow. "My lady. Where do you wish to go?"

She blushed delightfully. "To St Giles, if you please. I am trying to find a… a servant who I am worried about."

A servant?

"She lost her job, and I feel responsible," Lady Isabella added. "I am told that it is not safe for me to go alone to where she lives."

It was an odd request for assistance—a lady should not be concerning herself with the lower orders. But she wanted to go, and

75

he saw no harm in escorting her. "Very well. Anything to please a lady." He bowed over her hand again with an extravagant flourish, and laughed with her as she giggled. "Are we to walk?"

"No, I sent a footman to find a hackney." She turned to the maid. "Molly, where is Langton?"

"He's here now, my lady." Molly pointed at a carriage drawing up beside them. A young man jumped down and Luis inspected him with disapproval—a footman working for someone of Lady Isabella's status should be in livery with a properly powdered wig.

Langton opened the door and Luis wrinkled his nose as a smell of stale sweat, cabbage, and… yes, vomit, wafted his way. He could not ride in that, and nor could Lady Isabella.

"This is not good—"

"It will have to do, Senhor da Gama." The command in Lady Isabella's words surprised him—she had not seemed so forceful when they talked earlier. She climbed into the carriage, followed by her maid.

Getting in after her, he dusted the seat with his handkerchief before sitting down. If he'd known he would have to ride in a conveyance this filthy, he would not have worn these clothes. The footman closed the door, and the hackney rocked as he climbed up beside the driver.

Lady Isabella stared out of the window, looking distracted—worried, even—as the carriage wound its way through the traffic. The view changed from large, stone-fronted houses to smaller brick ones, and the roads grew narrower. They passed fewer polished carriages with matched horses, and more delivery carts and hand barrows.

"Are you sure you wish to go to this part of the town?" he asked. They were well beyond the areas of London he had explored—these streets were beginning to resemble the overcrowded and filthy areas around the docks.

"My footman knows the way," Lady Isabella said, her voice lacking the confidence it had held before.

London must be larger than he had thought, as it seemed to take a long time to reach their destination. Eventually they came to a halt, and Langton opened the door.

"This is as far as the carriage can go, my lady," he said, ignoring Luis. "The next streets are too narrow."

Luis stepped out with relief, and held his hand to assist Lady Isabella.

"I can take a message, my lady," Langton suggested. "You could wait here."

Lady Isabella's brows creased as she looked about her. Luis followed the direction of her gaze. Paint peeled from the doors of the dirty houses, and the wet cobblestones could hardly be seen for mud and other things he didn't like to contemplate. It smelled, too, although not as badly as the inside of the hackney. The people on the street were careworn, hunched under shawls or ragged coats.

"Langton, did you see Billy when you came before?" Lady Isabella asked.

"No, my lady. There was only a woman and a lot of brats at the address Miss Fletcher gave me. The woman said it'd cost, but she'd see Billy all right this once."

None of that made any sense to Luis.

"It's a few streets away," Langton went on. "What do you want me to say?"

"I wish to speak to her myself."

"Are you sure, my lady? It's not a good—"

"Your mistress has decided," Luis said impatiently. "She is under my protection."

Langton's mouth turned down at the corners, but he took a step back. "It's down there, my lady," he said, pointing to the entrance to an alley.

"Oi, I want my money before you go," the driver called.

"We will pay when we return," Luis said, holding his elbow for Lady Isabella to take.

"Not good enough. 'Ow am I to know you'll come back?"

Luis spun around, glaring at the driver. "You have my word as a gentleman."

"Bugger that," the man said. Luis jumped backwards as a gob of spittle just missed their feet.

How *dare* he?

Luis took a couple of paces towards the driver, raising his cane. "Hijo de puta! You do not—"

"Sir!" Langton stepped in front of him. "Sir, you will put Lady Isabella in danger. Look around you."

Luis almost hit the footman, but stopped himself in time. It would not do to brawl with one of Lady Isabella's own servants, no matter how insolent. A small audience of skinny urchins had gathered around them, and a little way down the street a group of men clustered before an alehouse.

"My apologies, my lady," Luis said. "I was thinking only of the disrespect to you."

"I can send Langton—"

"Nonsense. I will protect you, Lady Isabella." There was no need for her to change her plans because of the protests of a mere servant. He glared at Langton. "Pay him."

Langton pulled some coins from a pocket and handed them up. The driver bit one, then stowed them in a pocket. "There'll be more if you're still here when we get back," Langton said.

The driver shrugged and called one of the urchins over. Luis looked back as they moved off down the street, seeing the lad dashing into the alehouse. The man might wait, but would he be in a fit state to drive them?

That was a problem for later—he could always send the ill-mannered footman to find another carriage when they returned. And a cleaner one, this time.

Not liking the look of the men outside the alehouse, Luis gestured for Molly to walk next to Lady Isabella as Langton led the way. He fell in behind them. A few children kept pace with them, round eyes moving from Lady Isabella's garments to his own coat and breeches. He checked that his sword was loose inside its stick.

· · ·

Bella looked at the crowd of ragamuffins from the corner of her eye, not wanting to attract any more attention than they already had. The men's stares had seemed to bore into her as they passed the alehouse, but thankfully none of them had approached their little party.

"What do they want?" she asked Molly, keeping her voice low as she indicated the children. She pulled her skirts sideways to avoid a pile of refuse with a gaunt dog sniffing at it.

"Looking at your clothes, like as not, my lady. They'll not have seen anything as fine, not in these streets." Molly's lips were a thin line, turned down at the corners.

"Should I give them some money?" Bella's hand moved towards the slit in her skirt as she spoke.

"No!" Molly took a deep breath, then spoke in a whisper. "No, my lady. Don't let on you've a full purse, for heaven's sake."

"Why n—?"

"My lady, there's some as would steal the clothes off your back, never mind taking the money."

Bella swallowed hard. Molly had tried to dissuade her from coming in person—why had she not listened? Stealing jewellery she could understand, but to steal clothing from a person wearing it? Molly's chatter about village life had included the effects of poverty, but she'd never seen this degree of hardship with her own eyes. None of the villagers at church had been as thin and hollow-eyed as these children.

Not only children, she realised, taking more note of her surroundings. A woman stood in a doorway, barely sheltered from the drizzle. She was more gaudily dressed than the others, with lace around the edges of her low neckline. As they approached, Bella could see that the gown must once have been very fine, but had been mended too many times. The woman smiled and took a step forward as they approached. Senhor da Gama snapped something at her and she retreated again, scowling. Glancing behind as they passed her, Bella saw two men further back. They were smaller and less well-built than Senhor da Gama and Langton, but Bella shivered. It was the expression on their faces—smiles that were more like snarls—and the purposeful way they walked.

Senhor da Gama pulled on the handle of his cane and she caught a glimpse of a sword blade. He sheathed it again, but the action did nothing to reassure her—he was also worried about their safety.

Her actions had put Molly and Langton into danger, as well as herself.

"Langton?"

"My lady?" The footman slowed, but did not stop walking.

"Can we go back?"

Langton, too, took in the men behind and shook his head. "Best not, my lady. I can try a different way out of this area, if you wish."

"Yes."

Langton turned left at the next side alley, his pace picking up. Bella looked behind again as they neared another corner, relieved to see that the men were no longer there. Langton turned left again—that should take them back towards the cleaner streets where they'd left the carriage.

Her moment of relief vanished. The alley ahead of them twisted to the right. Langton slowed, looking about him, then came to a stop.

"I'm sorry, my lady. I don't know my way from here. We will have to retrace our steps some of the way."

"Can we ask for directions?" Although that might not be a good idea. The few people standing in doorways regarded them with sullen expressions.

"Those men," Senhor da Gama said behind her.

Bella turned, her heart thumping in her chest as the same two men turned into the alley and advanced towards them. They smiled, triumph and greed plain on their faces, and one of them licked his lips.

"I'm sorry, Molly," Bella whispered, her stomach feeling as if a lump of cold lead had settled in it. This was all her fault for not listening. She clutched Molly's hand and moved a few steps further down the alley, but then stopped. There might be just as much danger if they went on. Metal sang as Senhor da Gama drew his sword, and the two men came to a stop, their smiles fading.

"Keep an eye out the other way, my lady," Langton said, moving around her to stand next to Senhor da Gama. "Molly, if you can, run past them and back the way—"

Langton's voice broke off as four more men turned into the alley. One of them shouted and broke into a run, pushing his way between the two would-be assailants. Behind, the other newcomers swung cudgels.

"Thank God," Langton muttered.

Bella looked again—what was Langton thinking? These men only added to their danger, surely?

"That's Mr Archer, my lady," Molly whispered. "We'll be safe now."

Their two assailants turned to look behind them, then ran, pushing past Archer's men and disappearing down a side lane.

Bella swallowed bile in her throat, her knees threatening to collapse with relief. If it *hadn't* been Archer, they could all have been killed.

"This way, my lady," Archer said as he reached her, taking her arm without ceremony and setting off back the way they had come. Apart from being rather cleaner, Archer was dressed as scruffily as the others in this neighbourhood. Was this really Will's trusted man?

"Unhand her, man!" Senhor da Gama pulled on Archer's shoulder, but Archer shook him off with a glare and Langton grasped his sword arm.

"Don't, sir. You'll attract more attention."

Archer pulled Bella along, Molly hurrying beside them. A servant had never handled her so, but Bella was too glad of the rescue to mind.

"I am not afraid to—" Senhor da Gama protested behind them.

"Then you're a damned fool." Langton's voice carried clearly. "There's more of 'em in these houses, and we need to get Lady Isabella out of here."

The men with Archer were keeping a watchful eye on the houses lining the street, their expressions wary rather than threatening.

She would be safe. The knot of dread inside her vanished, even though they were not yet back in civilisation.

Archer's pace did not slow until they came in sight of their carriage. The driver took one look at Archer's face and handed a mug down to a boy still hanging around on the corner.

"Where to, guv'ner?"

"Davies Street," Archer said, opening the door. Bella climbed in without assistance, Molly following her.

"No." Senhor da Gama's voice carried through the door. "Grosvenor Square. Lady Isabella needs to be—"

"Davies Street," Archer said again. "We will walk from there. Get in, or be left behind. Your choice."

"How dare—?"

"Can we go now? *Please?*" Bella begged, leaning forward until she could see Senhor da Gama.

He muttered something she could not make out, but did get into the coach. Archer shut the door and climbed up with the driver before the coach moved off.

"Who *is* that man?" Senhor da Gama asked, his mouth tense in anger.

"He works for my brother."

"He *works*—?"

"He rescued us," Bella said firmly, resting her head against the greasy squabs and closing her eyes. She should thank Senhor da Gama for escorting her, even though he hadn't actually been much help. If Archer hadn't...

No, she refused to let her mind dwell on what might have been. She must think about a better way of contacting Fletcher instead. Would Archer know? Molly could ask him.

But all that was too much to think about now. All she wanted to do was to get home and feel safe in Marstone House. Aunt Aurelia would be back from her afternoon card party in an hour, expecting to find Bella fully rested and preparing for Mrs Roper's rout.

CHAPTER 10

"She did *what?*" Nick gazed at Archer, sitting at ease in the chair at the other side of the desk. "Not alone, surely?"

"No, sir. She had Molly Simons and Langton with her, and a foreign gentleman. A Senhor da Gama."

Da Gama again? He must ask Talbot if he'd found out anything yet, although he'd only enquired yesterday. If the gossips found out about the expedition, Lady Isabella would likely find herself returned to Marstone Park—he could not think that the earl would approve of such exploits. That would keep her out of trouble, but it would also remove any possibility of his being able to keep his word to Wingrave. Nor could he wish such a fate on her.

"Langton sent a message to me, sir, and I got there as soon as I could." Archer smiled, although there was little humour in it. "He'll go far, that lad—told the coachman to take a long way round to give me more time."

"It would have been better if he'd stopped her going," Nick said, then shook his head. "No, that's unfair."

"There's not much a footman could have done," Archer agreed. Nick listened to Archer's account. Taking da Gama with her showed some sense, even if he could have done little to help them if Archer had not turned up.

He pinched the bridge of his nose—he couldn't really blame her. Most gently bred young ladies would have no idea of the true dangers that awaited them in such a place, let alone one who'd been kept as isolated as Lady Isabella.

"Why did she go?"

"Langton said she was looking for a seamstress who had been turned off. She has some notion it was her fault, but Langton didn't know the reason."

"She didn't find what she wanted?"

"No."

"I hope you told her not to do such a thing again."

"No, sir. It's not my place to give orders to Lady Isabella. Lady Cerney could, but I'm fairly certain she knows nothing about the expedition, nor do any of the servants that might tell her."

Her aunt could stop Lady Isabella trying again, if she hadn't learned her lesson today. But he couldn't drop a hint to Lady Cerney about keeping a closer eye on her—she would want to know the reason, and that could result in Lady Isabella being returned to her father. Lady Cerney might overlook it in the interests of keeping Marstone's money, but he couldn't be sure.

"I told Langton and Simons not to accompany her again, and I doubt any of the other footmen would," Archer said.

"Even if she orders them?"

"I made it clear that Lord Wingrave's promise to employ anyone who lost their job for assisting her does not include helping her to put herself in danger. But the maid reckons Lady Isabella's not the type to put them at risk, so I don't think she'd try again."

"Thank you, Archer." Nick recalled the extra men Archer had hired. "Are you out of pocket for this?"

"Not yet, sir. Lord Wingrave left me with plenty of funds."

"Come to me if you need more."

Archer nodded, producing a folded piece of paper from his pocket as he stood. "Simons sent this, sir."

"Thank you."

Archer bowed and left.

Damn. He'd have to speak to her again, and she hadn't taken kindly to his mild warning about Senhor da Gama. From what he'd heard, Wingrave had been headstrong and foolhardy in his youth—his sister could be just the same. He had to make her understand the dangers of what she'd done. Unfolding the paper Archer had given him, he deciphered the untidy scrawl.

Rowt at Mrs Ropers tonite. Voxhal in 5 days.

Nick sighed. He'd told Mrs Roper he would attend her rout if he was free, but he was also promised to Gilbert, to discuss the progress of his latest report. He'd go to the rout first, and leave as soon as he'd spoken to Lady Isabella.

Nick arrived early, while Mrs Roper was still greeting guests at the door. She welcomed him with a smile and a murmur that Jemima was in the blue parlour, if he would like a word with her. He obediently made his way there, recalling that Miss Roper had seemed friendly with Lady Isabella. If his charge had already arrived, he might find her there.

He couldn't see her in the parlour, but he stayed to make the usual conversation with Miss Roper—discussing the number of people expected, the weather, and her thoughts on the play last night. They spent a few minutes on the relative merits of Sheridan and Shakespeare, then she asked him if he had been to the Royal Academy exhibition.

"Yes, indeed. I was much struck by The Night-Mare," he said, wondering what she'd made of that strange image.

Her face reddened. "I'm afraid Mama did not like me looking at that one. She said it was not proper for—"

"Good evening, Mr Carterton."

The interruption cut across Miss Roper's words, and Nick turned in irritation. Miss Quinn stood behind him, a coy smile upon her face.

"Miss Quinn." He bowed and turned back to Miss Roper. "I suppose it is a little—"

"Such marvellous paintings," Miss Quinn said. "I do so admire the skill of the artists."

Miss Roper took the second interruption in good part, one side of her mouth lifting. "I'm sure my mother will be needing me," she said. "I have enjoyed talking to you, Mr Carterton. I hope to see you at Lady Durridge's musicale the day after tomorrow."

Nick watched as she dipped a brief curtsey and walked away. When he turned back to Miss Quinn, the smile on her face looked a little forced. "I, too, admired the paintings," he said. "Excuse me. I've just seen someone I need to talk to." He bowed, and walked off before she could reply. Rude, perhaps, but no worse than the way she had interrupted his conversation with Miss Roper.

In need of a breath of fresh air, he made his way through the assembled guests to the floor-length windows. They opened onto a terrace across the back of the house, still damp from the earlier rain. The clouds had cleared, and the terrace might be useful for a private conversation.

He glanced at his watch and tucked it back in his pocket. He'd sent a note round to Gilbert saying he'd be late, but if Lady Isabella didn't appear soon, he'd have to go. He headed back to the central hall, looking into what must normally be a music room, then into a chamber with a long table of food. Finally, he spotted Lady Cerney talking to someone he didn't recognise. Lady Isabella stood beside her, looking... bored? Tired? That wouldn't be surprising, given what Archer had told him. If she'd been here all along, he'd wasted his time in idle conversation.

No, that wasn't fair. Miss Roper could talk sensibly, and he'd made a start on keeping his promise to his father.

Lady Cerney inclined her head towards him as he approached, then took the arm of the woman she was talking to and moved away. Lady Isabella looked after her in dismay.

"You appear to have been abandoned, my lady," Nick said, managing to keep his tone polite. Although he needed to speak to

Lady Isabella alone, he resented the blatant way that Lady Cerney seemed to be pairing them off, as well as the need to have this conversation at all.

Lady Isabella lurched towards him as someone jostled her from behind, and he put a hand out to steady her.

"Thank you," she said, meeting his gaze briefly before lowering her eyes. A blush coloured her cheeks. She had not been so shy before—or was that guilt? She must know that Archer would report to him.

"I hope you are well?"

Her lips compressed, as if she suspected he was needling her, but she inclined her head politely. "Thank you, yes."

It was his turn to take a step forward as someone pushed past him. Not only was this not a place for private speech, it was not a place for any kind of conversation at all.

"There is a terrace behind the house. Would you care to take a stroll on it with me?"

He thought she was about to refuse, but she squared her shoulders and nodded. Rather than offer his arm, he turned and shouldered his way through, hoping she could follow in his wake. When they reached the terrace, he breathed in the cooler air with relief.

"Are parties always like this?" Lady Isabella asked, gazing back into the room.

"Many of them. That's why I avoid them as much as possible." Ignoring her choke of laughter, he looked along the terrace. Two men stood at the far end talking, but they had the rest of the space to themselves. The hubbub of voices from inside ensured they would not be overheard.

"I hear you had an adventurous afternoon," he started.

The amusement left her face. "That is one way of describing it, yes."

"What did you hope to achieve by going into such an area? And accompanied by someone you know so little about?" He made an effort to keep his voice calm—it would not do to draw attention.

She lifted her chin and looked away. Nick waited, but it was clear that she wasn't going to answer.

"Do you realise the danger you put yourself in? And your maid and footman, too." Irritation, and the need to keep his voice down, sharpened his tone.

She scowled—there was no other word for that mutinous expression. "They could not have stolen much."

"Losing your purse should have been the least of your worries." A beautiful innocent like her, brought up as she had been, could not even conceive of being sold to a brothel. Damn Marstone.

"We came to no harm, Mr—"

"Only because Archer arrived in time." He would *not* think of what might have happened to them without Archer's help.

"Senhor da Gama and Langton had matters in hand." Although she, too, kept her voice low, there was no mistaking the truculence.

"Wingrave asked me to look out for—"

"You said he asked you to prevent my father forcing a husband on me. This has *nothing* to do with my marriage prospects." She dipped a small curtsey, and when she spoke again she was icily polite. "Excuse me, I must find my aunt." Without waiting for a reply she turned on her heel and stalked back into the house.

He rubbed his forehead. *That went well!*

There was no point in trying to resume their... discussion—he would end up losing his temper, or causing her to do so. And he was late for his appointment. He looked out over the garden. Damp be hanged—rather than push through the crowds inside yet again, he would find the gate onto the mews behind.

Bella stopped inside the doors, partially concealed by the curtains, and took deep breaths. She could not make polite conversation while she was still so angry.

How dare he reprimand her like that?

Because he was right, a little voice said. She closed her eyes, guilt beginning to replace the anger. He'd only spoken the truth, and she had berated him. Will, had he been in London, would have surely said much more, and with justification.

She leaned on the wall, wanting nothing more than to be in her bed. After the events of the day, and now the crush in Mrs Roper's rooms, she felt more tired than she'd ever felt before.

"Lady Isabella, why are you hiding in here?"

Her eyes flew open.

Lord Barnton stood before her, holding one edge of the curtain back. He bent forward to see behind the curtain, a frown creasing his brow. "Are you unwell?"

"No, my lord." He looked curious rather than concerned, and she didn't want to have to talk to him now. "I was a little overcome by the heat, but I am well now."

"A turn on the terrace would assist your recovery, my lady."

"I am perfectly recovered, thank you," she repeated, trying to stop her impatience showing in her voice.

"Then let me take you for some refreshment. A glass of lemonade would revive you."

"Thank you." Unfortunately, it would be too impolite to tell him to go away and let her think. She placed one hand on his arm, and looked about her for inspiration as they crossed the room. If she could start him lecturing her again…

A large black vase stood on a side table, decorated with golden pavilions, arched bridges, and strange, twisted trees. "That is a beautiful vase."

Lord Barnton raised a quizzing glass to scrutinize it, then tapped it gently with one fingernail. "It is British-made porcelain, Lady Isabella, not true lacquerware."

"But it is pretty, is it not?" Bella raised her eyes to his, trying for the innocent expression that had sometimes worked on Nanny after an incident in the nursery. "Why does its origin matter?"

"True lacquerware originates in the east, in…"

She had been terrified as Senhor da Gama and Langton faced those two men. She didn't want to imagine what could have happened if the others approaching had not been in Archer's pay.

Telling Mr Carterton he should only concern himself with her possible husband was splitting hairs, and she'd been rude to him.

She should apologise.

"...sap from a tree that grows only in that country. Imitations..."

Molly and Langton deserved an apology, too. She had put both of them in danger. They could have refused to accompany her, she supposed, but most servants would not disobey direct orders.

"...japanning produces an adequate finish..."

What would she have done if Langton and Molly had refused? Going on her own would only have been possible if she had persuaded Langton to give her the address. She could have made up some complaint to threaten his job if he did not tell her, but she dismissed that thought instantly. That would be as unfair as the way Fletcher had been treated. Worse, as Langton's refusal would only have been to protect her.

"...bought by persons of insufficient wealth to obtain the real thing, or too little refinement to wish for the genuine product."

Bella realised that Lord Barnton was awaiting an answer this time. "Thank you for explaining it to me, my lord."

He patted her hand where it still rested on his arm. "A pleasure, Lady Isabella." He bowed and walked away. He'd forgotten that he was going to get her some refreshment, but Bella wasn't sorry to see him go.

She still hadn't found Fletcher. She could persuade her aunt she needed another fitting at Madame Donnard's tomorrow, and see if Dawkins could tell her anything. That might work.

"Lady Isabella."

Bella sighed, then pasted on a smile and turned, wishing she'd asked Lord Barnton to take her to her aunt after all. The man before her was middle aged, with beady eyes, no smile... she searched her memory. "Lord Narwood." She made a small curtsey.

"All alone, Lady Isabella?" He ran his gaze from her face down her body, then slowly back again. Bella resisted the impulse to fold her arms across her chest.

"As you see, my lord."

She wasn't sure what she was supposed to do—Aunt Aurelia had left her as soon as Mr Carterton appeared, then she... well, being left alone after that was hardly her fault. She could not just start conversations with people to whom she had not been introduced.

"I should find my aunt. Excuse me."

"Dear me. Allow me to escort you." He held out one arm, and she had little choice but to accept his offer. "Your gown becomes you."

Bella was uncomfortably aware that her short stature made it easy for someone standing as close as he was to look down on her bosom. Of course, no gentleman would do so. No *real* gentleman, she thought, catching his head turning away abruptly as she glanced up at him. She made to remove her hand from his arm, but he put his own hand over hers, holding it in place.

"Did your father send you to school, Lady Isabella?"

"No, my lord. I was taught at home."

"You have older sisters, do you not? Did you accompany them to Town when they were presented?"

"No, I was... I remained at home."

Lord Narwood nodded, as if she had given the correct answer. His hand was still firm on her own. Where was her aunt? Bella looked around, but she could not see over people's heads.

"Are your sisters married? Do you have many nieces and nephews?"

Bella opened her mouth to answer but closed it again. From someone else, such a question might have led to a friendly conversation about families, but his eyes on her were cold. Assessing.

"My aunt may be in the retiring room, my lord. If you will excuse me, I will go and look." She had no idea where the retiring room was, but tugged her hand from his grip and made her way as quickly as she could out of the room. She needed to find someone she recognised. Anyone—even Lord Barnton— would be welcome to get her away from Lord Narwood and out of this noisy, jostling collection of people. At last she spotted Lady Tregarth.

"Bella, are you all right?"

"I'm looking for my aunt, my lady. Have you seen her?"

Lady Tregarth shook her head. "Not for some time—she was in the card room. From what I've heard of her, she's like to be there for some time yet."

"Oh." Perhaps she could find Jemima, and ask if there was somewhere quiet she could wait.

"It is too bad of her to abandon you like this," Lady Tregarth went on. "Shall I take you home? You can leave a note for your aunt."

"If you please, my lady. Thank you."

She would write a letter to Mr Carterton when she got home, and hope he would accept her apology.

CHAPTER 11

"Try again."

Luis scowled at the scrawny youth sitting across the battered table, who had introduced himself only as 'Ben'. Given the man's skills, Luis wasn't surprised he didn't want to give his full name. With a sigh, he pulled the locked box towards him again and picked up the tiny tools. He put one of them into the lock and twisted it gently.

"Feel it," Ben said. "Close your eyes, and see through your fingers."

It sounded stupid, but Luis closed his eyes anyway.

"Feel the bolt?"

Luis poked the tool in further. "I think so." He twisted it, hearing a quiet snick.

"Good, now put the—"

Luis swore under his breath as the door opened—he didn't need an interruption now he was getting somewhere.

"Can he do it yet?"

Don Felipe. Who else would walk into someone else's rooms without even bothering to knock?

"It's not something you can learn in an hour," Ben snapped.

Luis hid a smile as he turned to face Don Felipe. "I'm improving," he said. "I just need practice." Quite a lot of practice, but he wasn't going to tell Don Felipe that.

"Good." Don Felipe looked at Ben. "Leave us."

Ben muttered a curse as he slammed the door.

"Are you going to tell me why I need to open locks?"

Don Felipe sat on the chair Ben had been occupying. "Sir Edward Milton works in the Admiralty."

Luis sat up straighter, dropping the picklocks. This sounded like the business he was here for.

"He is known to sometimes take documents home with him for review. Documents we want sight of."

Luis nodded.

"Your relationship with his wife needs to be close enough for you to have access to their house. We will let you know when Milton is likely to have suitable documents at home. You will locate these documents, read them, and repeat to me what they say."

Remember whole documents?

"Why not send someone like Ben to steal them?" Ben would have little difficulty breaking into a house.

Don Felipe rolled his eyes. "If they are stolen, then Milton will know the information has been passed on. If what you report is of interest, we may steal one to be copied and then returned, but the chance of something being missed while the copying is happening is too great for us to do that with all documents. And before you suggest it, Ben cannot go because he cannot read fast enough with full comprehension."

"Won't Milton be in the house when the documents are there?"

"Possibly. But you should be able to learn your way about the house, find hiding places or arrange to leave a window unlatched." Don Felipe waved a hand as if such sordid details were beneath him.

Luis fiddled with the picklocks. He had no experience of... of burglary. About to suggest that Ben could help him, he thought better of it. It was a good idea, but mentioning it might make Don Felipe think he could not accomplish this task himself.

"So, I need to be more friendly with Lady Milton," he said. "Is that all?"

"Lady Sudbury. How are you progressing with her? You haven't been seen with her very often."

"Is her husband in the government as well?"

"No. How are you prog—?"

"Well enough," Luis said, annoyed at Don Felipe's manner. "What am I to do with her?"

"Bed her. Talk to her. Find out what her other lovers have told her."

Luis' brows rose. "How many does she have?"

Don Felipe shrugged. "The number is not important, but one of them is a Mr Trantor. If he is as loose-mouthed as we hope, you may get something of value there."

"Very well." He wondered how much of her chatter he'd have to put up with to hear anything useful. He wasn't even sure what Don Felipe would consider worth knowing, but he'd been told too many times that he'd be informed when it became necessary.

"Then there's the Stanlake girl." Don Felipe went on. "I have discovered she is daughter to the Earl of Marstone, and so is of some interest. However I wouldn't recommend seducing her—the brother's not averse to duelling, and considered a good shot."

"I can shoot—"

Don Felipe banged his hand down on the table. "You fool! If you get caught ruining the girl, I don't give a damn if Wingrave kills you. Your usefulness would be at an end. The point is not to draw attention to yourself by causing a scandal."

"What do you want from Lady Isabella? Information about her father?"

"No. He's old, hardly leaves his house, from what Lady Brigham says. It's Wingrave we're interested in, the heir. He's in France at the moment, something to do with preparing for the peace negotiations. But there are rumours that he is not merely a diplomat. Gain the girl's confidence. She may not know anything, but she could be a way to get closer to Wingrave when he returns."

Well, that part of his task should not be too difficult or unpleasant.

Don Felipe's chair scraped across the floor as he stood. "That is all. I will be observing your progress."

Luis clenched his jaws against a retort and took a deep breath as Don Felipe left. He'd come this far—it would not do to lose his temper with the man now. Another few breaths and he felt calm enough to tackle the locked box again. This time he heard a satisfying click as the internal bolt moved.

～

"Are you well, Bella?" Aunt Aurelia asked as Bella entered the breakfast room. "You are usually up much earlier than this." She had finished her own repast, and was busy with her usual sorting of calling cards.

"I am well, Aunt," Bella said, taking her seat and waiting while the footman brought her hot chocolate. In truth, she felt almost as tired as she had last night. She had not slept well, the menace of the two men who had followed them in St Giles interrupting her sleep. Waking from the nightmares, she had stared into the darkness above her bed. Had she even understood the true extent of their danger?

Molly had mentioned robbery or worse, and Mr Carterton had implied the same. What had they meant? She'd intended to ask Molly this morning, but by the time she'd written her letter of apology and asked Molly to take it to Langton, she was late for breakfast.

"Are you sure?" Aunt Aurelia put the cards down and regarded Bella intently. "You claimed you were tired yesterday afternoon, and you left the rout early last night. A young girl like you should have more stamina. I do hope you are not sickening for something."

"I'm well, Aunt." Yesterday afternoon's tiredness had partly been an excuse not to accompany her aunt on social calls.

Aunt Aurelia nodded and returned her attention to the cards. Bella drank her chocolate, and ate spiced rolls spread with butter and honey, beginning to feel a little better with some breakfast inside her.

"I have sent an acceptance to Lady Durridge's musicale this

evening. She invites all the best people, although it will not be the ideal place to attract suitors."

Bella sighed. Had her aunt ever attended an event—other than a card party—simply to enjoy herself?

"Then there is our trip to Vauxhall in a few days."

That sounded more interesting than routs and musicales.

"Hmm. Lady Yelland invites us to a ball next week." Aunt Aurelia put the cards to one side. "Will you be ready to dance if I accept that invitation? I will watch part of your lesson this morning, to see how you are getting on."

"I... I think I will be ready." She could remember the steps with Herr Weber, although she wasn't sure she had enough confidence to perform in public. But she had to try some time.

"Good. We should call on Lady Margate when we are out this afternoon. I hear she has returned to Town."

"Yes, Aunt." Bella suppressed a sigh. Lizzie and Theresa's letters hadn't said how boring a season would be, but perhaps with Will and his wife in Town their season had been more than a seemingly endless round of calls. "Didn't you say you would take me to the British Museum, and tell me which objects I should admire?" If only Will were here—a visit such as that would be entertaining.

The butler knocked and entered, holding out a silver salver with a sealed note. "My lady, there is a footman awaiting a response."

Aunt Aurelia's lips curved in a smile as she read the note. A satisfied smile, Bella thought, with foreboding. *Not Lord Narwood, please!*

"Mr Carterton invites you to a drive in the park this afternoon," her aunt said. "Mowbray, tell the footman the invitation is accepted."

That was quick—he must have written as soon as Langton delivered her note. If he'd accepted her apology, he might not be too angry with her.

"I suspect Marstone is after someone of higher rank than a baron, but he did not specify," Aunt Aurelia said. "Carterton would do if Narwood or Barnton do not come up to scratch."

"Must my husband be English, Aunt?"

"Hmm. I suppose you'd be living closer to Theresa if you could find a Scottish lord." Aunt Aurelia paused. "Isabella, you're not thinking of that Portuguese, are you?"

Bella felt heat rise to her cheeks.

"You'd do best to put him out of your mind. Marstone is not likely to accept a foreigner."

"He's the son of a viscount. Is that not high enough?"

"Not the heir, I understand, so almost certainly not. Is he like to offer for you, Isabella?"

Bella looked away. "I don't know, Aunt, but I do like him. I know you and father don't care whether I like my future husband, but—"

"Don't tar me with the same brush as my brother, Isabella. I am not so unfeeling. I would not see you wed to a man you detest, or are afraid of."

"Then why do you keep mentioning Lord Narwood?" Bella asked.

"What is wrong with him? He is older than you, to be sure, but that can be a good thing. He's not been in Town often, so I know little about him."

"I... It's the way he talks to me. Last night he was looking down my gown, and asking how many children Theresa and Lizzie have. He probably only wants an heir, and someone who will be obedient."

"Most men want an obedient wife, my dear. He knows far more of the world than you."

"Of course he does—even the scullery maids know more than I do! Apart from a few weeks in Town the first time Papa tried to marry off my sisters, I've never left Marstone Park. Even then I wasn't allowed out of this house. How am I ever to learn anything if everyone just tells me what to do all the time?"

Bella waited for a reprimand for raising her voice. It didn't come.

"I always said Marstone was a fool." Aunt Aurelia leaned over and patted Bella's hand. "Now, most men want an heir. What is different about Lord Narwood?"

"I... I don't know. He makes me feel..." She closed her eyes in frustration. "I can't describe it, but I know I don't like it."

"I will not encourage him, then. But once Marstone gets wind of his interest, you will find it hard to avoid him. You'd better make sure someone like Lord Barnton makes an offer first."

"Will Papa know?"

"Undoubtedly. Some of the staff will be reporting back. He'd be here to make sure we were doing his bidding if he hadn't made himself ill raging at me."

Bella nodded—sometimes her father's temper could be an advantage.

"He'll come to Town as soon as he's well enough to travel. Hopefully that will be some weeks. He was an obnoxious bully when he was a boy, and he's only got worse since."

It was a relief to feel she wasn't an unnatural daughter for fearing and disliking her father.

"Make sure you look your best this afternoon, Bella—Carterton's not the highest ranking of your suitors, but I think Marstone sees some political advantage to that match. Unless you've taken a dislike to him too?"

"No, Aunt." She didn't dislike him at all. In fact, she quite liked him when he wasn't telling her off or issuing orders—and he did have the excuse of acting in Will's stead. Thank goodness her aunt didn't know the reason for his invitation.

CHAPTER 12

*D*riving his phaeton to Grosvenor Square, Nick thought over Lady Isabella's letter. It had shown far more maturity than he'd expected—her apology had been handsome, and she'd given a concise but complete explanation as to why she'd ventured into such an area. The whole was a far cry from the overdone politeness with which she'd rejected his reprimand last night.

The letter also begged for advice, so he had to talk to her today even if it caused the aunt to think he was a suitor. If he didn't help her find the seamstress, would she try again on her own? The consequences of that didn't bear thinking about.

Lady Isabella came down the steps as he drew up outside. She gave a wary smile as his groom handed her into the phaeton, but didn't speak until they'd turned into Hyde Park. "Did you receive my note?"

"I did, thank you." He pulled the phaeton to a halt and told his groom to wait for him by the gate, then guided the horses towards one of the lesser-used drives. "I accept your apology. Do not look so apprehensive, Lady Isabella, I am not going to repeat what I said yesterday."

"You would have been justified in saying more," she said, her hands clenched in her lap. "Will would not have been as polite."

"Would he sympathise with your intent, do you think?"

"Yes, I think so." Her mouth set in determination as she looked up at him. "But I would try to help Fletcher whether or not he approved."

"She's only a seamstress," he pointed out, curious to see her reaction.

"She's a *person*, and it was my fault she was turned off. Should I ignore that?" She took a breath. "*Are* you suggesting I forget about it?"

"No. But your wish to help is rare amongst our class. Most have no idea how others live."

"I only know how people live in Over Minster. That's where my maid lives near Marstone Park, but I've never seen their homes. Molly's family aren't—" She broke off, biting her lips.

Nick cursed Marstone under his breath—if his guess was correct, Lady Isabella's only confidante since her sisters married had been her maid. "What will you do now?"

"I don't know. That is why I asked if you could advise me. Langton has the address, but I don't know what he'd do if Fletcher isn't there."

"Why didn't you just send him yesterday?"

She looked down at her hands again.

"You don't have to tell me," Nick said. "My help is not contingent on getting an explanation."

"It was partly because I didn't understand how dangerous it might be. I knew I might be robbed, so I took only a little money with me, and wore old clothes." She smoothed a hand across her gown—fashionably new, as far as he could tell, and flattering. "I didn't realise how much even my oldest gowns would stand out."

How could she?

"Molly said something about stealing clothing—I never thought people would do that. But you said something last night about robbery being the least of my worries. What did you mean?"

Good grief—he could not explain brothels to Lady Isabella. He let his hands drop, and the horses came to a stop.

She crossed her arms, her chin rising. "It is hardly surprising that I make mistakes, Mr Carterton, when no-one will *explain* things to me."

She had a point. "It's not a proper subject for me to discuss with you. With any lady," he corrected himself.

"So something bad might have happened to me, but I'm not allowed to know what it is?"

Nick sighed. Society would not approve of his telling her.

Hang society's rules.

"Do you know what happens between a man and wife?" He hoped he didn't have to explain that. To his relief, she nodded.

"Molly told me about it. It's the same as animals do."

He winced.

"Is that wrong?"

"Not exactly, but most people would not take kindly to such a comparison."

She shrugged. "Well, it sounds most uncomfortable and unpleasant."

It sounded ridiculous, to his mind, if one only described the mechanics. "It isn't, if—" No, he would *not* go into any more detail. He hoped she married someone who could show her there was far more to it than that.

She was regarding him expectantly, so he made himself continue with his warning. "But imagine being forced to take part in that act with men you do not know or like."

"As I would be if Papa marries me off to a suitor of his choosing?"

That gave him pause—the act would be carried out within matrimony, but he could see how it might feel little different from prostitution to the woman involved. "Worse than that. Lots of different men. Men like the ones who almost attacked you yesterday. If you are lucky, they may not hurt you, and some of them might even pay you."

She digested that in silence for a moment. "There was a woman in a fancy dress. She tried to talk to Senhor da Gama..." Her expression became grim. "Is that... is that what Fletcher will have to do if she cannot get another position?"

"Quite possibly. It is the last resort for many women, I'm afraid."

"I was right to want to help her, then. But what has that to do with me? Do you mean someone might force me to... to do that?"

"And worse," he muttered, not intending her to hear. Lady Isabella, unfortunately, appeared to have very good hearing.

"What do you mean?"

Damn it, why had he started on this explanation?

"Mr Carterton?"

"Your brother would have my head if he knew what I was saying to you. And you really do not want to know, Lady Isabella."

She said nothing in reply. Relieved at first, he took in her pursed lips and frown, and wondered if he should explain further. He set the horses in motion again with a flick of the reins and waited to see what she would say.

Bella had no doubt that whatever it was would be unpleasant hearing, and that Mr Carterton thought he was doing what was best for her. Everyone else thought they knew better than she did. In many cases—most cases—they would be correct. Men made the decisions for women because they knew more about the world, and made sure they stayed in charge by preventing women learning anything for themselves.

But she was here to help Fletcher. She must not let her resentment towards Mr Carterton—and men in general—prevent her from achieving that goal.

"What will you do if you find her?" Mr Carterton asked.

"Give her some money, I suppose." She didn't want to admit that she hadn't thought beyond that. His expression hadn't changed, but somehow she knew he didn't approve. "You are about to say that's the wrong thing to do, aren't you?"

"No, but it would be of only temporary assistance."

"She needs a new job." Fletcher used to be a lady's maid, but Bella already had Molly. Could she persuade Aunt Aurelia to employ her? No, and if she tried it was likely that the whole story would come out. "Would Lady Carterton provide a reference for her?"

"I'm afraid my mother died some years ago."

"Oh. I'm sorry."

"No need to apologise, Lady Isabella. I might be able to find someone who will—Lady Tregarth, possibly—but she would need to be sure she was recommending an honest worker. But the first thing is to find Fletcher."

He drove on in silence for a while. She hoped his frown was a sign of thought, not that he was still displeased with her.

"You said you wished to know more of the world, Lady Isabella?"

"Yes," she said, wary of what he might say next.

"I can try to find Fletcher. Do you wish to accompany me? As you pointed out, you know her better than your footman does. I can make arrangements that should keep you safe."

Bella gaped at him and then closed her mouth with a snap. After all the reprimands for putting herself and others in danger, he was now suggesting she repeat her action? She took a deep breath—she should not complain now that someone *was* offering to help her.

"There are conditions, though," he went on, before she could answer.

"Do exactly as I am told, I suppose?"

"Yes. And without argument or question."

That was nothing new, but she could understand the reason for obedience in these circumstances. "Very well."

"You will have to persuade your maid to come along, for propriety's sake."

That might be more difficult—she wasn't even sure that she should. But although Mr Carterton was not quite as tall or as broad as Senhor da Gama, something about him made her trust that he could keep her safe. And if she was safe, Molly would be too. "I can try."

"What pretext will you give this time?"

"Aunt Aurelia said she would take me to the British Museum, so I have more things to talk about. You could... I could say you had invited me to accompany you there."

"That could work. Say nothing yet. I need to make some arrangements, but I will let you know when I have a plan."

"Thank you, Mr Carterton."

"Wait until it's done before you decide whether thanks are in order." He shook his head. "I shouldn't be doing this. Now, the museum has an interesting selection of stuffed birds and animals from around the world, and you may talk about how different some are from the creatures you know of." He broke off and smiled here, his eyes crinkled in amusement. "You may *really* be interested in them, when you visit the museum."

She hoped he was going to invite her to go there with him in reality—he would be a much more entertaining companion than her aunt. But, after a brief hesitation, he started talking about tiny, brightly coloured hummingbirds.

Nick took a glass of wine from a footman and wandered through Lady Durridge's rooms, seeing who else was present at the musicale. He didn't normally attend such events, but this was a chance to further his acquaintance with Miss Roper as well as letting Lady Isabella know he had made the promised arrangements.

"Good evening, Mr Carterton." It was Miss Yelland this time, rather than Miss Quinn, but in Nick's mind there was little to choose between them.

"Miss Yelland." As he greeted her, he saw Lady Isabella arrive with Mrs Roper and her daughter. Where was Lady Cerney?

"…rout last night." Miss Yelland was still talking. "It was a shame I could not attend, but Lord Kidsgrove had invited my family to share his box at the opera."

"How lucky for you to have another musical evening," he said. If she was being courted by the Earl of Kidsgrove, he wondered why she was bothering with a mere heir to a barony. On the other hand, he was a couple of decades younger than the earl. "I hope you enjoy the singing, Miss Yelland. If you will excuse me, I must see Mr Gilbert about something."

He had no idea whether or not Gilbert was present, but Miss

Yelland did not follow him as he retreated to another room, remaining there until he heard the first strains of an aria.

Most of the chairs in the ballroom were occupied, so he leaned against the wall from where he could see the performer without having to peer past ostrich plumes and towers of powdered hair. His position also had the great advantage of being at the opposite side of the room to Miss Yelland and her mother.

For the first half of her evening's programme Lady Durridge had engaged Señora Lopez, a soprano Nick admired for her excellent vocal range. As a medley of folk songs succeeded the initial arias, Nick ran his eyes over the audience. Da Gama sat a few rows behind the Yellands, and appeared to be paying as little attention to the music as most of the audience. Talbot had sent a note that afternoon, reporting that although the visconde the man claimed as his father undoubtedly existed, no-one had heard of da Gama himself. He'd also reported that Lady Brigham owed a great deal to a moneylender, and requested that Nick take note of da Gama's activities. As if he didn't have enough to do already.

His gaze moved on, to find Mrs Roper and her daughter listening attentively, making a comment to each other now and then. Lady Isabella, sitting beside them, appeared entranced, a wide smile on her face.

Her gown became her well, but more attractive was her obvious enjoyment in the music. This must be the first time she'd heard a professional singer. She would enjoy the opera; perhaps Lady Tregarth could get up a party, and he could ensure that she didn't wander off with unsuitable men again.

He recalled his other purpose in being here as he turned his attention back to Miss Yelland, wafting a fan in front of her face as she peered around the room. On the face of it, she would be suitable as a political wife. She was poised and attractive enough to look at, but there was something unappealing about her nature. His gaze turned back to Miss Roper—she appeared to have a pleasant personality without any of the impetuosity that might make a wife difficult to manage. He would make more of an effort to talk to her when the opportunity arose.

Bella came back to reality as the applause died down and Lady Durridge announced a short break for refreshments.

"Well, Bella, I think you enjoyed that," Mrs Roper said. "Shall we all go for some lemonade?"

As they joined the throng heading for refreshments, Lord Narwood bowed towards her from the other side of the room. She looked away without acknowledging him, to see Mr Carterton approaching. She must mention Lord Narwood's interest to him, but this was too public a place.

"I've made arrangements to find your seamstress," he said, his voice only loud enough for her to hear. "Lady Tregarth will invite you to visit the museum with her tomorrow afternoon. Will your aunt allow you to go?"

"Yes," she whispered. Aunt Aurelia would be glad to be excused the duty.

Mr Carterton nodded, then spoke normally. "How did you enjoy the singing, ladies?"

"Oh, very much," Jemima said. She and Mr Carterton began to discuss other singers they'd heard as they all entered the refreshment room. It was the kind of intelligent conversation Bella wished she could have, but she had no knowledge of the opera. Or of much else, come to that.

A cold feeling between her shoulder blades made her turn. Lord Narwood stood behind her. "Lady Isabella," he said. His lips curved up at the corners, but she could not describe his expression as a smile.

Senhor da Gama approached before Bella could answer, a full glass in each hand. "Excuse me," he said, inclining his head towards Lord Narwood before turning back to her. "I am pleased to see you here, Lady Isabella. I took the liberty of getting you a glass of lemonade." He handed Bella one of the glasses, and a delicious shiver ran through her as their fingers touched.

"Thank you." Bella let out a breath of relief as Lord Narwood turned and stalked off. Mr Carterton was still talking to Jemima, so she took a few steps away, Senhor da Gama keeping pace with her.

"You seem no worse for yesterday's little... adventure," he said. "I'm sorry I could not have protected you better—I am not familiar with London and its ways."

"I am well, thank you." Bella felt slightly breathless. "Is Lisbon so different? I have been reading about it."

His eyes flicked away for a moment. "If your brother were not in France, he would have escorted you, I think. But let us not talk of such things. You looked as if you were appreciating the singing as much as I."

"Oh, yes." Bella's heart began to race at the way he smiled at her, his teeth flashing white against his olive skin. How lovely that they both enjoyed the same thing. She could ask him about Lisbon some other time.

"Señora Lopez is very talented. Do you sing, Lady Isabella?"

Bella shook her head, feeling her cheeks heat. "No. I mean, yes, I have been taught to sing, but I could not compare with the Señora."

He took her hand and bowed over it, raising it to his lips. "You have other attractions, my lady. I hope to see you again soon."

"And I, you." Bella watched him go, aware of a tingling in the hand he had kissed. A touch on her shoulder and Jemima's voice beside her reminded her she should not stare so.

"He is good looking, is he not?" Jemima said, a twinkle in her eye.

"Yes, indeed. But so are many others," Bella added, conscious of Mr Carterton standing nearby and recalling his advice to be wary of Senhor da Gama.

Jemima took her arm. "Come, let us return to our seats."

Mr Carterton took a step forward. "Lady Isabella, may I have—?" His words were interrupted by the sound of a bell ringing. Lady Durridge was summoning her guests for the second half of the performance.

"Excuse us, Mr Carterton."

He frowned as Jemima spoke—so briefly that Bella wondered if she'd imagined it. She pondered that expression as they took their seats for the rest of the performance. Had he been about to reprimand her again for talking to Senhor da Gama? Then the strains of a complex piece caught her attention and she concentrated on the music.

CHAPTER 13

*L*ady Tregarth's butler showed Bella into the parlour. Molly followed, carrying a bag that held a set of old clothes. Langton waited in the mews behind the house.

"You are nicely on time," Lady Tregarth said approvingly. "Did you have any difficulty getting away without Lady Cerney?"

Bella shook her head. "Not at all, my lady. She is at a card party, and may not return until late."

"Good. Come upstairs with me. You, too…?" She looked at Molly with raised brows.

"Molly Simons, my lady." Molly curtseyed and followed the other two out of the room. She'd protested at Bella's plan to return to St Giles, only agreeing when she found out that Mr Carterton and Archer would be in charge this time.

"Are you sure about this, Bella?" Lady Tregarth asked, when they were all in a bedroom with the door closed behind them. Hairbrushes and bottles of perfume were set out on top of a dressing table, and Bella guessed that it was Lady Tregarth's own room. "Carterton has persuaded me he can keep you safe, but to venture into such an area? It is not wise, not at all."

Bella explained once more.

Lady Tregarth sighed. "I suppose you will not be dissuaded; you appear to be as headstrong as your brother. But you must promise me you will do exactly as Carterton tells you, or his man Archer."

Bella nodded.

"And you, Molly?" Lady Tregarth asked the maid.

"Mr Carterton and Mr Archer will keep us safe, my lady. I'll do exactly what they say."

"All right, then. If… when you find the woman, bring her to me. I can help you to arrange something appropriate for her. Molly, please bring in the leather bag from my dressing room."

The bag contained two sets of clothing. Bella wrinkled her nose as Molly held up a drab brown skirt and bodice, worn thin or torn in places, streaked with dirt and smelling faintly of damp. She'd much rather wear the old clothes she'd brought with her, but she could see the sense in donning these rags.

"You may keep your own undergarments on," Lady Tregarth said. "Of course, if you don't want to go…?" She raised a brow.

"Help me undress, Molly," Bella said. She unpinned her stomacher —she was not going to be put off now.

Molly, too, was required to change. They fastened their gowns and donned enveloping caps that had once been white, then Lady Tregarth brought out a covered bowl. She removed the lid, revealing a brownish powder.

"Dried soil from the garden," she explained. "Carterton said you must not look too clean."

Bella stared at the powder and then dipped her hands into it. When Lady Tregarth was satisfied that she had finished, her face bore streaks of dirt, with more under her fingernails and in the creases of her knuckles, and she looked as though she hadn't washed properly for weeks.

"It's going to take a long time to get clean again," Molly said as they inspected themselves in a mirror. Bella was both shocked and impressed at the way they now resembled some of the people they'd seen in St Giles three days ago, albeit much better nourished.

"I'll send a note to Marstone House saying you'll stay here for dinner." Lady Tregarth said. "That should give you plenty of time. Carterton will meet you in the mews."

Mr Carterton was rather cleaner than Bella, and with less ragged clothing. She put her chin up as he ran his eyes from her head to her toes, but he didn't comment on her appearance. He inspected Molly in the same way before turning back to her.

"Are you sure you want to do this?" he asked.

This was her last chance to back out of the venture, but she would not do so on her own account. "Will Molly be safe?"

"There are no absolute guarantees in this world, but I will do my best to keep both of you safe."

Somehow his admission that he could not guarantee their safety carried more weight than Senhor da Gama's bravado. He had an air of knowing what he was doing. Bella glanced at Molly, who nodded.

"Then yes, please."

He regarded her closely for a moment. "Very well."

A battered hackney waited at the end of the mews, Langton already seated next to the driver. Mr Carterton opened the door and climbed in, not waiting for Bella to precede him.

"He looks better than we do, my lady," Molly whispered as Bella gaped at this unexpected display of discourtesy. "A man like that wouldn't be polite to the likes of us."

"Of course." Bella climbed in, feeling stupid for not having realised that herself. "You had better both call me Bella," she said, as the hackney set off. It would not do to have Molly calling her 'my lady' where they were going.

She didn't recognise the streets they were passing through, but when they alighted the road was as narrow and run-down as the one where they'd stopped last time. That their disguises worked was obvious as soon as they began to walk down the street, Bella next to Mr Carterton and Langton with Molly. Passers-by regarded them without curiosity, and went on their way.

Mr Carterton looked alert, but not nervous, and that gave Bella confidence. She had almost begun to relax when she noticed a man ahead of them, leaning against a wall and looking their way. Another was partly hidden behind him. They were dressed in a similar fashion to her escort, and she wouldn't have thought them menacing had she seen them on Piccadilly or Bond Street, but anyone taking an interest in them here could be a threat.

The men pushed themselves upright as Bella's party drew nearer, and Bella's tension eased as she recognised Archer. The other man was taller and considerably broader than anyone else in their party, and had a bent nose. Bella was glad he was on their side.

The large man nodded his head towards Mr Carterton, who returned the greeting.

"Jarndyce. Have you got anything for me?"

"Not much. I found the Dawkins you mentioned, but she don't know where Fletcher lives, just that it's around here somewhere. I didn't go on to the address you had, like you said."

"Lead on, then."

They followed Jarndyce along streets as cramped and noisome as before. When they stopped outside a door with peeling paint, Langton nodded as if he recognised the place. Bella examined the house as Archer knocked. The windows needed washing, but there was less rubbish outside than in most of the streets they'd passed along.

A thin woman opened the door, her faded gown covered in a stained apron, although her hands and face were clean. Tiredness was evident in the lines around her eyes.

"We've come to see Ruby," Jarndyce said.

"What for? Can't be about the rent, Mr Jarndyce, she's not behind. What'll I tell—?"

"We're not here about the rent. We'll wait inside." Jarndyce pushed the door open as he spoke, forcing the woman to move backwards. He stepped into the dim hallway, the others following behind. The corners of the woman's mouth turned down, but she merely shrugged and headed for the back of the house.

The passage was cramped with six people waiting in it. Bella sniffed—a sickly scent in the air mingled with something more stomach-turning, as if someone had upset a chamber pot and not cleared it up.

"Smells like the paregoric my grandad used for his rheumatics," Molly said. "Plenty of laudanum in it."

The sound of a small child crying came from behind a closed door, then a louder wail. Curious, Bella pushed the door and peered around it, almost gagging at the stench. Rows of babies lay on the bare floor, each one wrapped in a thin blanket. A few were crying, but most appeared to be asleep. Slightly older children sat against the wall—most of these were dozing, too. The rest looked at her with blank eyes.

Bella stared, bewildered, until she felt a presence behind her. "I'll explain later," Mr Carterton said, low-voiced. "Come back into the hall."

She stepped back, and he reached around her to close the door. The smell still lingered, and Bella put a hand to her mouth, hoping she wasn't about lose her breakfast.

"I'm up to date, Jarndyce." The shrill voice came from a plump woman, advancing on them down the hall. "You've no business barging in like this."

"I want to find Sarah Fletcher, Ruby, and I got this address for her."

"Well, she ain't here. And if you find 'er, you can remind her she still owes me for the last weeks."

"Where does she live?"

Ruby shook her head. Bella caught the glint of a coin as Jarndyce held it up. "You help us find her, and we'll pay what she owes. And I know how much you charge, Ruby Doyle, so don't try anything on me."

Ruby sniffed. "In Saddler's Alley, last I heard. Had a nice little room on the ground floor."

"I know it," Jarndyce confirmed.

"But she ain't there now—I went to look when she didn't bring Billy in, nor my money."

Billy was a child? Perhaps the baby was Fletcher's younger brother.

"That'll be two shillings, Mr Jarndyce."

Jarndyce handed the coins over. "There'll be another two if you find her and send word to me."

"Do yer own searching. I ain't got the time to go looking for drabs like 'er. Now be off with the lot of yer."

The door slammed behind them as they left. Bella had so many questions, but Mr Carterton was talking to Jarndyce. She could wait—the important thing now was to find Fletcher.

Nick stopped at the corner of Saddler's Alley—a street indistinguishable from the others they'd walked along. He looked down at Lady Isabella. "We'll let Archer and Jarndyce find out where your Fletcher has gone. They'll do much better alone than with four people trailing after them."

Although she'd agreed to follow his orders, he was relieved when she nodded. He hadn't been sure she could keep to her promise. He still couldn't fully understand the impulse that had led him to offer his escort, although part of his reason was the justice of her complaint that she would never learn about the world if no-one was prepared to tell her anything. Showing her was better than merely explaining, and after this trip she would have a much better idea of the dangers of venturing into somewhere like St Giles.

"Mr Carterton?"

"Yes?" He kept his eyes on Archer and Jarndyce as they knocked on doors further down the street.

"Those babies, why were they there? Why did the house smell of paregoric?"

"Ruby looks after them while their parents work. The laudanum in the paregoric stops them crying."

"Poor little mites," the maid said, shaking her head.

"Does that happen in Over Minster?" Lady Isabella asked the maid.

"Not that I know of, m... er, Bella. There's more like to be grandmas to watch the little ones, or older sisters what don't work.

And they can take babies out to the fields with them if the weather's not too bad."

"The children at Ruby's will be put to work as soon as they're old enough," Nick added, looking at her. "As climbing boys for chimney sweeps, or trained as pick-pockets or thieves."

She appeared to be mulling that over, her brow creased. "The laudanum cannot be good for them, surely?"

"If it wasn't that, it would be gin," he said. "It's cheaper than feeding them properly and keeping them clean." The air in the room had almost choked him, and he'd been in these places before. The sight and smell must be well beyond Lady Isabella's experience.

"Oh. Fletcher left him… Billy… there?"

"I reckon Fletcher didn't have no choice," the maid said. "That Madame Donnard wouldn't have let her have Billy at work, no matter how quiet the mite was."

The maid had the right of it. With relief, he saw Jarndyce approaching—that would put an end to explanations for now.

"Found where she lodges, guv." He jerked a thumb over his shoulder, to where Archer waited half-way down the street. "What now?"

"I'll go in with Archer," Nick decided as they all walked down the street. "No offence, Jarndyce, but you're rather alarming."

Jarndyce grinned, as Nick knew he would. "It all helps with the job."

"Stay here, La… Bella," Nick said as they reached the doorway. "You've got Jarndyce and Langton—you'll be safe."

Lady Isabella opened her mouth, but just nodded.

They trod quietly up the stairs, their footsteps drowned by a shouted argument in a room on the second floor. On the top landing, Nick waved Archer to stand back, and pressed his ear to the door. If Fletcher had resorted to prostitution, interrupting her with a client would likely lose her the money for that transaction. Hearing nothing, he tapped on the door.

"Miss Fletcher?"

Still with his ear to the door, he heard footsteps.

"Who is it?" The voice was high, nervous.

"I've come from Lady Isabella." Nick kept his voice low.

"What for? I didn't steal from—"

"Miss Fletcher, we are here to help. Please, could we have this discussion inside your room?"

A bolt scraped, and the door opened an inch. All Nick could see was a slice of face with too-prominent cheekbones and eyes with dark shadows.

"What do you want? Why would Lady Isabella send you?"

Fletcher was distrustful, and who could blame her?

"She feels she was partly responsible for you losing your position, and she wants to help. Will you come with me?"

"You're not here to collect the money Madame said was hers?"

"No, Miss Fletcher. She—Lady Isabella—is waiting outside. Can I bring her up?"

"She's *here*? No, it's not right for someone—"

"Miss Fletcher? She is waiting downstairs." He didn't want to leave Lady Isabella outside any longer than he had to.

Fletcher sighed. "She'd best come up."

"Fetch her and the maid, Archer. Leave Jarndyce outside, though."

Archer hurried down the stairs. Nick waited on the landing; Fletcher didn't move away from the door until the two women appeared.

Bella tried not to stare as she and Mr Carterton followed Fletcher into her room, leaving Molly to wait on the landing. The seamstress looked even thinner than before. The ceiling was low, sloping in odd angles, with a tiny window that let in little light. A small table stood beneath the window, crowded with a pile of white fabric, scissors, a pin cushion, and spools of thread. A bundled blanket on the bed had a little head sticking out of it—Billy, sound asleep. The furnishings made plain that this was the only room Fletcher inhabited.

"Won't you sit down, my lady?" Fletcher pulled out the single chair.

Bella sat. Mr Carterton remained standing in the middle of the room—the only place he could stand upright.

"You should not be here, my lady." Fletcher examined the tattered and dirty clothing Bella wore, but did not comment.

"Nor should you," Bella stated. "If I hadn't asked you to stay and advise me, you would still have your position."

Fletcher looked down at her hands.

"That is true, is it not?"

Fletcher finally nodded. "Madame overheard me telling Dawkins I had enough money to pay... pay what I owed, and when I wouldn't tell her where I got it, she accused me of stealing."

That was what the new seamstress had said. "Why didn't you tell her?"

Fletcher looked at her with hopeless eyes. "She'd say I'd stolen it from her, because I was working for her when I came to you."

"That's not fair," Bella protested, but there was nothing she could do about it now. "Will you come with me, Miss Fletcher? And bring your brother?"

Fletcher's eyes widened, and Bella caught a sudden movement from Mr Carterton out of the corner of her eye. Billy was not her brother, then. She'd heard stories from Molly about village girls needing hurried marriages before a baby arrived; that might be the case here, with a man who would not do the decent thing.

"Bring Billy," Bella amended. "I don't know what we can do, but I will not let you starve." Nor would she let Fletcher sell herself.

Fletcher glanced at Mr Carterton, then back to Bella. "Thank you, my lady." She moved over to the table and folded up the fabric—a half-made shirt—wrapping it in a shawl together with a worn chemise hanging on a peg behind the door. Bella took the bundle, with only a token protest from Fletcher, leaving the woman to carry her son as they made their way down the stairs again.

Billy was suspiciously quiet as they all walked back to where the hackney waited, not stirring even when it started to rain. Bella pulled her shawl tighter as they hurried the last few steps and clambered into the carriage. Mr Carterton spoke to Jarndyce, and Bella saw coins changing hands before the big man touched his cap and walked briskly away.

Bella had questions, a great many, but it seemed indelicate to question Mr Carterton about the challenges facing the poor in front of Fletcher. She would have to wait.

CHAPTER 14

*M*r Carterton sent Bella straight into the Tregarths' house when the hackney pulled up in the mews, and Lady Tregarth whisked her upstairs. Once in Lady Tregarth's room she stripped off the dirty clothing, relieved to be rid of it. But the smell seemed to linger in her hair and on her skin, and she wanted nothing more than to immerse herself completely in hot water. Even then, she suspected the fetid stink of the room where the children were kept would stay with her for some time.

"Where's Fletcher?" she asked Molly as she washed her hands and face in the hot water Lady Tregarth had provided. She pulled a fresh chemise over her head and commenced the task of getting the dirt from beneath her fingernails.

"The housekeeper took her off," Molly said, combing out Bella's hair and attempting to restore it to its previous style.

"The boy—do they always sleep so soundly?"

"Things'd be easier if they did," Molly said. "When I was looking after our little ones, they was always making a fuss. I reckon Billy was given gin or laudanum, same as them others. No, hold still, my lady, do!"

"Sorry," Bella said. Somehow, Fletcher dosing her own child

seemed much worse. At least the child hadn't smelled as if he had soiled himself, not like the ones at Ruby Doyle's place.

"I don't reckon Fletcher had a choice there, neither," Molly went on. "If the babe was crying too much, other folks in the building would complain."

"Oh. Molly, do you think the baby is a—?"

"You'd have to ask Fletcher, my lady," Molly said. "But even if it was her fault she had the little mite, she's tried hard to look after him. There's some as would just let him die, or leave him at a workhouse. She'd have made a living for herself much easier without him."

Bella managed to keep her head still this time. She didn't need to look at Molly—the maid's tone had made it clear that she was serious. She struggled to believe that someone would be so desperate as to murder a baby, even though she knew it must be true. But why did Molly think a workhouse was a bad idea?

"There, my lady." Molly put the comb down and straightened Bella's fichu. "It'll take me a little while to get myself clean. Lady Tregarth said for you to join her downstairs when you're ready."

Lady Tregarth was not alone in her parlour. The other woman was familiar—Bella had been introduced to Lady Jesson during that first hectic day of morning calls, but had only exchanged a brief greeting. Lady Jesson had a friendly face, with light brown hair and laughing eyes. She wasn't much older than Bella, perhaps in her mid-twenties.

"Lady Isabella, I'm intrigued to meet you again," Lady Jesson said, as Bella made her curtsey and sat down.

"I'm afraid Maria saw you as you went upstairs," Lady Tregarth said. "I explained what you were doing."

"Oh."

"Don't worry, Lady Isabella. It sounds most interesting." Lady Jesson paused, her eyes on Bella's face. "I can see that 'interesting' is not the right word. It is commendable to wish to help."

Bella glanced at Lady Tregarth, unsure of how much she should say.

"Maria will not repeat anything that you wish to keep between us."

"I never knew babies would be kept like that," Bella said. Seeing the poverty in the streets on her first trip had been shocking enough. The babies, and the tiny room where Fletcher lived…

"Mr Carterton asked me to pass on his apologies for leaving without speaking to you," Lady Tregarth said.

Bella felt a pang of disappointment. She'd wanted to thank him for finding Fletcher, and also for telling her so much that others would not. She must be sure to thank him for his help next time they met.

"But he did tell me—tell us—what you'd seen," Lady Tregarth said. "My housekeeper is making sure Fletcher and her son are cleaned and fed, but we need to decide what is to be done with them."

"I don't know what to do, my lady. I'd employ her if I could, but I already have Molly. And there's Billy as well…"

"She cannot stay here, because Billy has no father," Lady Tregarth said. "My housekeeper talked to her, and thinks it is not Fletcher's fault. However it is not good for the other staff to have an unmarried mother and her babe around the place—it sets a bad example."

"You would employ a seamstress?" Lady Jesson asked Bella.

"She was a lady's maid." Bella described her encounters with Fletcher.

"I thought you looked better dressed than when we first met," Lady Jesson said. She turned to Lady Tregarth. "Send Fletcher to me—I could use her advice. I'll talk with her, and I may be able to do something if she is as she seems. If we can find somewhere for Billy first, there shouldn't be a problem with my staff."

"Thank you, Maria. That will be a great help."

"Lady Tregarth…" Bella paused, not sure how to word the question, or even if Lady Tregarth was the right person to ask. "Molly said that some women in Fletcher's position would have left the baby at a workhouse? Why didn't Fletcher do that?"

Lady Tregarth's lips turned down at the corners.

"I… I'm sorry, my lady, if that is not a proper question." Bella hoped she had not offended her hostess.

"It is a question too few people ask," Lady Tregarth said. "You would have to ask Fletcher herself, but I can think of a couple of reasons. One is that the local workhouses usually send infants into the country to be looked after. I imagine Fletcher would not want to be separated from her child unless she had no other way of providing for him."

Bella wondered what happened to the children, but didn't feel she could ask Lady Tregarth to give too many details. "You said a couple of reasons, my lady?"

Lady Tregarth rubbed her forehead and sighed. "Isabella, do not let Lady Cerney or your father suspect you have been talking about such things." She waited until Bella nodded before going on. "Most parishes will try to locate the father of an unborn child and make him contribute to supporting it."

That seemed sensible.

"But it appears that Fletcher did not conceive the child willingly," Lady Jesson put in. "All the more reason to make the man support it, you might say. But he will claim that she led him on, or give some other excuse, and the *men* in charge of the workhouse are likely to take his part. She could end up being branded a... a loose woman."

"That's not fair!"

"No, it is not," Lady Tregarth said. "Unfortunately that is the way of the world." She turned to Lady Jesson. "Now, Maria, Isabella is staying to dinner—do you wish to?"

"Yes please." Lady Jesson smiled at Bella. "I've heard rumours about your brother's efforts to thwart your father's plans a couple of years ago. You can tell me more—if you wish—and how you are getting on in society. I heard that Lord Narwood and Lord Barnton are both taking an interest in you, much to the dismay of Miss Yelland and Miss Quinn."

"They're welcome to them," Bella muttered.

Lady Jesson laughed. "Perhaps they deserve each other. Well, you have not been about in society much. I'm sure I can help you find someone better."

~

When Nick returned to Brook Street, Lord Carterton was sitting in the parlour, dozing in his chair with a newspaper discarded on the floor beside him. Nick crossed the room to pick up the paper, wondering whether he should wake him or not. If he needed his sleep, should he be in bed?

A lump rose to his throat as he contemplated the lines on his father's face, and the pallor of his skin. Father had been nearly fifty when Nick was born, so it was inevitable that he would die when Nick was still relatively young. Inevitable, but hopefully not imminent, not just yet.

Let him sleep, Nick thought as he crept out of the parlour. He asked Mowbray to have a bath sent up and went to his room. A soak in hot water would help to relieve some of the remaining tension of the expedition. He'd been in St Giles many times before, but never with the responsibility of looking after a pair of young women.

They'd both taken things remarkably well, although Lady Isabella had clearly been shocked. The maid, too, although not nearly as much; Nick guessed she'd seen poverty in her home village, but to him it seemed much worse when there were so many crowded together, and at the mercy of unscrupulous landlords.

Father was awake when Nick returned to the parlour, and seemed ready for a conversation. "Did you enjoy your drive?"

Nick pulled up a chair and poured them both a small brandy. "Yes, I did." In a way—they had rescued two people from a hellish future. There were so many more, though.

"Who were you with? I've heard you're seeing the youngest Marstone girl."

"I'm not courting her, Father." Someone so headstrong would be completely unsuitable.

His father did not reply, but merely gazed at him and waited.

"Wingrave, her brother, asked me to keep an eye on her while he's away on business."

"She has a father and an aunt," his father prodded.

Nick sighed—he should have known he would not get away with such a brief explanation. "You know what Marstone's like. He'll marry her off according to what he sees as his advantage, without reference to her own wishes."

"A most unpleasant man," Lord Carterton agreed. "And I suppose the aunt will do as Marstone commands. What are you doing to help?"

"Not much," Nick had to admit. "Merely keeping in touch and seeing who is showing an interest."

His father's brows rose. "And if Marstone does pick someone unsuitable?"

Nick ran a finger around the top of his neckcloth. "I'm not sure. It depends who it is."

"How did you help Wingrave get rid of…what was his name? The one he picked a couple of years ago for Lady Theresa?"

"Drayton. I helped Wingrave win money from him at cards—that gave Wingrave something to use against him. But that wouldn't have worked with a better player, or less of a drunkard."

"Hmm. Marstone might pick a decent man, then—"

Nick snorted in disbelief.

"He did pick you for Lady Elizabeth," Lord Carterton pointed out. "All you'd have to do in that case would be to point out to the man that he'd be getting an unwilling bride."

If only things could be that easy.

"Well, you can address the problem if the need arises, but come to me, Nick, if I can help. There is not much I could do personally, but not all my friends have yet turned their toes up. I might be able to find a weakness that you can use."

"I will, thank you."

"So what did you talk about with the Marstone girl?" His father was nothing if not persistent once he got an idea into his head.

"It wasn't a drive in the park. I… well, I escorted Lady Isabella into St Giles, to find—"

"St Giles? Good grief, boy, what were you thinking to do such a thing? What in heaven's name did she want to go there for?"

Nick explained, omitting all reference to Fletcher's bastard child. His father's frown increased as the tale proceeded.

"Nick, it's bad enough you venturing into those places, but to take an innocent young girl…" He shook his head. "Spirited lass, eh?"

Nick shrugged. Spirited she was, but she had also been affected by what she'd seen. He hadn't wanted to talk to her in front of the seamstress, and Lady Tregarth had taken her away as soon as they set foot in the house. He hoped that Lady Tregarth's trust in Lady Jesson was justified—Wingrave would certainly be displeased if the expedition resulted in gossip about his sister.

He needed to reassure himself that she was none the worse for the expedition. Lady Tregarth would know—he'd send her a note later.

"So if you're not courting her, who *are* you considering?"

"Miss Roper. Of good family, and makes sensible conversation. I'm taking her for a drive tomorrow."

"Good, good. Let me know how you go on, Nick. Pass me the paper before you go, will you?"

As he left the room, Nick suppressed the thought that sensible conversation wasn't always interesting.

CHAPTER 15

"I met Lady Jesson again at Lady Tregarth's house yesterday," Bella said, sipping tea while her aunt carried out her usual morning sorting of the invitations and calling cards she'd received.

"Jesson?" Aunt Aurelia's eyes narrowed in thought. "Jesson is a baron, if I recall correctly. A bit wild, from all accounts."

"She has invited me to drive with her this afternoon."

"That is good. Lady Tregarth must approve of her, and it will allow you to be seen. Better than Miss Yelland or Miss Quinn. Spiteful cats."

Bella blinked at the unexpectedly candid statement.

"I've heard some of the things they say about you, Bella," Aunt Aurelia added. "I'm not unobservant, or stupid, you know."

"Yes...I mean, no." She cleared her throat. "Aunt, may I use the calèche? Lady Jesson..." Maria had been very honest with her yesterday about the state of her finances, but it didn't seem right to repeat any of it to her aunt.

"Not a feather to fly with, I know." Aunt Aurelia nodded. "I will not be needing it, so you may as well give the coachman something to do. Now, you have a few more days until Lady Yelland's ball—it would not do to make missteps in public."

"I have been paying attention to my lessons, Aunt." She was

looking forward to dancing with someone other than Herr Weber, and to wearing her new ball gown. Would Senhor da Gama be there?

"You must be sure to dance with Lord Barnton, and Mr Carterton. They seem the most likely men to make an offer for you." She poked at a letter on the table, its seal broken. "Your father wants a list of your suitors."

Bella's anticipation faded. Could she not be allowed to enjoy herself for a time, without being reminded that the purpose of all this was to find a husband?

"I'll omit Lord Narwood, if you wish."

"Please."

"Although if he's seriously interested, it's possible he's written to Marstone. We'll know soon."

Bella pushed away the remains of her breakfast. She wanted to see Mr Carterton to thank him for yesterday's expedition, and she should tell him about Lord Narwood's interest at the same time.

Why didn't Papa just put an advertisement in the newspaper? *One daughter, with dowry. Available for marriage to man of suitable status.*

"It does feel grand to be riding in a carriage like this," Molly said as Langton descended from the rear step to knock on Lady Jesson's door. Aunt Aurelia had insisted that Molly accompany her as far as Lady Jesson's house. Bella was wondering if she should ask Molly to wait here, when the door opened wider and Lady Jesson came out, followed by her own maid. It wasn't until they both climbed into the carriage that Bella recognised Fletcher. She wore the same drab garment as yesterday, but her face looked different. The lines of care had faded—she almost looked happy.

"Have you arranged something?" Bella asked, leaning her head close to Lady Jesson so her father's coachman could not hear.

"The wet nurse I used for the boys lives nearby," Lady Jesson replied, her voice as low as Bella's. "Billy is with her for now. Fletcher is going to be my personal seamstress for a while."

Bella glanced at Lady Jesson's redingote—her friend did not appear to be in need of new clothing.

"Oh, this is several years out of fashion," Lady Jesson said, allowing her voice to rise to normal levels. "Fletcher can update my wardrobe and make some new gowns for much less than I would pay at a mantua-maker." She glanced at Fletcher, sitting opposite. "I suspect they will suit me better, as well."

Fletcher smiled. Bella turned her head away, swallowing hard. The things Fletcher had coped with made her own troubles seem less desperate. She was right to have helped her, even if she hadn't gone about it in the safest way.

"Her advice to me was very useful."

"You need not be without it," Lady Jesson said. "We will be great friends, I'm sure. You must call me Maria."

"Thank you."

"I've brought Fletcher along so we can take a look at current fashions. We will dissect everyone's appearance ruthlessly..."

Bella chuckled. This drive promised to be much more fun than being put on show by her aunt.

"...and both you and I will learn the tricks that will best suit us."

An hour later they had circled the park several times, discussing hair powder and the height of one's coiffure, the shape of stomachers and necklines, colours, and patterns. Fletcher had been silent at first, but Molly had asked her how to achieve different styles, and she had soon gained confidence. Bella had spotted Lord Barnton riding in the distance, and was happy that he had not noticed them. Mr Carterton, too, was enjoying the sunshine, driving a phaeton with Jemima Roper by his side—she fleetingly wondered what they were talking about, before Maria drew her attention to the tallest plumes she'd yet seen on a bonnet. Her enjoyment was only dimmed a little by the sight of Senhor da Gama standing by a carriage with the same lady she'd seen him with a couple of times before. As she watched, Senhor da Gama bowed, and the carriage drew away.

"What is so fascinating that two of you must needs stare at it?" Maria asked.

Bella turned to see that Fletcher, too, was looking at the carriage.

"That was Lady Milton, I think," Maria added.

"Yes, my lady," Fletcher said. "She was my last mistress."

The woman who had taught Fletcher some of her sense of style. "Is she the one who turned you off, Fletcher?" Bella kept her voice low.

"She had no choice, my lady. No-one will have a maid who's with child, and the master would have believed the footm—" She broke off. "She gave me a reference, but that wasn't any use when I was increasing and then had a babe to look after."

Fletcher still felt some affection for her previous mistress, it seemed, in spite of the circumstances.

"Who was that with her?" Maria asked. "I'm sure I've seen him before."

"Senhor da Gama," Bella said. "The son of a Portuguese viscount."

Maria raised an eyebrow.

"Lady Brigham introduced him to society," Bella said, not understanding why she felt defensive. "He said Lady Milton was a family friend."

"I didn't hear of any Portuguese connections when I was working there," Fletcher said, then bit her lips as if afraid she'd spoken out of turn.

"Hmm," Maria said. "I always thought Sir Edward didn't pay her enough attention. Spends too much time at Whitehall, from what I've heard."

"What's at Whitehall?" Molly asked, to Bella's relief. Will had mentioned Whitehall in some of his letters, but she hadn't known what he was referring to.

"It's where a lot of government offices are," Maria explained. Bella pressed her lips together and looked away—that was something she should have known, if her father hadn't kept her shut up at Marstone Park all these years.

Bella turned her gaze back to Senhor da Gama. Another open carriage pulled up beside him, and the lady in it extended her hand over the side. Senhor da Gama bent over it.

"That's Lady Sudbury," Maria said. "*Not* another family friend, I suspect."

Lady Sudbury turned to look back at Senhor da Gama as the carriage set off again, raising a hand in farewell.

"She could be," Bella said, with an odd feeling that she was trying to justify something that was wrong. "Many men kiss a lady's hand, do they not?" Senhor da Gama had kissed *her* hand.

Maria did not answer Bella's question. "I've seen enough fashions for one day," she said. "I mean to let Fletcher off in Bond Street to buy some fabric, if your coachman will allow, that is. And you must join me for tea before you go home."

Relieved at the change of subject, Bella happily agreed.

Nick read through his conclusion one last time, then shuffled the pages of his final report into order. Outside, the sun shone on the people and carriages in the street; he was due to call on Miss Roper in an hour, which gave him enough time to deliver the report to Gilbert on the way.

Miss Roper was ready when he arrived, dressed in a deep green redingote that brought out flecks of green in her eyes and set off her dark hair. They exchanged the usual pleasantries, and Nick escorted her out to his phaeton.

It wasn't far to Hyde Park, and their conversation during the drive started with the usual subjects—the weather, her enjoyment of the musicale, other entertainments that she planned to attend.

Nick stopped listening as he reined the horses in at the back of a crush of stationary vehicles around the park gates. "Finch, get down and find out what's going on."

The groom jumped down and hurried off.

"I'm sorry, Miss Roper, you were saying...?"

"Nothing of import, Mr Carterton. Oh, look, the carriages are beginning to move."

Nick tried to spot Finch in the crowd still milling around the gate, but couldn't see him. He could not remain here without becoming an obstruction himself, so he flicked the reins to start the horses moving, drawing to a halt again a little way beyond the gates. Finch found them there before Nick had run out of things to say about the most recent opera he'd seen.

"It was a poor woman with a child, sir, trying to beg from the carriages. A gentleman attempted to push her away, and she fell." He shook his head. "She's a bit cut and bruised, sir."

Nick felt in his pocket and handed the groom some coins. "See she gets some help. Wait here when you've finished. I'll pick you up on the way back."

Finch set off back to Park Lane as Nick drove further into the park. "Do you ride, Miss Roper?" he asked. Could that be something they had in common?

"A little, when we are in the country, but I prefer being in a carriage."

Oh, well.

"Papa says it is too expensive to stable riding horses in Town."

That was honest, at least. "Where is your family's home?"

Nick listened as she described a house near Cambridge, with more enthusiasm for its proximity to the city than for the surrounding countryside. That was a shame—he loved the position of his father's house on the High Weald and enjoyed the time he spent there.

"Do you enjoy riding, Mr Carterton?" she asked, after an awkward pause.

"Very much. When I'm in Sussex, particularly." Given that she didn't care for the activity, what more was there to say? He could describe Oakley Place, he supposed, but it didn't sound as if she would enjoy living there if…

No, that was getting too far ahead of himself. Much too far.

"It was good of you to help that woman, Mr Carterton."

Nick glanced at her—although her words were approving, her tone had been uncertain. She was looking at the horses, not at him.

"It will help for a little while," he said.

"Why does she not go to the workhouse? Mama says that is why we pay poor rates, to have such people taken care of. She says I should not give money on the street, as it only encourages them to beg and cause a nuisance to decent people."

Like mother, like daughter?

"What is *your* opinion, Miss Roper?"

She gazed at him for a moment without speaking. "I... I suppose she is right. I had not really considered it."

Nick nodded. That was what any well-bred young woman was supposed to say. The aim was obedience to parents, and then to a husband—so why did he find her answer unsatisfying?

"Does your father take an interest in politics?" He asked the question, even though he guessed what her answer would be.

A small crease formed between her brows. "I don't know. He would not discuss such a subject with me."

As he'd expected.

"He spends a lot of his time at his club, I think." She glanced at the sky. "Do you think it will come on to rain? The clouds are thickening."

They didn't look like rainclouds to Nick. Nevertheless, he took the hint, agreeing with her as he turned the phaeton back towards the gate. He felt a trifle guilty at his relief in drawing the expedition to a close. They had conversed well enough at the musicale, about singers —perhaps he should accompany her to a museum or gallery, where they would have something in front of them to discuss.

"So, is Miss Roper the most beautiful woman you've seen?" Lord Carterton asked, as the dishes were removed and Hobson set the port decanter on the table.

Rather taken aback by this direct approach, Nick wasn't sure what to say. It was her calm demeanour and pleasant manners that had drawn him to her, not her features, attractive though they were.

"I see she is not," his father said. "That is promising."

Nick set his glass down. Was his father's mind beginning to wander? "How so?"

"A match based mainly on physical attraction is unlikely to be a happy one."

"I'm not about to offer for her, Father. A week or so isn't long enough to make such a decision."

"It can be. It only took me a couple of meetings to decide that Catherine was right for me, and I never regretted that, even though we had no children."

Nick found it difficult to imagine his father as a young man, courting his first bride. "What about...?" Should he ask? It mattered to him that his own mother had also been a good choice. "How long did you take to decide on Mama?"

"A little longer," his father admitted, "but that was an excellent decision, too. She was so much younger than me, I wanted to be sure. Now, tell me more about Miss Roper."

"She would make a good wife. She wouldn't cause scandals or gossip, or outspend her allowance, I think. And she's punctual."

"Good heavens, boy, you sound as if you're appointing a secretary!"

"You wanted me to marry and get an heir, Father." He had expected his father to be glad he was getting on with the business of choosing a wife, not to criticise the woman he was considering.

"I want you to be happy, Nick, not simply to choose someone who can tell the time! If you're going to do that, I can interview some candidates for you and inform you which you should accept."

Father looked serious, but Nick caught the twinkle in his eyes. "Point taken," he said, with a smile.

"Joking aside, my boy, if your feelings for the woman are so tepid, do not offer for her. I want you to make a suitable match, but that means one in which you can be happy. Lady Isabella sounds a much more interesting woman."

She was attractive, certainly, but he shook his head. "Too impulsive, Father."

"Hmm. Well, I am not so desperate for an heir I would see you rush into something that is not right for you."

Nick took a mouthful of port. He was relieved that his father wasn't pressing him to make a decision, but he did have to marry at some time. Miss Roper was the only potential wife he had met so far who seemed to meet his requirements in any way. She would organise his household well without bothering him, and leave him plenty of time for his own pursuits.

"I recall Somerton—you won't remember him, Nick. Chose a wife because she was sensible, but..."

Nick listened to his father's rambling story, relieved that tonight's interrogation seemed to be over.

CHAPTER 16

*N*ick called on Lady Tregarth the following day, surprised to find Lady Isabella also present when he was shown into the parlour. She did not appear to be suffering any ill effects from their expedition as she greeted him with a smile, the cream and primrose stripes on her gown adding to her cheerful air.

"I thought it would be better for you to talk to Isabella yourself," Lady Tregarth explained, once the normal greetings had been exchanged and the tea tray brought. "You will be pleased to know that Fletcher is settled with Lady Jesson."

That was good news. "Are you recovered from your trip, Lady Isabella?"

"Yes. I have to thank you, sir—I could not have done it without your assistance."

"You are welcome." He had made a better job of it than that Portuguese, although the man's sword-wielding had probably cut a more dashing figure. "I hope your brother doesn't find out—I hardly think he would approve."

She smiled, a glint of mischief in her eyes. "I won't tell him if you don't."

He could not help but laugh.

"Mr Carterton..." The twinkle had gone from Lady Isabella's eyes, and she looked serious. "What do you know of Lord Narwood?"

"Narwood? I don't know him, I'm afraid. Is he taking an interest?"

"I fear so. I... I cannot like him."

He didn't enquire further—her expression was telling enough. Her dislike was clearly more than the boredom she felt when with Barnton.

"He is in his forties," Lady Tregarth said. "Wealthy enough, as far as I know, but I have heard little about him. I will enquire."

Nick took a breath—he had hoped Wingrave would return before he needed to take any real action. "As will I," he promised. He could start by asking his father.

"Thank you," Lady Isabella said. "Could I ask you some more questions?"

Lady Tregarth chuckled. "Do not look so dismayed, Mr Carterton. Isabella only wants information; she is not planning another expedition."

"Ask, then." He trusted he would not have to discuss anything too improper.

"I was wondering how you knew a man like Jarndyce. What is his occupation?"

He hadn't expected that, but he saw no harm in explaining. "Jarndyce is a rent collector. As you can imagine, his size is a great encouragement to those who are reluctant to pay." He'd meant the comment in jest, but her quick frown showed she had not taken it that way. "He does have a heart, Lady Isabella, and does his best to help those who cannot pay through no fault of their own." But not those who'd wasted their money on drink or whores.

"How do you come to know him? Does he collect rent for you?"

"I do not own any such properties. I was introduced to him by Thomas Gilbert; he is a member of parliament who has recently got a bill passed to improve the running of workhouses. He asked me to analyse information that men such as Jarndyce, and others, provide about the conditions in St Giles and Seven Dials."

"Why are you interested, Mr Carterton? You told me yourself that most people of our class are not concerned about the poor."

That was a more personal question than he'd expected, but his reasons were no secret. "I used to play with some local lads when I was a child. One of them… well, his mother had to resort to the workhouse after his father was transported for poaching on a neighbouring estate."

She nodded, her brow still creased in thought. "But poaching is illegal, so why…? I mean, people are supposed to obey the law."

"Too many mouths to feed," he said. He watched the corners of her mouth turn down as she filled in the rest of the story for herself.

"They can't win," she said, then took a deep breath. "How did you know Lady Tregarth would help?"

"Maria and I contribute to several charities to aid the poor," Lady Tregarth put in. "Mr Carterton advises those charities from time to time."

Nick awaited Lady Isabella's response with interest. Miss Roper, he was sure, would change the subject at this point, if the conversation had even progressed this far. Would she have cared about the fate of a scarcely known seamstress?

"Lady Tregarth said that babies are sent away from workhouses into the country."

"Yes, it is thought they will be healthier out of the smoke and disease of the city," he explained. "Unfortunately, that is often not the case and many of them die. Then there is the recent practice of sending children off to be apprenticed, often to distant parts of the country, where their parents may never see them again. All in the name of keeping the costs down."

"Is that what Mr Gilbert's bill is for—to increase the money?"

Nick glanced at Lady Tregarth, still surprised by the interest Lady Isabella was showing. He'd expected her involvement to end with the rescue of her seamstress.

"I can explain, if you have another appointment, Mr Carterton."

"No, thank you, I am quite happy to talk on the subject. I do not wish to bore either of you."

"I do not mind," Lady Tregarth said. "And Isabella wants to know."

Half an hour later, with a throat dry from talking, Nick finally took his leave. He'd ranged from corrupt contractors to the differences between indoor and outdoor relief, and explained the plans for introducing guardians to ensure proper use of funds in the workhouses. Lady Isabella had listened intently, and asked questions that showed she had understood most of it.

It was only as he walked home that he recalled the note from Lady Isabella's maid five days ago—there was an expedition to Vauxhall planned this evening. He should go, to see who might be courting her —and he had yet to pass on Talbot's warning about the Portuguese. Would she enjoy an evening at the Pleasure Gardens as much as she'd enjoyed the theatre and the musicale?

As he entered the Handel Piazza at Vauxhall, Nick could hear Lady Cerney berating a waiter for poor service. She sat at the back of the supper box, with Mrs Roper beside her. Nick grimaced at the sight of Lord Barnton in the party—he'd had the misfortune to be subjected to the man's lectures on several occasions. Miss Roper listened with apparent interest, but Lady Isabella was looking out across the piazza, her attention on the people passing by.

He approached the box as the hapless waiter left at a trot.

"Carterton!" Lady Cerney said, the gleam of speculation in her eyes making Nick feel wary. "You are acquainted with Lord Barnton, I think?"

"Indeed," Barnton said. "Evening, Carterton."

"Join us if you wish," Lady Cerney went on. "I'm sure that sluggard waiter will be back soon."

"Thank you."

Lady Isabella moved down the bench, and Nick sat. Lord Barnton picked up the bottle on the table and topped up Lady Cerney's glass. "Do have some more wine while we wait, my lady. Mrs Roper." The two young women had glasses of what looked like lemonade in front of them.

"Is this your first visit here, Lady Isabella?" Nick asked. "Are you enjoying it?"

"It's wonderful," she said, eyes sparkling with excitement. "But I wish we could walk around. Jemima tells me there's a cascade that mimics a waterfall."

"Indeed there is." He pulled out his watch. "Although it will not be in operation for another hour or more."

"I would be happy to show you the triumphal arches, Lady Isabella," Barnton offered. "Or would you like to view the paintings in the Saloon?"

Nick hid his amusement at the brief flash of dismay that crossed Lady Isabella's face. "The triumphal arches, please," she said firmly. "Jemima, will you come, too? Aunt, may I go?"

"I don't see why not, as long as you all stay together."

"I will join you, if I may," Nick said. Lady Isabella might not take too unkindly to his warning about da Gama if he rescued her from one of Barnton's improving lectures.

Barnton took Lady Isabella's arm, and Nick offered his to Miss Roper. They had not gone ten paces when Barnton stopped by the statue of Handel.

"You have heard of Handel, I assume, Lady Isabella?"

"Of course, my lord." Lady Isabella pointed at the plump cherub sitting at the composer's feet. "Is that his son?"

"My dear Lady Isabella, that should more correctly be called a putto. It represents the inspiration..."

Nick shook his head as Barton continued. How was she to enjoy the evening if they could not walk ten yards without a lecture? Miss Roper, standing beside him, was again listening with concentration. He supposed Barnton's discourse might be interesting, if only it were not delivered in such a pompous manner.

"Handel's rehearsal for the Music for the Royal Fireworks was carried out here," Barnton finished, "witnessed by thousands of people."

"How fascinating," Lady Isabella said, and Nick's lips twitched at the hint of sarcasm he detected. "Did you attend?"

Nick suppressed a snort of laughter as Barnton scowled down at her. "That took place over thirty years ago, Lady Isabella."

"Shall we go and see the arches?" Nick interjected, hoping to fend off another lecture.

Bella took Lord Barnton's arm again as they set off down the walk, wishing she could change places with Jemima. Mr Carterton had talked for half an hour or more this morning, about workhouses and the poor, without losing her attention. Why was it so much more difficult to listen to Lord Barnton? The topics were interesting, but she always felt he was condescending to someone of lesser intellect by imparting his greater knowledge.

But she was with him now, and must make the best of it. The surroundings were beautiful, the path illuminated by the many lanterns suspended in the trees. They were bright enough to hide the stars, but looked like huge stars themselves. The strains of music coming from the central orchestra enhanced the magical effects.

Bella looked into the supper boxes they passed, trying to make out the paintings on the back of each one.

"Each box has a different image," Lord Barnton informed her. "They depict…"

She sighed—could she not be left to simply look, and enjoy the music?

"…British life and traditions. There are other paintings…"

Her heart sped up as she spotted Senhor da Gama in one of the boxes. He had his back to her, and was facing Lady Milton, but she would know him anywhere. *Was* Lady Milton only a family friend, or was she something more?

"…scenes from Shakespeare's plays…"

Maria Jesson and her husband were sitting with them. Bella looked away, trying to focus on what Lord Barnton was now saying about the arches. Senhor da Gama was nothing more than a friendly acquaintance—it shouldn't matter to her who he was with.

"…canvas and wood, but the effect…"

141

"Lady Isabella!"

Bella released Lord Barnton's arm and turned. Maria was following them.

"Lady Jesson." Lord Barnton looked down his nose at her, his mouth a thin line. "I am showing Lady Isabella around the gardens."

"I'm so sorry, my lord." Maria curtseyed, looking serious to anyone who did not know her. "But I wanted to give Lady Isabella a message."

"I do not approve of gossip, madam, and you are—"

"Lady Jesson is my friend, Lord Barnton," Bella interrupted, taken aback by his hostility.

"She is—"

"Come, Barnton," Mr Carterton said behind them. "Miss Roper and I would be interested to learn more about these arches."

Lord Barnton glared at Maria, then took up a position next to Jemima. "The paintings on the arches…"

"Poor Jemima," Bella said quietly, linking arms with Maria and walking on. "One never has to think what to say to Lord Barnton. And I learn so much…"

"…whether or not you wish to! But how heroic of Carterton," Maria giggled. "Perhaps you should encourage him as a suitor?"

Mr Carterton? No, he was not interested in her—no more than a brother would be.

"Why does Lord Barnton dislike you so?" Bella asked.

Maria shrugged. "I do have a bit of a reputation as a gossip." She glanced sideways at Bella. "But I do not repeat things about my friends, or anything that would be damaging or is untrue. Lord Barnton was on the point of making an… arrangement… last year, when gossip reached his inamorata that made her back out. For some reason, he thinks it was me."

"Gossip spoiled his marriage plans?" Bella could understand him being bitter at that.

"Er, not exactly. The… the woman who backed out was—still is—a well-known opera singer. Barton was furious when she took up with someone else."

"Oh."

"It is quite common, you know, for men of our class to keep a mistress." She put her head closer to Bella's. "Just think, if you were married to Barnton, wouldn't you be happy if he spent a lot of his time elsewhere?"

Bella bit her lips and nodded. Maria was trying to distract her, she knew, but it wasn't working. "Why did you come after us?"

"I saw you look into our box. Bella, I know you like Senhor da Gama, but he is definitely pursuing Lady Milton. And he's been seen with Lady Sudbury several times, too. I don't want you to be hurt."

Bella could not deny what she had seen. "I thought he liked me," she said, just managing to keep a wobble from her voice.

"He may, but when a man is... befriending three women..." Maria sighed. "Bella, he is using at least two of you, possibly all three."

"Using?" Using *her*? She swallowed against a lump in her throat—she'd thought Senhor da Gama liked her for herself.

"I don't know what he wants, Bella. A dalliance, perhaps? From what I know of Lady Milton, he'll be out of luck with her. Fletcher speaks highly of her, too. She's lonely, but I don't think she's foolish enough to risk her marriage."

"What about Lady Sudbury?"

"Oh, he'll have no trouble there. She's..." Maria broke off and bit her lip.

"No-one tells me anything," Bella protested, even though she knew she was being unfair.

"Very well. Lady Sudbury is known for having numerous lovers. Sudbury doesn't care."

"Oh."

"Has Senhor da Gama said anything... significant to you, Bella?"

"Nothing about courting me, no." Although the way he gazed into her eyes sometimes had led her to think he might... or hope he might. "He said that Lady Milton was a family friend."

"Fletcher hadn't heard of any Portuguese connections," Maria reminded her. "And he's not acting as if she's *only* a friend."

Bella sighed. "So that may not have been true—probably *isn't* true. But what could he want from me?"

143

"Your dowry?"

Bella blinked back tears as she looked away.

Maria laid a hand on her arm. "If it's any consolation, I think he *does* like you, Bella. It's possible that he may not be using you at all."

"It's silly to repine," Bella said, taking a deep breath. "Papa would never approve of a match." That didn't stop her from feeling hurt, though.

"What have you talked about with him?" Maria asked.

"Paintings... all sorts of things, really." He'd been amusing to talk to—what they talked about hadn't mattered.

"Hmm." Lady Jesson tapped her chin with a finger. "If he was really after your dowry, why would he risk being seen with another woman like that? It has put you off him a little, I think."

Bella nodded miserably.

"And why Lady Milton? If he were Spanish, or French, I might be suspicious—Sir Edward is something in the Admiralty. But she is also an attractive woman—there need be no other reason he is pursuing her." Maria glanced behind them. "I think we have conferred long enough. Do think about what I have said, Bella, next time Senhor da Gama approaches you."

"Are you ready to return, ladies?"

Bella turned to find that only Mr Carterton and Jemima stood behind them.

"I think Lord Barnton has imparted his stock of knowledge for the evening," Mr Carterton said, only a twitch of his lips betraying his amusement.

"You were most generous, sir, to listen on our behalf." Maria curt-seyed with a smile. "But, yes, I should return to my husband."

They walked back down the avenue in companionable silence, Maria leaving them as they passed her supper box. Bella could not enjoy the lights and the music as she had earlier; her mind was on what Maria had said. What did Senhor da Gama really want with her?

She tried to put that question from her mind when they reached their box. Lord Barnton was already there, looking rather disgruntled. Bella felt a brief stab of guilt—she hadn't been polite to him. She didn't want to marry him, but he might be the only alternative to Lord Narwood. She should endeavour to make up for her deliberate obtuseness earlier.

As Jemima slipped into the bench to sit next to her mother, Bella sat down next to Lord Barnton, ignoring his raised brows.

"My lord, I was sorry to have missed your explanation of the arches," she said. "Won't you tell me about them?"

Nick was in two minds whether to rejoin the party, but Lady Isabella's words decided him. He wasn't about to sit through Barnton's lecture again, not when there was little chance of having a private word with her. Instead, he set off back towards the triumphal arch—he hadn't missed Lady Isabella's hesitation when she noticed Senhor da Gama, and the man had still been in that box when they passed it on their return. If he couldn't warn Lady Isabella about the Portuguese, he could try to satisfy Talbot's request to know more about what the man was up to.

He wasn't sorry to be free of the company. Conversation with Miss Roper had been pleasant, but had lacked any spark, and he had once more run out of things to say that he thought might interest her. His conversations with Lady Isabella were making him realise that it was possible to discuss more serious matters with some women, and at the same time her sense of the absurd was very refreshing.

When he reached the box, he saw that da Gama was now alone in it with a woman he didn't recognise. Fawning over her, too—he was toying with that woman's affections, or with Lady Isabella's. Or both, Nick supposed. Tamping down his rising anger, he walked on a few paces, looking for somewhere he could stand to watch.

He settled on standing beneath one of the trees across the walk from the box, just beyond the pool of light from a nearby lamp. The people strolling in pairs or larger groups were too engrossed in each other to take any notice of him. It didn't sit well with him to spy on others like this, but Talbot had asked him to, and it was also to protect Lady Isabella.

All he could see of da Gama was his back, but from his posture he was gazing into the lady's eyes. Her head was dipped, listening, then the Portuguese put his hand out—to take hers, Nick guessed. But the lady was having none of it; she pulled her own hand away and sat stiffly upright. Nick smiled without humour as some hand-waving from da Gama was followed by further stiffening from the lady. She spoke; Nick couldn't hear the words, but her expression made it clear that she was giving da Gama a setdown. Da Gama stood, made a bow and stalked off.

Nick's satisfaction at the thwarting of the Portuguese faded when he saw the lady raise a handkerchief to her face. She should not be left alone, but he didn't know her. Lady Jesson had been with her—he should be able to find her and send her back to her friend before he went home. He still hadn't passed on Talbot's information, but after this evening that might no longer be necessary. He should still keep an eye on da Gama, though. Lady Isabella deserved to have someone who cared for her, not a womaniser like the Portuguese.

CHAPTER 17

*M*olly straightened the gown Bella had donned for her final dancing lesson, and started to brush her hair. "I heard the housekeeper telling the maids to get Lord Marstone's room ready, my lady. He's expected this afternoon."

Bella twisted around, ignoring Molly's tut. "My aunt didn't say anything about him coming."

"A letter came yesterday, from what I heard. Now hold still, do."

Bella watched in the mirror as Molly skilfully piled her hair on top of her head, arranging a couple of long ringlets to fall over her shoulder. One of her new gowns was laid out on the bed, ready for calls with her aunt this afternoon. She'd been looking forward to wearing it, but now it seemed only an advertisement in silk, a pretty package aimed at selling its contents. That was all her father was doing, the only reason he was funding her wardrobe.

If Lord Narwood had written to Papa, would she even be allowed to go to her first ball?

"Molly, can Langton get a message to Mr Carterton?" She had no idea what Mr Carterton could do, but he had promised to help.

"Already done, my lady." Molly's reply interrupted her thoughts. "And Langton'll do his best to listen to any talk."

"Do you know the servants' passages here?" She might be able to eavesdrop herself.

Molly shook her head. "No, my lady, nor yet the routines, not properly. You're like to get caught if you try. I'll see what I can find out for you, but the housekeeper keeps a close eye on things." She stood back to regard her handiwork. "There, that's done."

"Thank you."

Bella remained seated in front of the mirror as Molly left the room, gazing at her reflection. She looked very different from the ignorant and uncertain girl who'd arrived in Town only a fortnight ago.

She was not going to submit to her father without a fight. Although she still lacked confidence in many things, she'd stood up to spiteful comments. She'd also attracted the attention of three men—even if she disliked two of them and the third was likely to be using her. But, most importantly, she had some friends.

Aunt Aurelia would be sorting out her invitations soon. Bella hurried downstairs to the library, pleased to see that Langton was the footman on duty in the hall. She found paper and pen in a desk drawer, but hesitated. Lady Tregarth had said she was soon to visit her daughter, who was expecting another child—she might have already left Town. But Maria Jesson would be more helpful in any case. She wrote a quick note to Maria and then wrote another from Maria to herself, inviting her to call. She could show that to her aunt if necessary.

"Please get it sent as soon as you can," Bella whispered as she handed the first note to Langton.

"I'm on duty here until noon, my lady," he said. "I'll need an excuse to…" His gaze moved away from her, and when he looked back there was a trace of amusement in his normally impassive face. "Could you knock over that vase?" He inclined his head towards a large arrangement of lilies on a table.

The vase made a satisfying crash as it hit the tiled floor. Bella wondered if it was valuable, but didn't really care.

The butler hurried through the baize door.

"I'm so sorry, Mowbray, I had a little accident," Bella said. "Get it cleaned up, Langton. I'll need your attendance in a couple of hours, as well."

"Yes, my lady."

~

"What the hell are you doing still in bed at this hour?"

Luis turned over and squinted at Don Felipe through gritty eyes. After Lady Milton had sent him off last night, he'd wandered around the gardens for a while before heading off to find a tavern. The English ale was not to his taste, but he'd wanted to get drunk.

"Get dressed and be above stairs in ten minutes."

Luis winced as the slam of the door speared his brain.

Damn. Someone had already reported last night's failure to inveigle his way into Lady Milton's house. He supposed it was no use asking who had been watching.

"You have failed your main task, you young fool," Don Felipe said, as Luis stepped into the room. He was sprawled in an armchair, his legs stretched out in front of him. Luis ignored the lower chair the older man indicated, and leaned on the wall instead.

"Anyone would have failed. She is an honourable woman." He'd got drunk to try to forget the anger and disappointment in her face when she'd sent him off. He'd felt both respect for her and a certain amount of guilt, even though her rejection put his own goal further from his reach.

"Rubbish. Her husband neglects her; she should have been ripe for the plucking."

"She is lonely, yes, but—" Luis closed his mouth. He'd failed with Lady Milton—there was no need to pass on what he knew of her to Don Felipe.

"There's still Lady Sudbury, and the Marstone girl. How are you getting on with them?"

"Don't you know? I thought you had watchers everywhere."

"Mind your manners, you ignorant bastard. You're here—"

149

"Don't call me that!"

Don Felipe's lips thinned. "If you want people to stop calling you that, then seduce the Sudbury woman and get the information I need. She should be no problem. I will arrange what you want only when you have helped me to achieve my own goals."

"I did my best with Lady Milton! It's not my fault you picked on someone who would not..." Luis broke off and took a deep breath. Don Felipe's implacable expression told him he would get nowhere with that argument. "I will call on Lady Sudbury today."

"See that you do. And the other—find out what the brother is doing in Paris. Seduce the chit if necessary, that'll—"

"You told me *not* to do that before."

Don Felipe shrugged. "You've failed with the main prospect, so your usefulness is already reduced. Do it, but don't get caught—that will give you something to hold over her if she's reluctant to tell what she knows. The threat of scandal and a public shaming is a powerful incentive." Don Felipe glared at Luis. "The end justifies the means," he added, when Luis did not immediately respond.

He supposed it did. All this would be worthwhile if he got what he wanted. "Very well."

"Good." Don Felipe stood, advancing until he was within a few steps of Luis and thrusting his face forwards. "I am not against you, you fool, but I want your side of the bargain delivered." He left the room without waiting for an answer.

Luis groaned and then called for Mrs Hathersage to bring him some coffee. If he was to start his seduction of Lady Sudbury, he needed to bathe and shave, and get rid of this aching head.

Maria Jesson was still at breakfast when Bella arrived. "I'm sorry to interrupt you," Bella said, hesitating in the doorway.

"Nonsense," Maria said. "Come and have some chocolate while you tell me what is wrong. Tompkins, bring another cup and plate." She waited until the footman had poured a drink for Bella and left the room. "Are you upset about Senhor da Gama?"

"Senhor da Gama?" She had been, last night, but the news about her father had driven him from her mind.

"I went for a walk about the gardens with Jesson after I left you yesterday," Maria continued. When we returned to the box, Lady Milton was most distressed. It seems…" She pressed her lips together.

"The senhor upset her?" Bella guessed.

"I'm afraid so. He tried to seduce her." Maria leaned forwards and patted Bella's hand. "Come, you knew he wasn't only courting you."

Bella swallowed hard and nodded. She had more important things to consider at the moment. "My father is coming to Town. Today, most likely."

"Ah. Oh dear. That's rather short notice."

"Aunt Aurelia knew yesterday. She had a letter, but all she said about it was that Papa wanted a list of my suitors. This morning, she said she hadn't wanted to worry me."

Bella wasn't sure whether she trusted Aunt Aurelia, but not knowing of her father's arrival had allowed her to enjoy last night's excursion to Vauxhall. Until she'd seen Senhor da Gama.

"Do eat, Bella, unless you have already had breakfast. I always think better when I'm not hungry." Maria took another spiced roll then pushed the platter towards Bella.

Bella had not felt like eating that morning, so she took a roll and started to break it into pieces.

"It won't do you any good on your plate," Maria pointed out. She waited until Bella had eaten a few mouthfuls. "Do you think Marstone wants to hurry matters along?"

"I don't know. He wants a list of suitors, and it will only have Lord Barnton on it. And possibly Mr Carterton."

"Not Lord Narwood? I haven't had chance to find out much about him yet."

"Aunt Aurelia said she wouldn't include him." Bella pushed her plate away. "But if Papa's already had a letter from him, he'd probably accept. Barnton is still only the heir to a viscount." And he might not offer for her—he'd seemed quite taken with Jemima last night.

"Hmm. And Carterton only a baron's heir. So you might be pushed into marrying Narwood."

"Mr Carterton isn't a suitor," Bella stated. "He's only…" She closed her eyes—she wasn't supposed to tell anyone about Will's request, but Will wasn't here and she needed more allies.

"He's quite attentive," Maria prompted.

"He's acting in Will's stead," Bella said, making up her mind.

Maria's brow creased. "There is some speculation about Wingrave's absence, as he was in Town when your sisters came out. People generally assume he's at home with his wife. Can he not help you?"

"I don't… I have no way of contacting him. He only told me he was away on business." A brief memory came, of Senhor da Gama saying Will was in France. How could he know that?

"Mr Carterton said I should think of him like a brother," Bella went on. "He must be about the same age as Will, so he's ten years older than me, at least." He did have friendly eyes, although his gaze didn't give her the same melting feeling as Senhor da Gama's. But then the senhor's admiration was a lie.

"He's about my age, thank you very much." Maria sniffed and put her nose in the air, but Bella could still see a dimple. She giggled despite her worries.

"I didn't mean any offence," she said. "How do you know how…? Oh, in Debrett's, I suppose."

"He's only six or seven years older than you, Bella. That's not old at all. Men think they've grown up when they leave school. Some have, to be sure, but…" She shook her head. "Someone a little older than you would make better husband material. He'd have had time to settle down a bit." Her look became wistful, and Bella wondered if Maria thought that she herself had married someone too young.

"But that is beside the point," Maria went on, her tone matter of fact once more. "If your father has any sense, he'll not rush things. You've hardly been in society yet."

"The theatre, a rout, and a musicale. And yesterday's trip to Vaux-hall. Not really enough to sell myself, you think?"

Maria choked on her hot chocolate.

"It feels like that," Bella protested.

"I know what you mean, but for goodness sake do not put it like that to anyone else." Maria set her cup down. "Barnton really wouldn't do for you, you know, if you are going to say such things."

"He's not as bad as Lord Narwood."

"Hmm. Have some more food while I think."

Bella took another roll and started pulling it to pieces.

"If your father does want to rush things, I think there are a couple of options," Maria said at last. "Perhaps more, if your aunt would co-operate."

"Aunt Aurelia is enjoying being in Town at my father's expense," Bella said. "She might."

"Good. In that case, one thing to try is for her to tell your father you have another suitor, richer or higher ranking than Narwood."

"But I haven't."

"I know, but Marstone won't. Or at least, not immediately. I will consult a peerage later and work out who it might be. You are going to Lady Yelland's ball tomorrow, are you not? If your father tries to keep you close, she can say you need to be there to fix his interest."

"How do you know who'll be…? Oh, you mean my aunt will have to lie about it."

Maria regarded her, tilting her head to one side. "Do you think she will mind? She will also benefit from the deception."

"I don't know." Bella didn't like telling untruths herself, but they seemed a necessity unless she was to submit to her father's will. "That wouldn't work for long, though, would it?"

"It might buy you some time."

She would keep it in mind. "What other options do I have?"

"Ask Mr Carterton to marry you." Maria took a sip of her choco-late as if she had not just said something outrageous.

"*Ask* Mr… I can't do that!"

"Not even if the alternative is marrying Narwood?"

153

Avoiding that was surely worth the embarrassment she would feel, both at asking and at the likelihood of being rejected.

"From what I've heard, he's on the lookout for a wife," Maria added. "He's been escorting Jemima Roper around. A lovely girl, but rather quiet."

"They would be well suited," Bella said, although the thought did nothing to cheer her. Quite the opposite.

"Do you trust him, Bella?"

"Yes." She felt… comfortable, safe… when she was with him. She'd dreamed of finding the love evident when Will mentioned his wife, but she wasn't likely to be given the chance.

"You may not actually have to marry him; discussing a betrothal would delay things and give you a chance to meet someone else."

"But an honourable man would not court me if it was known that Mr Carterton had spoken to my father. It's not fair to ask him either, if he is courting Jemima."

"Hmm, you have a point. Never mind."

"You said several options," Bella reminded her.

"Run away—go and stay with your brother in Devonshire. Although while your father is still alive he is your legal guardian and could have you brought back."

"No. Once he'd got me back I wouldn't be allowed out of my room until he'd got me married."

"My final idea is even more risky."

"Well?" Bella asked, impatient to know more.

"Put yourself out of the marriage market by compromising your reputation."

Bella's mouth fell open. Had Maria really suggested that she…?

"You only need to let people *think* you have done so," Maria clarified.

"Oh. But if everyone believes… I mean, I might never be able to marry." That option wasn't inviting, either. She was sure Will would let her live with him, but she'd still be dependent on someone. Depending on a husband—the *right* husband—was different.

"That's the risk," Maria said. "But the only people who need to think you have done something improper are your father, and whoever your father is trying to arrange things with."

"If Lord Narwood wants an heir..." Bella said, trying to think of the implications. "If he thinks I might be... might have..."

"Exactly. That would work with Barnton, too. But even if an heir is not the primary reason for his approaches, most men want to be the first." She shrugged. "Unfair, I know, and the problem with that strategy is that he could well put it about that you were no longer untouched. Rumour might eventually die down, but it could take some time. However, you are an earl's daughter with a substantial dowry, and young enough to wait for a few more years before marrying."

"I don't want to be married for my dowry," Bella said. None of the options before her was attractive.

"Worry about that if the time comes," Maria said briskly.

"Papa might marry me off anyway."

"That's another risk."

Bella shook her head. "I don't think that would work. Who would I say it was? Papa might try to force him to marry me."

"Think about what I've said," Maria suggested. "Something else may occur to me, or to you."

"The best idea is your first one—to pretend I have a suitor with a higher rank than Narwood." Although her father may not necessarily demand a high-ranking suitor, or why would he have pursued Mr Carterton for Lizzie two years ago? She didn't know what her father really wanted—other than unquestioning obedience, of course.

"There's a peerage in the other parlour somewhere," Maria said, putting her napkin on the table. "Let us go and select a suitable..."

"Victim?" Bella suggested, managing a smile.

CHAPTER 18

"*L*ord Gilling?" Aunt Aurelia said. "I didn't know you'd met him."

Bella sighed—she should have broached the subject while they were still in Marstone House, but she hadn't wanted any of the servants to overhear. Now her aunt was too busy gazing at a display of elaborate hats in a shop window.

"If Papa arranges my betrothal as soon as he arrives, he won't need you here any longer, will he?" Bella asked. "You said he was in a hurry."

Her aunt stared at her, an arrested expression on her face.

"And he'll stop paying your bills," Bella added. "I might still need a chaperone, but he could use my governess for that." Unless Papa had turned her off.

Aunt Aurelia took her arm and walked along the street until they reached a less crowded spot. "Start again, Isabella."

"Papa wants to see me wed as soon as possible—you told me so on the journey here." She waited until her aunt nodded. "If there is a marquess interested in me, he might—"

"But there isn't."

"No, but he won't know that. He'll only know what you tell him.

Unless he has friends who will—"

"Friends? My brother?" Aunt Aurelia grimaced. "Even if he did, they'd spend their time criticising the government, or their servants, not talking about possible suitors. Is Gilling in Town?"

"Lady Jesson says so." Bella held her breath until a smile spread across her aunt's face.

"I like the plan. You met while I was taking you on morning calls, I think. And you must let me know anyone else with whom you've conversed. The more on my list, the better." She cast one long, regretful, look back towards the hat shop. "Let us see who is in Mrs Roper's salon this afternoon."

Bella looked around as she followed her aunt into Mrs Roper's parlour—the only people she recognised were Jemima and Lord Barnton, talking together at the far side of the room. Mrs Roper came over to them, accompanied by a man of about Will's age.

"Lady Cerney, may I introduce Sir Andrew Belton? Lady Isabella Stanlake." She smiled and moved off to greet another new arrival.

Bella squared her shoulders and curtseyed.

"I haven't seen you before, Lady Isabella," he said, as Aunt Aurelia moved away. Apart from a rather long nose, his appearance was unexceptionable.

"I have been in Town only a couple of weeks, Sir Andrew." She strove to look interested as the conversation took its usual course—whether she was enjoying her season, whether she had been to many events. The only new question was whether she rode.

"I do, but I don't have a mount in Town at present. My father may arrange for one when he arrives."

"Who is your father?"

"The Earl of Marstone," Bella said, irritated to see his rather languid air sharpen as she spoke.

"If you cannot ride at present, would you care to drive with me in the park one day?"

"I would be delighted."

Sir Andrew smiled and bowed his head before moving off to speak to someone else. Bella added him to her mental list of suitors. She found an empty sofa, and looked around as she sat down. Lady Brigham was talking to her aunt. Bella's pulse accelerated as she wondered if Senhor da Gama had accompanied her. After what she'd seen at Vauxhall, she shouldn't want to meet him again, but she did.

Yes, there he was, over by the window—and he was coming towards her.

"Lady Isabella, how lovely to see you again" He sat beside her, half turned so he could look into her eyes. "You are looking as beautiful as ever."

His admiring expression was just the same, but the knowledge that he had been bestowing that same gaze on Lady Milton the night before robbed it of its usual effect. "I am happy to see you, sir." She lowered her eyes and smiled, as if she was flattered.

"I hope you have fully recovered from our excursion," he said.

"Why, yes, thank you." She still wasn't very good at starting conversations, but she recalled the guidebook she'd found in the library. "I have not been able to see much of London myself—how are you finding it? It must be similar to Lisbon in many ways."

"Ah… I am not familiar with Lisbon, I'm afraid."

"It is your capital city, is it not? Have you never been there?"

"My home is in the far north of the country, Lady Isabella, and my family do not care to travel to Lisbon."

That seemed odd. If Senhor da Gama could travel all the way to London, surely he must have been able to visit his own capital city. Theresa lived in Scotland now, at her husband's estate, but she'd met him in London.

"What is it like where you live?" she asked. Vastly different from Hertfordshire, she was sure, and it was interesting to learn about other places, no matter who was telling her.

Nick breathed a sigh of relief as he was shown into the parlour—Lady Cerney was here, so Lady Isabella would most likely be present too.

He could spend a little time with Miss Roper and check on Lady Isabella without having to brave any other gatherings this afternoon. Then he swore under his breath as he spotted her—she was listening with rapt attention to da Gama.

That damned Portuguese again! What did she see in him?

He shook his head—he was here for a purpose, and Talbot might be interested in what da Gama was saying. He went to sit on an empty chair behind the sofa where the two of them were talking. The people either side of him nodded a greeting, but returned to their own conversations.

Hills... da Gama was saying something about hills.

"...more than I have seen in your England. There are vineyards on some of the countryside, but there is also good hunting for me and my brothers. My father's house..." He paused. "House is not the right word... palacio, perhaps?"

"You live in a palace?"

Da Gama laughed. "No, not so big as that. Casa grande is a better description. Big house."

"Oh, like Marstone Park," Lady Isabella said.

"Is that where you live? With your brother and sisters?"

Nick frowned as da Gama's voice sharpened.

"No, they are all married," she said. "Theresa lives in Scotland, and Lizzie in Yorkshire. That is in the north of England."

"And your brother?"

"He normally lives in Devonshire. But you told me he was in France, Senhor da Gama. Did you meet him there?"

Nick wondered if he had heard correctly. There was a pregnant pause, then da Gama answered.

"No, I have never been to France. Do you go to Lady Yelland's ball tomorrow?"

"I... I believe so."

"May I have the honour of dancing with you?"

"Thank you, yes."

Nick caught movement from the corner of his eye—da Gama had taken his leave.

"If you wish to talk, Mr Carterton, there is now a space on this sofa." Lady Isabella was looking over her shoulder, regarding him with a strange expression—something between annoyance and amusement, if such a thing were possible. Embarrassed at being caught eavesdropping, he hoped his face had not reddened. Damn Wingrave for putting him in this situation.

"Thank you." He took the place just vacated by the Portuguese.

"Have you come to reprimand me again for my choice of... friends?" Lady Isabella spoke while he was still thinking how to broach the subject.

"I... er...Your brother did ask me to act in his stead while he was away."

"In France?" Thankfully, she spoke quietly.

"Yes. But that is not commonly known. It would be better if you did not repeat it."

She nodded, to his relief.

"Your brother, had he been in Town, would have made the same enquiries about your friend as I have."

"He was introduced by Lady Brigham, a family friend of his," she objected, but without the heat he remembered from the first time she'd made that point.

"There is more than one moneylender pressing Lady Brigham for repayment."

Her expression made it clear that he didn't need to explain the implications.

"And although the visconde he claims as his father undoubtedly exists, no-one that... none of the people of whom enquiries were made have heard of a son by that name."

"Thank you for informing me, Mr Carterton."

About to ask that she end her friendship with the man, Nick hesitated. She had not ripped up at him as he'd expected.

"Forewarned is forearmed," she added. "I'm glad you are here, sir, for I have a favour to ask of you. Lady Yelland's ball tomorrow night will be the first time I dance in public. Would you dance the first with me? Then I can concentrate on my steps without fearing I am being rude to my partner."

"It would be a pleasure." And it would be, albeit a silent one if she was minding her steps. He hadn't intended to go, but how could he refuse her request?

"I would have asked Will, had he been here, but you did say you were to stand in his place."

"I will look forward to it, Lady Isabella." He was surprised to find himself wishing that she would look at him in the intent way she'd regarded the Portuguese earlier.

Bella followed Aunt Aurelia up the stairs, her stomach knotted in anticipation of what her father might say. Papa had gone straight to his room when he arrived, but a message to the dining room had dashed her hopes of avoiding him until the following day.

"Typical of my brother," her aunt said again. "There is *no* reason why we could not have this interview after we finished dinner."

Papa's valet awaited them outside the door to the earl's private suite. "Lady Cerney—"

"Send them in, Chambers. Stop blathering out there!" Her father's voice sounded slurred to Bella's ears.

Chambers swallowed, but did not move. "My lady, his lordship's physician said it was imperative that he not be angered."

Aunt Aurelia looked down her nose at the valet. "I'm sure he did. You have done your duty by informing me, so stand aside."

The valet bowed, and they entered the room. Papa sat by the fire, his legs wrapped in a blanket despite the room being over-warm. His cheeks looked sunken, even though the rest of him was as fat as ever, and one side of his mouth drooped downwards. Bella had never seen him looking so unwell.

Aunt Aurelia took the remaining chair without waiting to be asked to sit. "Chambers, bring a chair for Lady Isabella," she ordered.

"Damme, Aurelia, stop giving orders in *my* house!" The earl examined Bella from head to toe. "She appears well enough turned out—as she should be, from the amount you've spent. I want an accounting of your activities, and to know when I can expect to be approached about Isabella's marriage."

The tension in Bella's shoulders relaxed a little. Her main worry, that Lord Narwood had already written to him about a marriage, seemed to be unfounded.

"Well, Aurelia?"

The valet arrived with a chair—it was a hard, upright chair, but as Bella sat she realised it had the advantage of allowing her to look down on her father. In spite of her determination not to submit to his wishes, she kept her back straight, her hands folded meekly in her lap.

"Isabella has a number of suitors," Aunt Aurelia began, her eyes flicking towards Bella. She counted off the names as her aunt recited them and, in some cases, gave exaggerated descriptions of their wealth or status. If any of those men did offer for her, Papa would find out how inaccurate some of her aunt's descriptions were—but if she was lucky that would cause further delay.

"And Isabella has only been to a few events so far," Aunt Aurelia finished, without mentioning Lord Narwood. "There is time yet for her to make—"

"What has taken you so long? It's weeks since she came to Town, and you've spent a tidy sum on her clothing. Is that all you have to show for it?"

"I hardly think more than half a dozen potential suitors is a paltry number for less than a fortnight in Town, particularly with a viscount's heir and a marquess in their number. If you'd bothered to keep her fashionably clothed, she could have been in society for more of that time, instead of spending a week being fitted for the gowns you failed to provide. Then there is your lack of forethought in not ensuring she knows how to dance."

"Pah, don't make excuses, woman. If you'd done what I'm paying you for, I could have applied for a special licence and have the whole business settled within a couple of days."

Thank goodness Aunt Aurelia *hadn't* done what her father wanted.

"And write a list of these potential suitors—I need to think which you should encourage."

"Very well." She stood as she spoke. "Come, Isabella, let us see if our dinner is still edible."

Bella was thankful that her aunt seemed to be following their plan, but how long could this reprieve last?

CHAPTER 19

*L*uis leant closer to the window—it *was* Lady Brigham entering the house. He hadn't seen Don Felipe arrive, but Lady Brigham would not be here unless his employer was, too. Cracking open the door to the hall, he saw Mrs Hathersage escorting her to the upper room.

He pulled his coat on and glanced in the mirror over the mantel-piece to straighten his cravat, guessing that he would shortly be summoned to account for yesterday's activities. It wasn't long before Mrs Hathersage descended the stairs, but she headed straight for her own rooms rather than asking him to go up.

Luis scowled—he'd had enough of being ordered about like some lackey and kept in the dark about what he was doing. Slipping off his shoes, he ran up the stairs and tiptoed along the corridor. The door of Don Felipe's room was closed, but when he crouched down to put his ear near the keyhole, he could make out some of what was being said.

"...talk with the Marstone girl yesterday afternoon. Lady Sudbury was with one of her cicisbeos in..."

"Damn fool hasn't tried—"

"Be fair, Don Felipe. With the number of lovers that woman has, da Gama probably has to join a queue."

Luis nodded to himself at this unexpected support. Lady Sudbury had welcomed him when he called, but he'd only been at her home a few minutes when Mr Trantor arrived to take her to the Park.

"...did you promise the boy?"

Luis muttered a curse as Don Felipe's voice became an incomprehensible murmur—he must have moved further from the door.

"Really?" Lady Brigham's voice carried more clearly. "Can that be done in Spain? ... not possible ... out of wedlock."

"... thinks it can be, that's what matters ... irrelevant if he doesn't do what he's asked. We'll get him up to explain himself in a minute, but first tell me..."

Don Felipe's voice faded again. Luis backed away from the door and hurried back to his room. It would not do to be found on the stairs when Mrs Hathersage answered the bell.

As he put his shoes on, he puzzled over what he had heard. All he wanted was his rightful name and inheritance, but Lady Brigham seemed to think that was not possible. But what would she know? She was English, and surely Don Felipe would know more about Spanish law?

Mrs Hathersage knocked on his door, and he climbed the stairs once more—this time without making any effort to be silent.

"I will be calling on Lady Sudbury again tomorrow," he reported. "I talked to Lady Isabella this afternoon, but I do not think she knows anything about Wingrave's activities. She didn't even know he is out of the country."

Don Felipe tapped his chin with one finger. "Nevertheless, you will ask again. Particularly if you still have got nothing from the Sudbury woman by the time Wingrave returns from France. You will persuade her to find out what he has been doing."

"It should not take too long to get close to Lady Sudbury," Luis pointed out.

"True, but it may take some time for useful information to be obtained via that route. You will also start playing cards in some of the clubs I enrolled you in. I may wish you to befriend someone there, and it is better for you to be known before you approach him."

"If I am to gamble, I will need more money. I may not always win."

"Naturally." Don Felipe looked down his nose. "But do not lose too much. I will give you no more than fifty guineas at this time. And you will need to keep a clear head."

"Is that all? If so, I have a ball to prepare for."

Don Felipe waved a hand. Luis made an effort to keep his expression bland as he left the room. It wasn't his fault that Lady Milton had resisted his advances, and now he was to be given a new target. Don Felipe could keep giving him new tasks and finding excuses not to repay him for his efforts. And if Don Felipe had been lying to him all along, he'd been wasting his time here. How could he find someone here to consult on Spanish law without raising suspicion?

Luis closed his eyes. He could give up now and go home, before his father worked out the real reason for his absence. Or…

His spirits rose a little. If he couldn't get what he had come to England for, perhaps he could aim for something else. An earl's daughter was not a small prize. He'd noted Don Felipe's warning about Lady Isabella's brother and his duelling, but Wingrave was not in the country. Besides, he wasn't planning on ruining her.

Nick arrived at Lady Yelland's ball as the opening minuet was starting. The butler, when questioned, did not recall Lady Cerney being announced, so Nick took up a position near a pillar to one side of the huge ballroom to await their arrival. The first cotillion was well under way by the time he spied Lady Cerney in a group of people near the edge of the room, with Isabella behind her.

"Such a pity she is so short," Miss Yelland said beside him. Nick muttered something rude under his breath; he hadn't noticed her approach.

"Really?" Nick said, irritated by the woman's proprietary air. "I think she looks very well." She didn't merely look well, she was beautiful, in a confection of pink and warm ivory that set off her creamy skin and the delicate blush in her cheeks.

"A large dowry will make up for many shortcomings," Miss Yelland added, and he dragged his gaze back to her.

"Even yours?" Nick asked, at the end of his patience with her. "She cannot help her height. You, however, have chosen to be spiteful. Excuse me." He didn't wait to see, or hear, her reaction.

Damn—while Miss Yelland had been talking to him, someone else had approached Isabella. A man more than twice her age and, from the stiff way she held herself, not someone she was pleased to see. Could that be Narwood?

As he neared them, the man held one hand out as if waiting to lead her onto the floor.

"My apologies, my lady," Nick said, coming to a halt beside them. "I was delayed."

Isabella's posture relaxed as she put her chin up. "As I told you, Lord Narwood, I already have a partner for my first dance." Lady Cerney, standing beside her, gave a nod and walked off—to the card room, Nick suspected.

Lord Narwood's hand dropped. "The next one, then, Lady Isabella."

"I am..." Her words tailed off as Narwood bowed and moved off while she was still speaking. "I suppose I'll have to dance with him now."

"I'm afraid it would be rude not to," Nick said. He could see why she did not like the man.

"If I tread on his toes enough times he might go away." The words were little more than a whisper, but Nick was standing close enough to hear.

"I pray you do not wish to practise that aspect of your dancing on me."

Her lips were pressed together, but with a curl to them—hiding a smile, he guessed.

"I should guard my tongue, should I not?"

"Not with me," he said. Her honesty was refreshing. Enchanting. "Come, it is time to take our places."

She was silent as they moved through the first figures and changes, her lips moving occasionally as if she were reciting the patterns. That was the only sign that she was new to this, as she made no mistakes. Gradually, as the dance progressed, she looked about her more.

"You are doing well," he said.

She smiled—a wide smile of enjoyment mixed with triumph. It reminded him of the pleasure his sisters' children showed when mastering a new skill, but she was far from a child. Very far from it, he thought, admiring the way the cut of her gown accentuated her figure as she turned.

He lifted his gaze to her face as the dance brought her closer again. The fun had gone out of her expression.

"Did you find out anything about Lord Narwood?" she asked.

"Not much," he admitted. "He needs an heir, and isn't well-liked." He'd heard a little in his club, and his father had known the man slightly. Opinion agreed that he was a bit of a cold fish who hated being contradicted—exactly the kind of man Wingrave had asked him to protect his sister from. He sounded far too much like Marstone himself.

"Unfortunately, that's nothing I could use to put him off—or put your father off him. I will see if I can find out more," he promised. He would talk to Talbot tomorrow. "Has Narwood approached your father?"

"No, but if he does…" She gave a quick pout before the dance took them apart. "My father wanted a list of my suitors," she went on as soon as she was close enough to speak privately. "I got my aunt to invent a few to give us more time."

If this wasn't a matter that would affect her whole life, he'd be amused. As it was, he found himself impressed by the initiative she'd shown.

"Is there no-one on the list you would be happy to marry?"

Was *he* on it? He had been, briefly, a suitor for her sister's hand two years ago; Marstone might accept if he made an offer now. Looking into her blue eyes, he thought it wouldn't be such a bad fate.

No, not bad at all.

The final bars of the music sounded before she could answer, and everyone made their bows and curtseys. Aunt Aurelia was nowhere in sight, but Mrs Roper sat fanning herself at the edge of the room, her daughter by her side.

"Thank you, Isabella." He bowed over her hand as they reached the Ropers. "No-one would know it was your first dance," he added quietly, and was rewarded with an uncertain smile. He wondered if he had said something wrong, until he saw Narwood approaching.

Narwood led Isabella into the next set. Nick could watch, or he could keep an eye on Narwood by taking part.

"May I have this dance, Miss Roper?"

Unwilling to meet Lord Narwood's eyes, Bella looked down the lines of dancers. She recognised no-one else, but as the music started and she took her first steps, she spied Mr Carterton and Jemima in another set. They made an elegant pair, Mr Carterton's well-fitting dark coat contrasting with Jemima's pale gown. She should feel happy for her friend being courted by someone like him—shouldn't she?

"I hear your father is in Town," Lord Narwood said.

Bella had to take his hand for a turn; it was cold in hers, and he held onto her fingers a little too firmly. Quite unlike the pleasant warmth of Mr Carterton's touch.

"Yes, my lord."

"Why did he not accompany you at first? He is only just arrived, I think."

"He was not well." What business was it of his?

"Tell me about your education, Lady Isabella. What were you taught at home?"

"I'm sure I was taught the usual things." His mouth thinned as they moved apart in the dance, and she took a deep breath as they came back together again. "Excuse me, but I am new to society, as you know. Is it not more usual to discuss the musicians, or the crowds in the ballroom?"

"Do such things interest you?" The lack of expression in his face was chilling.

"Not really, but I do not see how my childhood could be of interest either."

"Your lessons did not include being polite to your superiors, I see."

Bella's jaw clenched—she did not trust herself to answer. If he'd already judged her impolite, she was losing nothing by not answering him. Instead, she kept her eyes on the other dancers as they worked their way up the set.

"You are young enough to learn from suitable instruction, I suppose," Lord Narwood said the next time the dance brought them together. To Bella's surprise, he didn't look angry, or even annoyed. His gaze felt like an inspection, lingering on her face and then her chest, and the corners of his lips curled upwards. "Schooling you would not be a hardship. In fact, I think I would enjoy it. I will write to your father tomorrow."

Bella's mouth fell open, and she only remembered where she was when someone bumped into her. Murmuring an apology, she hurried to regain her proper place in the set.

How easily a few words could ruin her evening. Narwood had one of the highest ranks of the men on Aunt Aurelia's list, apart from the marquess she'd never met. Given her father's unseemly haste to see her wed, she thought he would agree to such a match without waiting to see if her imaginary courtship with the Marquess of Gilling came to anything. He'd talked of a special licence—she could find herself wed before Mr Carterton had a chance to help her.

She must find Maria Jesson after this set—some of the strategies she had discounted the day before were beginning to seem more attractive. It appeared that Narwood felt no need to talk to her further, having made his decision, so for the rest of the dance Bella concentrated on not scowling in public and minding her steps. After what seemed an age, the dance was over. Lord Narwood bent over her hand before placing it on his arm and returning her to Mrs Roper.

"I will see you soon, Lady Isabella," he stated, making one final bow and heading for the door. Mrs Roper watched him go, her brow creased, then turned to Bella.

"Are you...? Did he...?"

Bella shook her head. "He only said he will write to my father tomorrow."

"It would be a good match," Mrs Roper said, although she sounded uncertain. "And so soon in your season, too. Oh, here is another of your suitors."

Expecting to see Lord Barnton, Bella was pleased to find Senhor da Gama approaching.

"May I have the honour?" He bowed, gesturing towards the dance floor.

Bella looked to Mrs Roper—the nearest she had to a chaperone at the moment.

"Your aunt approves, I think." Mrs Roper said.

"If you don't mind, Senhor da Gama, I would prefer something to drink." She couldn't concentrate on her steps while her mind was turning over possibilities.

"By all means. Shall I bring you something, or escort you to the refreshment room?"

Bella rose. "Let us walk."

He held out one arm, and they set off slowly around the edge of the ballroom.

"You do not look happy," Senhor da Gama said, covering her hand with his own.

"I am not."

He made a murmur of encouragement, and squeezed her hand gently.

"I am about to be betrothed." It was probably unwise to confide in him further, but she wasn't sure that she cared now.

"Ah, to the one you were just dancing with?"

Bella nodded.

"He looked very… stiff."

Stiff, uncaring, and worse… She couldn't work out why Lord Narwood was interested in her. "It would be like continuing to live with my father," she said bitterly. "Except with—" She waved a hand in frustration. There were some things she really couldn't bear to think about doing with Lord Narwood.

"Ah, yes. Your father, you do not like him?"

"No."

They passed into the anteroom. A long table down one side held arrays of filled glasses and platters of food, with liveried footmen waiting to serve guests. Small tables filled the rest of the space— mostly empty this early in the evening. Bella sat down, and Senhor da Gama brought her a glass of something orange-coloured and sweet.

"I would help you if I could," he said, sitting opposite and leaning over the table to take her hand. "Is there anything I can do?"

His warm grasp felt comforting, and Bella had to remind herself that he wasn't to be trusted. "My father wants me married, and Lord Narwood has the kind of rank that Papa requires."

"I suppose the younger son of a visconde would not do? We would deal well together, I think, Lady Isabella."

Bella froze—had he just proposed marriage to her? His expression was concerned, pleading almost—and he did have lovely brown eyes.

Remember Lady Milton. And Lady Sudbury.

"This is rather sudden for you," he said. "Perhaps I should not have said it."

"Oh, no," Bella breathed. "I... I need some time to think." He was a deceiver, so the plan that was beginning to form in her mind would not be unfair.

More people came into the anteroom, including Miss Yelland on the arm of a finely dressed older gentleman Bella did not recognise. Miss Yelland's brows rose as she looked towards Bella, then her nose tilted upwards and she looked away.

"No-one must know," Bella added in a whisper.

He smiled. He really was good at pretending sincerity.

"Meet me later, my lady, when you have had time to think about it."

"Where?"

"The ladies' retiring room is down a little corridor off the ball-room," he said. "Anyone will direct you. But three doors further down that corridor is a parlour. It will be empty."

How did he know that?

"I will watch," he went on, "and join you there if you leave the ballroom."

"We should not be seen together for too long," Bella suggested, taking a sip of her drink.

"You are right, to my regret. I will escort you back to Mrs Roper."

"Thank you." Bella gave him her best smile, blushing at the answering gleam in his eyes. Now she needed to find Maria—she could not carry out her plan alone.

CHAPTER 20

*L*uis headed for the card room after leaving Lady Isabella with her chaperone. Lady Sudbury had arrived and he didn't want Lady Isabella to see him flirting with the woman. Best to stay out of sight for a while.

An hour later, having kept himself inconspicuous by losing a little, but not too much, he ventured back into the ballroom. Lady Isabella was dancing, but she must have been watching for him as she caught his eye and inclined her head before returning her attention to her partner. When the set came to an end she made her way to the edge of the room, and left through the door that would lead to the retiring room.

At last, things were going well for him. She would not have slipped away like that if she had decided to turn him down. He waited a few minutes before following.

The parlour was dark, lit only by the glow from flambeaux beyond the windows. He'd checked earlier that the doors onto the terrace were unlocked, in case he could persuade her to leave with him tonight. What better way to escape secretly than across the gardens? And if she rejected him, he could ask her to walk with him there instead—there were plenty of couples taking the air who could observe them together and report a scandalous embrace. She would have to accept him then.

"Lady Isabella?" It was as well to check there was no-one else using the room for clandestine purposes.

"I'm here, Senhor da Gama." Her voice was little more than a whisper. The pale glimmer of her gown guided him to her place on a sofa near the empty fireplace. "Can we have some light? There are candles on the sideboard."

"I'm afraid I have no tinderbox, my lady." He advanced to stand before her. "May I call you Isabella? And you must call me Luis."

There was silence for a moment, and he wondered if he was being too precipitate. But no, she had willingly met him in an empty room.

"You may, Luis."

"Thank you." Going down on one knee might be too dramatic, so he drew up a chair to sit in front of her, leaning forward with his elbows resting on his knees. The sofa faced away from the windows, so he could make out little of her expression.

"Will you come away with me, Isabella?"

"Where will we go?" She sounded hesitant—he had not yet won.

"We will find a priest to marry us, of course." He didn't want to go to Scotland; there must be somewhere nearer. But there was no hurry. Once she'd run away with him they would have to be wed to save her reputation.

"Where will we live afterwards?"

So many questions. "Querida, we will be together. I will look after you, you will see. Will you marry me?"

Nick bowed to Miss Roper as their second dance together came to an end. "May I escort you in to supper?"

"I'm afraid I have already made arrangements." She gestured with her fan to a young man approaching them. "Mr Enfold invited me earlier."

He bowed as she left with her escort, rather relieved that he didn't

JAYNE DAVIS

need to entertain her through supper. Now he should ensure that Isabella had a suitable escort. He suppressed a curse at the memory of her heading for the refreshment room on the arm of that damned Portuguese—it appeared she had not heeded the warning he'd given her yesterday. She should not be throwing herself away on a charlatan like that.

The ballroom was rapidly emptying, and he couldn't see her anywhere. In the supper room, he wove his way between the tables, trying to pick out the cream and pink of her gown amongst the rainbow hues of the guests. He spied Lady Cerney, but she was sitting with a group of women her own age. Miss Roper and her escort sat at a table in the middle of the room, with her mother and another woman. No Isabella.

He didn't notice Miss Yelland until she was too close for him to escape.

"Are you looking for your short friend?" Miss Yelland made no attempt to hide the disdain in her voice this time.

A retort about seeking pleasant company rose to his lips, but he resisted. The woman was already hostile enough.

"She left in the direction of the retiring room some time ago," Miss Yelland said. "I do hope she comes to no harm in my father's house."

Her insincerity was obvious.

"That Portuguese viscount, or whatever he is, went out the same way not five minutes afterwards. Neither of them has reappeared." She laid a hand on his arm. "You should give up there, my dear sir. There are others more worthy of your attention."

"Thank you, Miss Yelland. I will look for her in the gardens." That was the most likely place for a couple to be together.

"But I…"

Her voice faded as he turned on his heel and strode away. He wasn't going to give her the satisfaction of seeing the effect her words had on him. Isabella couldn't really have gone willingly to somewhere private with Senhor da Gama.

Could she?

· · ·

176

Bella felt a fleeting impulse to accept Luis' offer—surely anything would be better than marriage to Lord Narwood? But who knew what this man would be like once he'd got his way?

"I thank you for asking, Luis, but I think I had better not."

There was enough light from the flickering flambeaux outside for Bella to make out his frown. He had not expected that answer.

"But Isabella, why did you come here if you were going to say no?"

He did sound puzzled, and she wondered if she had misjudged him.

"To find out what you really want," she said.

"You. I want you. Have I not just said so?"

"Would you still want me if my father casts me off?"

There was a brief silence. "He would not do that. The shame of having a daughter with a compromised reputation... No, he will want us to marry." He sounded as if he were trying to convince himself.

"No-one knows we are here," Bella pointed out, wondering if he had arranged for someone to discover them together.

"Can I not persuade you, my lady?"

"No." Bella spoke firmly. "Apart from anything else, I want a husband who would be faithful to me." He made a sound of protest but she carried on talking. "It is unfashionable, I know. I cannot believe you sincere, sir, when it is only a few days since you were trying to entice Lady Milton into something improper."

"I... How do you know about that?"

Bella sighed. Something within her had been hoping that Maria was mistaken, but he had not denied it. "Does it matter?"

"No." He stood up. "I'm sorry, we would have dealt well together, I think. Perhaps you will walk with me in the gardens for a while? I can tell you more about my country, if you are interested." He held his hand out as he spoke.

Bella made no move. Leaving this room was not part of her plan, nor was being alone with him. After a moment he bent and took hold of her hand.

"Come, let us walk together, and then part as friends," he said, the too-firm grip on her hand belying his seductive tones.

Bella resisted the pull, her breath coming fast as she twisted her hand out of his grip. "No, thank you. I prefer to remain here." *She* was in control here, even if he didn't know it yet.

"You liked me well enough only a few days ago."

"That was before—" She bit the words off. There was no point in bringing up Lady Milton again. But she did have a feeling that there was more to him than a mere fortune hunter.

"I still don't see why you want to marry me. My father may force us to wed if we are discovered, but he won't give you my dowry."

"I will be part of the English aristocracy."

"Why is that important? You are already part of the Portuguese aristocracy."

His mouth became a straight line, and he reached towards her again. Heart racing, Bella slid away and scrambled to her feet. It was time to show her hand, but she felt safer when she had put the sofa between them. That sudden move had frightened her.

"Maria!"

He froze, then spun around at a rustle of fabric from the far end of the room. "Mierda!"

"Well, this is interesting," Maria said as she emerged from the shadows.

"You! You have been poisoning her against me."

"Not at all."

Bella had to admire Maria's calm as her friend sat down on the sofa. Her own legs felt rather wobbly.

"Come and sit down, Bella. I don't *think* he's stupid enough to try something when there are two of us here, and a lot of people within screaming distance." Maria stared at Luis until he shook his head.

"Bella saw you with Lady Milton at Vauxhall," Maria went on. "That is how she knows. Now, if anyone comes, the three of us are having a nice little talk about your homeland." She glanced around. "I think the excuse would be more convincing if we were not sitting in the dark. Senhor da Gama, I'm sure you will find a tinderbox some-where if you look."

Luis turned, but headed for the door, not the fireplace.

"Oh, don't leave, please," Maria said. "Unless you wish me to inform the world that you are not what you seem."

He stopped, then turned slowly back. "I am exactly who I seem," he stated. His voice sounded overloud, to Bella's ears. Did he have something more to hide?

Maria shrugged. "People aren't interested in the truth. Any salacious titbit will spread. Light some candles, if you please."

There was a long silence, and Bella wondered if he was going to leave anyway. Then he muttered something under his breath and started to look for a tinderbox, feeling along the mantelpiece and then peering into the bookcase beside the chimney breast.

"Are you all right, Bella?" Maria asked, keeping her voice low. "Should I have shown myself earlier?"

"No," Bella said, "I don't think he meant to hurt me." Only to impose his will, like other men.

"Do you wish to return to the ballroom?"

"No. It would be better if someone discovered us here, would it not?"

"Probably." Maria smiled. "I think we might learn something more about our Portuguese friend while we wait."

Luis found what he was looking for, and lit candles on the mantelpiece and on a sideboard near the door.

"Do sit down, Senhor da Gama," Maria said. "You caused distress to one of my friends at Vauxhall, and tonight you have behaved in a deceitful and underhand manner with Lady Isabella. I don't know Lady Sudbury well, but…"

Her voice tailed off as he collapsed into the chair and put his head in his hands.

"Are you quite well?" Bella asked, feeling a little sorry for him now the tables had been turned.

He sat up straight. "I meant no harm to you, Lady Isabella."

Bella opened her mouth to protest but then closed it again. He hadn't forced her to meet him alone, and she *was* using him for her own ends. That didn't excuse his intent to ignore her refusal, but she wasn't blameless either.

"Senhor da Gama, why are you in England?" Maria asked. "There must be similar society in Lisbon."

Bella watched as he fidgeted in his chair. Something was nudging at her memory, something to do with ships. How odd.

"I... I wish to see the world," he said, unconvincingly.

Not ships, but a painting of a sea battle, at the Royal Academy exhibition. He had reacted strangely when she'd said she was glad he wasn't Spanish. And what had he said earlier? 'I am exactly who I seem', yet he knew so little about Lisbon. And how did he know that Will was in Paris?

She might be wrong, but she asked anyway. "What *is* your name, Senhor da Gama? Your true, Spanish name."

CHAPTER 21

*L*uis stared at Isabella. How did she know? How *could* she know?

"You *are* Spanish, aren't you?"

The other woman looked puzzled for a moment. "Ah, that could explain why you were so keen to..." She cast a quick glance at Isabella. "To befriend Lady Milton, because of her husband's position."

They had no proof, but that was no help. Don Felipe would not speak in his defence—he was a fellow Spaniard, and must have false papers too. Luis eyed the window, his muscles tensing. He could be across the room before either of them moved, and certainly before a scream could summon assistance.

"Senhor da Gama, I strongly suspect you are up to no good here, but I will not have you arrested if you give your word to leave England," Lady Jesson said. "However, if you run now, I will raise a hue and cry immediately."

It would take time for these women to persuade anyone he was worth chasing, and he could be long gone by then. But even as that thought crossed his mind, Lady Jesson unfastened her diamond necklace.

"He stole this," she said to Isabella. "Put it in your pocket." She turned back to him. "A reward for the return of my necklace would encourage pursuit, then we will have plenty of time to find out why you are here."

She was right, unfortunately.

"Why do you want me to stay? Why not just have me arrested?" It took some effort not to squirm under Lady Jesson's gaze.

"I am curious about who is paying you."

He shook his head. "I did not come here for money. I wanted—" He stopped and drew in a deep breath. These women could still see him arrested and hanged; it was stupid to tell them everything.

"What did they promise you?" Isabella asked.

"Your chance to be part of society here in London is gone, Senhor da Gama," Lady Jesson added. "You could repay some of the distress you have caused to Lady Isabella by satisfying her curiosity."

What harm could it do now? They might even sympathise a little.

"My title," he said. "The title I should have had from birth. My father was prevented from marrying my mother."

"Ah. Born on the wrong side of the blanket," Lady Jesson said. "So you were brought up in poverty and now you want riches."

"I said I was not doing this for money." Did they not listen? "No, my mother's father gave me to foster parents. My father found me when I was only a few years old, and I grew up with his other children. But I was his first-born—I should inherit his money and title, not be fobbed off with a few vineyards with which to make a living!"

There was silence in the room for what seemed like a long time. Then Isabella spoke, her voice strained. "Senhor da Gama, did… does your father treat you well? Does he like you, or even love you?"

Luis shrugged. "Well enough. He gives me the same attention as my half-brothers and sisters."

"You fool." Isabella put her head in her hands, and when she looked up again tears glittered in her eyes. "I would give anything for a parent who cared about me, who regarded me as more than just a problem to be dealt with. I would rather have such a parent than a legitimate birth. And you…" She broke off with a choke. "You are already treated far better than most illegitimate children, yet you are prepared to lie and cheat and seduce for something of so little value as a title! To disinherit your brother, too. Would your father be proud of you if you succeeded?"

"Bella." Lady Jesson put her arms around the girl. "Do not upset yourself. He is being a fool, in more ways than one. I don't know the law in Spain, but in this country he could never inherit his father's title."

"That was the promise Don Felipe made," he said, although he was becoming increasingly doubtful that Don Felipe would arrange what he'd promised even if it were possible. "He is a distant relative, and so I believed him when said he offered to…"

No, he must not say any more.

"Did you really want to marry me, Luis, or were you attempting to have some hold over me?" Isabella turned away, leaning her head on Lady Jesson's shoulder, and guilt settled heavily in his guts. Although he would have married her, he would still have been using her for his own ends.

Don Felipe's ends, whatever they were, did not justify this. Nor did his own wish for advancement.

"I would have treated you well," he said, but his words were lost as Lady Jesson spoke.

"Well done, Senhor da Gama, or whatever your name is." Her voice dripped with sarcasm. "That is two of my friends you have hurt within a few days."

"I didn't mean… I didn't think they would—"

"It appears you didn't think about much at all." Lady Jesson broke off, her head turning towards the door. Now she'd stopped talking, he could hear voices in the corridor. Voices getting louder.

Nick opened the next door along the corridor, but the room was in darkness. "You're wasting my time," he said to Miss Yelland, no longer trying to conceal his irritation. He had spent a good twenty minutes walking around the gardens, interrupting several courting couples in the process, but there had been no sign of Isabella or da Gama. He could not ask if anyone had seen her for fear of causing the very scandal he was trying to avert.

Miss Yelland had been waiting for him when he returned to the house, and the equally annoying Miss Quinn had joined her friend. What it had to do with them he didn't know—spite or jealousy, he supposed—but he couldn't shake them off without making a fuss.

"They… she must be in one of these rooms, Mr Carterton. You didn't find her in the garden," Miss Yelland pointed out.

"She hasn't reappeared in the ballroom," Miss Quinn added. "I was watching out for her."

"That is good of you."

She smiled, his sarcasm escaping her. Had the two of them conspired to have Isabella discovered in a compromising situation?

"Try the next one," Miss Yelland urged, walking on down the corridor.

Nick sighed. "As you wish."

This room *was* occupied. The candles flickered as a cool draught blew into the corridor, but there was enough light for him to see Isabella standing near the fireplace with someone else. Lady Jesson.

"Ah, we have found them." Miss Yelland pushed past him, her head turning as she gazed around the room. "Oh, there is no-one else here."

"Who were you expecting to see?" Lady Jesson asked. Beside her, Lady Isabella's lips curved into a small smile.

Nick hurried across the room to the curtains fluttering by an open door. He stepped out onto the terrace, but he couldn't see anyone who might have just left the room.

"Thank you for assisting me, Miss Yelland," Nick said, coming back into the room. "I'm sure you will be wanting to get back to the ballroom now."

All four women ignored him.

"Senhor da Gama…" Miss Yelland waved a hand. "That Portuguese. I saw him coming this way soon after Lady Isabella left the ballroom."

"How observant of you," Lady Jesson said, her tone politeness itself.

Like Miss Quinn, Miss Yelland seemed impervious to sarcasm. "He was here, wasn't he? That's why the window is open." There was a gleam of satisfaction in her eyes. Nick couldn't understand why Isabella didn't seem concerned about the gossip these two interfering women could spread, even though Lady Jesson had been present.

"Why yes." Isabella finally spoke, sounding surprisingly calm. "I felt a little overwhelmed—it is my first ball, you know. Senhor da Gama was entertaining us with descriptions of his home country."

"You didn't leave with—"

"Miss Yelland," Lady Jesson interrupted, "before you decide to spread false rumours about Lady Isabella, I suggest you consider some of the activities you have indulged in this season that you might not wish to become common knowledge."

Miss Yelland's jaw dropped and she stared at Lady Jesson.

"What things?" Miss Quinn asked, turning her inquisitive gaze on her friend.

"I don't know what you're talking about," Miss Yelland said, raising her chin. "Come, Celia, our assistance appears to be no longer needed."

Miss Quinn followed her friend out of the room, casting only one curious glance over her shoulder.

"Mr Carterton, would you be so good as to order my father's carriage?" Isabella said. "Maria will escort me home."

"I will come with you," Nick said. Perhaps he could find out what was going on.

"Thank you, but there is no need. It isn't far, and there will be both a coachman and a footman with me."

"There is every need," Nick said, annoyed at the feeling they were keeping something from him. "Your brother entrusted your well-being to me. Now you have put yourself in a position where scandal could ruin your marriage prospects."

Isabella smiled. "Yes, that is convenient. I do know what people might say, but Maria was with me the whole time."

"That wouldn't stop the likes of Miss Yelland speculating..." Nick looked at Lady Jesson. "Did I hear you threatening her? What you said could be tantamount to blackmail, in fact."

"Is it blackmail to prevent her doing something underhand?" Lady Jesson asked. "Besides, I have no scandalous information with which to do so."

"But you said… you implied that you had." Isabella was looking as confused as he felt.

"Yes, I did, and now I know she does have a secret. I don't know what it is, but that doesn't matter as long as Miss Yelland thinks I do know."

"Good grief!" Nick wondered if he should introduce Lady Jesson to Talbot—their minds seemed to work in similarly convoluted ways.

"It would not do for you to escort me home, Mr Carterton," Isabella said. "The coachman will tell my father, and he will assume you are one of my more enthusiastic suitors."

Looking at her flushed face and determined expression, Nick felt an odd fluttering in his chest. Why shouldn't he be one of her suitors?

"When we were dancing, Lord Narwood said he would write to my father," Isabella went on. "If there is any useful information to be had, the matter is becoming more urgent."

"Yes, of course, I'll see what I can do."

"The carriage, Mr Carterton?" Lady Jesson prompted. "Could you also inform Lady Cerney that Bella has gone home and that the carriage will return for her?"

"Very well."

He needed to give this some thought. The idea of having Isabella as a wife was becoming increasingly attractive, but he didn't want her to be forced into a marriage with him just to avoid Narwood. He wanted a wife who'd chosen him freely.

It wasn't until he'd handed the two women into the coach that he wondered what Isabella had meant by saying a potential scandal might be 'convenient'.

~

Luis turned into his street, but paused at the corner, unsure what to do. He brushed at the marks on his breeches from scaling the garden wall, swearing as he succeeded only in smearing the mess further.

Lady Brigham would not have reported to Don Felipe yet, and she only knew that Luis was trying to befriend Isabella. No, Lady Jesson was the problem. He was convinced that she would do as she had said, and inform the authorities if he showed his face in society again.

He might have a day or two's grace, but Lady Brigham or Don Felipe would soon realise that he was avoiding the very places he needed to be to work on Lady Sudbury. They had bought his co-operation with a false promise; he would be even more stupid to believe they would give him any assistance to return home once he was of no further use to them.

Don Felipe had been very convincing in his initial letter—a letter that he was told to keep hidden from his father. He'd told a sad a tale of a mother ruthlessly abandoned in favour of a more prestigious marriage, and himself sent as a baby to a poor family to hide his existence from the world and from his father's new wife. Later letters had fed his resentment before offering the enticing possibility of claiming what was 'rightfully his'.

A sick feeling of shame filled him—how could he have believed Papá would willingly abandon his mother like that? Abandon him as a baby? Papá *hadn't* abandoned him, but treated him as a valued son.

He'd believed Don Felipe's story and his promises because he'd wanted to.

And what would Papá say about his attempts to seduce two respectable women? Not to mention his idiocy in believing Don Felipe without even checking whether such a thing was possible.

He should go home. There would be plenty of time on the voyage to decide how he could explain his absence to his father.

Back in his room, Luis pulled his trunk from beneath the bed, thankful that Mendes was not in the habit of attending him at night. The trunk was far too small to hold all his new clothing—he would buy a bigger one tomorrow and then find an agent who could book his passage home.

Did he have enough money?

He sank onto the bed with a curse. He'd already spent or lost over half of the cash Don Felipe had given him the day before. This was not going to be as easy as he'd hoped. Running a hand down the velvet of the elaborate coat he still wore, he wondered how much he could sell it for. This, and the other fine suits, might be enough to buy his passage home. He would work out the details in the morning.

Pushing the trunk back under the bed, he began to undress. It would take time to make his arrangements, and he must give no clue about his change of heart to Don Felipe until he was ready to leave. Not even then, he reflected, trying to think it through. Don Felipe would not want his spying activities made public—not in England, and not in Spain, either. Was the man ruthless enough to have him killed to ensure his silence? He couldn't risk it.

Was Don Felipe even working for the Spanish government? Luis cursed himself again. Don Felipe was unlikely to have told him if he'd asked, but the question hadn't even occurred to him.

No-one must know that he had failed tonight.

CHAPTER 22

*T*he confrontation came shortly after noon the next day. Bella had spent part of the morning packing some of her plainest gowns in a small trunk, and writing letters for Langton to take to Archer and Maria Jesson. She didn't know what was to happen, and it was best to be prepared. Then she was due to make yet more tedious calls with her aunt. She was waiting for Aunt Aurelia in the hall when the butler appeared.

"Lord Marstone wishes to see you in his study, Lady Isabella."

"I am on my way out, Mowbray. Can it not wait?" Even as she spoke, Bella knew it was futile. With a sigh, she pulled at her bonnet ribbons.

Her father sat in a chair by the blazing fire with a glass of brandy to hand on a nearby table. Bella took the seat facing his. Her determination to stand her ground did not prevent her heart beating uncomfortably in her chest, or dispel the sick feeling in her stomach.

"Lord Narwood has written to make an offer of marriage to you." He lifted a paper in his right hand, his left lying unmoving in his lap. "Aurelia did not mention his name yesterday. Why did I not know about this?"

"You would have to ask Aunt Aurelia, Papa."

"Hmpf." He flapped the letter. "A viscount is below my station, certainly, but it has the advantage of getting you off my hands quickly. He has wealth, and political influence." He stared at Bella, then smiled. "Yes, it will do nicely. Ring the bell. Mowbray can summon Staverton to write the contract and apply for a special licence. Narwood is as keen to see this deal made as I am."

Bella fingernails dug into her palms. She hadn't wanted to use the scene she'd set up last night, but she had no choice. Even if Mr Carterton could find some way of dissuading Lord Narwood, there wouldn't be time to put it into effect.

"Papa, Lord Narwood only wants to marry me because he needs an heir."

"What of that? That is why most men marry."

Could she really do this?

She thought of Narwood's cold gaze, the way he inspected her person, and felt again that cold shiver.

Yes, she could. Life as a spinster was far preferable.

"Papa, what would happen if Lord Narwood discovered...?"

"Discovered what? Come on, out with it, girl!"

Bella looked at her father's scowl, and swallowed against a lump in her throat. She had never rebelled like this before, and wasn't sure what he might do. "That his heir was not of his blood." It came out little more than a whisper.

"What? What have you done?" Her father's face turned red. "Mowbray! Mowbray!"

Bella winced at his shout, but sat still.

"My lord?" Mowbray stood by the door.

"Fetch Lady Cerney. At once!"

Mowbray bowed, closing the door behind him.

"Well, girl?"

Before she could speak, her father took a shuddering breath and then coughed, his face becoming darker, almost purple.

"What is it now, brother?" Aunt Aurelia hurried into the room, still clad in redingote and bonnet.

He jabbed a finger towards Bella. "I want an explanation of... what this slut has... just told me." His voice was weaker than before, with pauses as he gasped another breath. "I was paying you to... introduce her into society... not to let her comp... compromise herself."

"She has not." Aunt Aurelia didn't even glance at Bella. "Don't be ridiculous."

Her father slapped his hand onto the arm of his chair. "She told me that—"

"Do you really wish all the servants to know, Marstone?" Aunt Aurelia gestured towards the door, where the butler still stood. "Mowbray, tell the coachman we will not be needing him."

"An explanation, madam." Papa was recovering his breath now. "Damme, Aurelia, I'll not... not pay your bills if this is true."

"Isabella has been chaperoned at all times." She glanced at Bella, raising one brow. "I have no notion when she could have done any such thing."

"Chaperoned by *you*, Aurelia? That... that is what I am paying you for."

"By me, her maid, or the mother of one of her friends." She tilted her head, her lips pursed. "You agreed to reimburse me for intro-ducing her to society, not for acting as some kind of nursemaid."

"I paid you to arrange a suitable match. I have had..." He broke off to wheeze again. "I've had an offer from someone who was *not* on your list."

Aunt Aurelia turned to Bella. "Narwood?"

Bella nodded. "He told me he would last night."

"You did know!" Papa glared at his sister. "Why did you not—?"

"I gave you a list of suitable prospects. Narwood is not suitable."

"I will be the judge of that."

Aunt Aurelia shrugged. "What, exactly, do you think Bella has done?"

He glared at Bella. "Tell her."

Bella looked down at her hands.

"Perhaps Isabella wishes to tell me in private?" Aunt Aurelia rose. "Excuse us. Come, Isabella."

"Aurelia! Do not walk away—" Her father pushed himself out of his chair as he spoke, lurching forwards before one leg buckled and he grabbed at the chair Bella had just left. He clung to it, almost falling to the floor.

"Calm yourself, brother," Aunt Aurelia said. "Mowbray, his lordship needs assistance!"

She didn't wait to see what the butler did, but led the way across the hall into the parlour. Bella looked over her shoulder to see that Papa was being helped back into his chair, then hurried after her aunt.

"Now, Isabella, what have you done?"

"Miss Yelland and Miss Quinn found me in a private parlour with Senhor da Gama at the ball last night." That was almost true—they certainly suspected that Luis had been there.

"What happened?"

Bella didn't reply. She had not anticipated her aunt questioning her in detail.

Aunt Aurelia sighed. "Marstone is likely to refuse to pay my bills now whether or not you wed Narwood." She smiled, her eyes remaining cold. "Although he's already paid some of them. The problem with buying loyalty, as he does, is that the loyalty vanishes when the payment stops. Now, did that Portuguese attack you?"

"No." She didn't think he would have done, even if he had forced her to go into the garden with him. "But Papa thinks I may be enceinte."

"Why does he think that?"

"I implied it."

Aunt Aurelia stared at her for a moment then, to Bella's astonishment, leaned back in her chair and began to laugh. "Good heavens—I never dreamed you were as much of a schemer as Wingrave."

Bella did not share her aunt's amusement. "I am only determined not to be married to Lord Narwood, Aunt."

"Yes, well, I cannot blame you for that. What is your plan?"

"Only to make it plain that if a marriage is arranged with Lord Narwood, there will soon be gossip about the... about whether he will be the father of his first child. Lady Jesson will take care of that."

"Lady Jesson? I don't know her well, but I didn't think she was the type to ruin your reputation."

"I will ask her to. And once it becomes known, Miss Yelland and Miss Quinn will take great delight in confirming it."

"Those cats?" She shook her head. "Isabella, no respectable man will have you if this becomes known."

"I know; Maria warned me that might happen. But Aunt, if someone won't take my word that nothing happened, I wouldn't want to marry him."

Aunt Aurelia regarded her closely and gave a quick nod. "It is your life, after all, and no doubt Wingrave will support you. But if I back you up, Marstone may insist you marry the Portuguese. Are you prepared to be shunted off to Portugal?"

"He won't want that."

"Why not? I…" She put up a hand as Bella started to speak. "No, I don't think I want to know."

Bella pressed on. "Are you going to confirm my story?" Her aunt could still spoil her plan.

"Isabella, if you come out of this well, put in a good word for me to Wingrave, will you? I could do with some assistance with the bills I've run up while I've been in Town."

"I don't think Will has a lot—"

"If he hasn't now, he will when he inherits. I presume you need me to confirm that you may be in an interesting condition, and that Lady Jesson is a known gossip?"

"Yes, please."

"Come, then."

Papa scowled at them as they resumed their seats in the study.

"I'm afraid it is quite true, brother," Aunt Aurelia said. "However, I should be able to contain any possible scandal if Isabella does not come to the notice of society for a while. If there are… unfortunate consequences of Isabella's little indiscretion, you—"

"Little indiscretion? The girl has shamed our family name."

"Oh, come, brother. It happens all the time."

"Not in my family. It is insupportable." His voice rose to a shout. "If

I had my strength, I'd...I'd..." He broke off, gasping for breath as beads of sweat appeared on his forehead. He reached for the glass on the nearby table, but knocked it to the floor. "Aurelia, get... get Mowbray. Now."

Aunt Aurelia shrugged, and pulled the bell.

"I think his lordship needs a doctor," she said dispassionately, when the butler arrived.

"I need Isabella locked into her room," her father gasped. "See to it, Mowbray, on pain of dismissal."

"If you will step this way, Lady Isabella?" Mowbray held the door for her.

Bella hesitated, but her aunt said nothing so she followed the butler into the hall.

～

"How's the courtship going?" Lord Carterton asked as Nick walked into the parlour. "Have you been taking that... that punctual woman driving again?"

Nick poured himself a glass of brandy and sat down, not quite ready to discuss the way his ideas—feelings—were changing. But there *was* something his father might be able to help him with.

"No—I've spent the whole afternoon trying to find out more about Narwood," he said. "He's about to make an offer for Isabella."

"Ah. Any success?"

Nick sighed. "No." He'd just returned from seeing Talbot. The spymaster knew of Narwood, but had nothing that Nick felt could be of use. "He's wealthy enough that a few losses at cards wouldn't bother him. If there is any scandal to be found, I doubt he'd care— in fact, he seems the type to be proud of a by-blow or two, or having several mistresses at once." He took a sip from his glass, the spirit warming his throat but doing nothing to soothe his thoughts.

"Hmm." His father looked at him over his spectacles. "I sent a few notes to friends after you asked me about him yesterday. It seems there is some question about how his first wife died. No evidence, though, and it might be merely gossip."

Gossip or not, Nick had to do something to extricate Isabella from the proposed marriage. It was bad enough that she disliked the man—with good reason—but he could not let her be married to someone who might have harmed his previous wife.

"Even if there were evidence, Father, it would do no good. By the time anything could be done, she'd be wed to him."

"What about her brother?"

Talbot had also said that Wingrave was almost finished with his investigations in Paris and could be back in England within a week, but that was no help.

"He might return soon, but I can't wait that long."

"You'd better run off with her, then."

Nick choked on a mouthful of brandy. He wasn't sure whether Father had been joking, but as he regained his breath, his mind cleared and he felt a sense of calm. He'd toyed with the idea that he could be a suitor for Isabella without really taking it seriously, but now Father had put it into words it felt... perfect.

For him, at least—he was fairly sure that Isabella only regarded him as a brother. But he could not elope with her; she deserved choice in her marriage.

"I'll take her to Wingrave's place in Devonshire," he said. "There should be no scandal if she's chaperoned." Lady Jesson would help, he was sure.

"Marstone would still have the legal right to have her brought back," Lord Carterton pointed out.

"He would, yes, but I'm sure Wingrave has enough loyal servants—not to mention his wife—who could keep her safe until he returns."

Father nodded, and picked up his newspaper. Nick stared into his brandy glass, swirling the amber liquid gently. Perhaps not Lady Jesson—with her reputation for gossip, it might be better if she stayed in London to divert any speculation. Would the housekeeper be a sufficiently respectable chaperone if he rode alongside the chaise?

He started to make a mental list of the arrangements needed.

~

Later that afternoon, Bella was summoned to her father's bedroom. Aunt Aurelia sat in a chair near the window, and two men stood near the bed. Bella recognised one as Staverton, her father's secretary. The other was short and rotund. Her father lay in the bed, propped up on pillows and wearing a nightcap instead of his usual wig.

"You will not excite his lordship," the unknown man intoned. "I cannot guarantee his continued health if he is made to feel any strong emotion. That would be most deleterious."

"For heaven's sake, Smythe," Aunt Aurelia said, "I don't need a physician to tell me that. My brother is an adult—it is entirely up to him whether or not he loses his temper."

The physician sniffed, looking as if he were going to argue, but Aunt Aurelia glared at him and he inclined his head and stood back.

"Come here, girl." Bella was shocked at how weak her father's voice sounded, even though he no longer appeared to be short of breath. "You have disgraced—"

"You will wait outside, Smythe," Aunt Aurelia insisted, her voice drowning out Papa's. "And you, Staverton. You will be summoned if you are needed."

Bella was grateful for her aunt's intervention. This interview was going to be unpleasant enough without having strangers present.

"I must protest, my lady. His lordship needs—"

"This is a private family discussion, Mr Smythe."

"This way, sir," Staverton said. Smythe sniffed, and the two men left the room.

"If you have finished interfering, Aurelia...?"

"For now, brother." Aunt Aurelia moved to a chair close to the bed. Bella had not been invited to sit, but she didn't mind—she was beginning to get the feeling that her aunt had the upper hand here.

"Isabella, you have disgraced the name—"

"Let us not have that rigmarole again, Marstone. Just tell her what you've decided."

"I will conduct my own business in my own house, madam!"

"Not if you make yourself ill before you've got to the point."

In spite of her situation, Bella had to bite her lips to hide a smile. She didn't succeed—Aunt Aurelia raised a brow in her direction but said nothing. Her father didn't seem to have noticed.

"Yes, well. I don't want to wait the months it would take to find out if she is breeding or not, and Narwood may well ask for an annulment if he finds she is not a virgin."

Bella's amusement vanished. She had told the lie herself, but it was dispiriting to find how readily her father believed it of her.

He turned his head towards her. "You must marry the perpetrator of this outrage, Isabella. I might be able to salvage something from your aunt's incompetence. A visconde's son, I understand."

"So he said, Papa."

"So he said? Do you not...?" He broke off, taking several rasping breaths.

"He is about to leave the country," Bella said, before her father could carry on.

"What? He can be summoned back. I'll get... I'll get Staverton onto it right away. What is his full name?"

"I don't know. He called himself Senhor da Gama."

"What do you mean, called himself?" A vein began to throb in her father's forehead, and a sheen of sweat appeared on his skin.

"I believe he is actually the illegitimate son of a Spanish nobleman."

"What?" Aunt Aurelia's voice was quiet, but it shook slightly. Bella glanced at her, to see she was suppressing laughter. "That seems most appropriate, brother. You married your son off to a woman of dubious parentage, after all."

"You stupid woman, I did not do that knowingly! Charters deceived me. Good God, am I to be surrounded...?" He broke off. "Get Staverton back in here," he croaked. "That fool physician can stay out of my way until I've given my orders. You, girl, you go to your room now. You'll be taken to Marstone Park and kept there until I can find someone—anyone—who'll give you his name. One of the men on your aunt's list will do, if he's been alone with you at all. Even if I have to pay him! I'll not have you besmirching my family's—"

"Come away, Isabella," Aunt Aurelia said, taking Bella's arm and urging her towards the door. With an uncertain glance at her father, Bella followed.

"Aurelia, come back here! I've *told* you not to walk away while I'm talking to you."

The door to the sitting room burst open, and the physician hurried over to the bed. "My lord, calm yourself. You really must not excite yourself so!"

"Get Staverton in here, now! I want—"

Aunt Aurelia closed the door behind them and accompanied Bella to her bedroom. The footman who had been guarding her door kept pace behind them and cleared his throat as her aunt followed Bella into her room.

"Er, excuse me, my lady."

"Yes? What is it?"

"His lordship said no-one was to talk to Lady Isabella."

Aunt Aurelia stared at him until he shuffled his feet and stood back.

"Sorry, my lady."

Aunt Aurelia closed the door rather harder than was necessary and crossed to the window, beckoning Bella to follow her. "I wouldn't put it past that insolent lackey to listen."

Bella sank into a chair, feeling less distressed than she'd expected. Perhaps it was because she had anticipated this outcome. Molly and Langton had already smuggled her small trunk out of the house and taken it to Maria, along with the letters. Now all she had to do was to get out of the house unseen. She had to leave tonight. Here in London she had people who would help her—it would be far more difficult to escape once she'd been taken to Marstone Park.

"Isabella, I cannot let you run off unprotected." Aunt Aurelia sat on the window seat.

What? How did her aunt know?

"You are thinking of that, aren't you?"

Bella nodded. There was little point in denying it.

"I cannot take you home with me—Cerney would not like to get involved in a dispute with Marstone."

"Papa could have me brought back, anyway."

"Yes. He has the right, in law. You'd be better at Wingrave's place in Devonshire. Marstone would still send someone to bring you back, but he'd have a fight on his hands. However, much as I sympathise, I am not prepared to escort you such a distance, particularly as Marstone is likely to send that secretary of his after us. He may not be able to force us to return with him, but he could make enough fuss to cause more scandal."

"I understand, Aunt." She shouldn't feel disappointed at her aunt's words—she had not been expecting to receive help from that quarter.

"Had you planned beyond telling my brother that you might be in an interesting condition?"

Bella opened her mouth to answer, but wondered how much she trusted her aunt.

Aunt Aurelia sighed. "Isabella, I have as little love for that man as you. Even if I betrayed you to him, I doubt he'd give me the money he promised. But I will not let you risk yourself on a long journey alone."

"I won't be alone, Aunt."

"Who will go with you?"

Bella still hesitated, but what had she to lose? Will *had* promised to employ anyone who lost their position through helping her.

"My maid, and one of the footmen. One of Will's men is in Town as well, and I think Lady— That is, I think Will's man has received a message that I need to escape."

"So you only need help to get out of the house?"

Could it really be managed so easily?

"Aunt, could you complain about that footman's insolence?" She pointed to the door. "If Langton can be assigned to guard me instead, that is all you need to do."

"Tonight?" Aunt Aurelia nodded. "Yes, the sooner the better, I think." She patted Bella on the shoulder. "Do take care, my dear."

CHAPTER 23

"*I* am afraid Lady Isabella is not at home to visitors," the butler said, as Nick stood at the top of the steps to Marstone House.

He was early, so it was unlikely that Lady Isabella had already left the house. "Is she unwell?"

"I am not at liberty to say, sir."

"I will see Lady Cerney, then." Nick took a step forward, forcing the butler to move aside.

"Very well, sir."

Nick gazed at a portrait of some Marstone ancestor while he waited, trying to think what he should say. He really needed to see Isabella and find out if she wished to be taken to Devonshire before he made further arrangements. Lady Cerney might at least confirm whether Isabella was still here.

"If you would step this way, sir?" The butler led the way upstairs. The curtains in the room he was shown into were only half drawn, but there was enough light to show that this was a bedroom, not a parlour.

"His lordship wished to see you, sir," the butler said, then bowed and left.

Nick scanned the room, only then noticing Marstone in the bed, his head and shoulders supported on a mound of pillows.

"What do you want with Isabella, Carterton?" Marstone's voice was a mere croak.

Nick knew the earl had been ill, but he hadn't realised how unwell he was.

"Sit down, man, don't loom over me like that." The testy voice was accompanied by a brief wave of a hand towards an upright chair near the bed.

"I called to enquire whether she wished to drive with me this afternoon." The truth, if not the whole truth.

"You've been seen with her a few times recently, I understand." Marstone's words came out somewhat slurred. "What are your intentions? Are you courting the chit?"

Nick hesitated. Did that question imply that Marstone was not planning on Narwood for a son-in-law?

"No, I am not." Not yet.

The image of her sharing his life, and sharing his bed, had been in his mind most of the night, but didn't want to court her in earnest until he could free her of the threat of an unwanted marriage. He didn't want a wife who'd married him just to escape someone else.

"Really?" There was an unpleasant half-smile on Marstone's face that made Nick feel uneasy. "You have been seen with her on numerous occasions, Carterton, and you attempted to see her here today. Why, if you are not courting her?"

The truth was unlikely to make things worse for Isabella than they already were. "Wingrave asked me to stand in for him while he was away, to ensure she wasn't made to marry against her wishes."

"You...? He asked...?" Marstone's face turned a shade of dull red, but to Nick's surprise there was no furious outburst. The earl took a deep breath and continued. "I might have known he would meddle somehow. Nevertheless, you *have* been seen in company with her, Carterton. She'll have a good dowry, a large one. A barony is not as high as I'd like, but people will readily believe you—" Marstone's words cut off abruptly, but his gaze was still fixed on Nick.

Nick's attention sharpened. Marstone hadn't stopped because he was unwell; he had thought better of what he was going to say. Had gossip already spread about her tryst with da Gama last night? Or had *he* been made the subject of the gossip?

"We'll see what Isabella has to say about you. I'm sure there's something to be done." Marstone reached out and rang a little bell on a table by the bed. A door at the far side of the room opened, and a man entered—the earl's valet, from the look of him.

"Get Mowbray to bring Lady Isabella here," the earl ordered.

"Very good, my lord."

Nick walked over to the window. He could leave now and avoid the coercion he suspected Marstone was about to apply, but he needed to know that Isabella was all right. It wasn't long before the butler entered the room, stopping just inside the door. "The house-keeper is fetching the spare key to Lady Isabella's room, my lord."

"Spare key?"

Marstone's words echoed Nick's thought and his jaw clenched. Marstone was keeping his daughter locked up? He made an effort to relax; he must remain calm if he was to be of any assistance.

"Er, yes, my lord. The footman on duty overnight is absent, so we cannot enter the room."

"The footman's gone?" Marstone pushed himself up, and the valet dashed to rearrange the pillows behind him. "Fetch Lady Cerney. Now!"

Nick stepped into the shadow of a curtain; Marstone seemed to have forgotten his presence.

"What is it now, Marstone?" Lady Cerney swept into the room, swathed in a loose robe and shedding a fine cloud of hair powder as she moved.

"Where is Isabella?"

"How would I know? I'm not her maid." Far from being worried or surprised, Lady Cerney appeared to be amused. Marstone didn't answer, sitting with his eyes on the door. The silence was heavy, ominous.

"Well?" Marstone barked as a footman appeared in the doorway.

"Lady Isabella's room is empty, my lord. No-one has seen her since yesterday evening."

She hadn't run off alone, surely? Nick's anger turned to a sick feeling in his stomach.

"Gone?" In a sudden burst of energy, Marstone flung the bedclothes back and swore as he tried to disentangle his legs from the sheets.

"Do take care, brother, or you will fall." Lady Cerney's tone did not match the concern in her words, and she made no move to assist the earl.

Marstone pushed himself to his feet and stood for a moment, swaying and breathing heavily. "Mowbray, get Staverton up here, now." The butler hurried off, and Marstone turned to his sister. "What do you know about this, Aurelia? You can forget having your bills paid."

"That was made plain yesterday. Why you think I owe you any further co-operation, I have no idea."

"You... you..." Marstone took a step towards Lady Cerney, then staggered. Nick hurried forward as the man began to collapse, and helped him to sit back on the bed.

"Should you not send for help, my lady?" Nick asked, wondering at her lack of concern, but the valet hurried in as he spoke.

"I think you had better get him back into bed and send for the doctor again," Lady Cerney said to the valet. "Damn fool. He's been warned not to lose his temper." She turned to leave.

"My lady?" Nick hurried after her, and she paused in the corridor. "Am I to understand that Lady Isabella has run away?" Wingrave would never forgive him—and rightly so—if harm came to his sister. But this was no longer about his word to Wingrave.

"I assume so. She assured me she would have her maid and footman with her, and one of Wingrave's men." She met Nick's gaze, a challenge in her eyes.

"You let her go?"

"What should I have done?" Lady Cerney asked. "My brother was going to incarcerate her at Marstone Park again until he could marry her off. She said she had made arrangements."

Why hadn't she come to him? He felt a stab of pain that she did not trust him to help her.

"I expect she's heading for Wingrave's place in Devonshire," Lady Cerney went on. "She'll be safe enough there for a while."

"If she gets there." He must go after her. If Archer was involved, why hadn't *he* sent word? "Excuse me, Lady Cerney."

The post-chaise rattled along the road, the houses and occasional buildings giving way to rougher countryside. Bella shifted uncomfortably at the weight of the child on her lap.

"I'll take him, my lady," Fletcher said, and Bella handed Billy over gratefully, smoothing the dull blue fabric of her skirt.

"You mustn't call me that," she reminded the seamstress.

"No matter," Archer said, from the other end of the seat. "As long as you don't do it when anyone else is around."

"Yes, Mr Fletcher."

Archer looked like a respectable merchant, and Fletcher's clothing was of good enough quality for her to pass as his wife. Bella's mob cap covered most of her hair, and her plain gown and cloak had been borrowed from one of Lady Jesson's maids. 'Mr and Mrs Fletcher' were travelling to Bath with their young son and servants. Poor Molly and Langton had been relegated to the outside seat at the back of the chaise. Thankfully the air was warm, even though drizzle still greyed the sky.

"Hounslow Heath." Archer indicated the scrubby grass and stands of trees. "We should be safe enough in daylight, though."

"Oh, I read about highwaymen," Fletcher said, bouncing Billy on her knee.

Bella still marvelled at the difference between this cheerful woman and the haggard seamstress she'd first met.

"There was one who asked a lady to dance, and only took some of her money," Fletcher went on.

"Du Vall," Archer said. "Over a hundred years ago, that was."

Bella let the discussion of legendary robberies flow past her, returning her gaze to the passing scenery. She wriggled her shoulders; the undergarments she wore felt rather scratchy. She was used to smoother fabrics, but Maria had pointed out that she would be staying at several inns during the journey, and it wouldn't do to raise suspicion by having undergarments that were too fine. Her father would send Staverton after her, and possibly others, as soon as her escape was discovered, but he would be looking for a young lady with a maid and footman, not a respectable steward and his wife, travelling to Bath with their child and nursemaid.

She hoped Maria's footman had delivered her note to Mr Carterton this morning. It had felt wrong to set off without letting him know, but her father's threats had stopped her doing so. Father would easily find out that he had been seen with her as often as any of the others on Aunt Aurelia's list—more often, in fact. If he also helped her to run away, Father would use every means he could to force a marriage. She was not going to submit to that—she wanted to choose for herself.

It wouldn't be fair to Mr Carterton, either. He was courting Jemima Roper—and even without that, he had only been seen so much with her because he was standing in for Will. He'd told her to think of him as a brother, and a man did not wish to marry his sister.

That was a pity, though; if her father did win in the end, Mr Carterton was by far the best of the men she'd met. No-one had as nice a smile as Luis da Gama, but Mr Carterton's came close, and there was no comparison between the characters of the two men.

Archer had passed from tales of highwaymen to smugglers and their battles with excisemen. Bella listened for a while, and would normally have been fascinated by such things, but her mind kept returning to her own flight. It was late morning, and if she hadn't been missed yet she would be soon. How long would it take her father to guess where she was going? Would Staverton overtake them on the road and recognise Langton and Molly? Possibly not—Archer had pointed out that most lords and ladies, and ambitious men like Staverton, took little notice of those beneath them.

A rider went past, breaking into a trot to overtake the chaise. Bella relaxed a little when she didn't recognise him.

"Best not to look, my... Mary," Archer said. "One of his lordship's men might recognise your face."

Bella looked away from the window. "I'll take Billy again," she said. Anyone looking for her would surely take little notice of a woman with a child on her knee. She enjoyed the feeling of the small, trusting body in her arms and wondered, with a lump in her throat, what it would be like to hold a child of her own. A child with a father who loved them both, who would discuss things with her and not merely give orders.

They changed horses without incident a couple of times, and stopped for dinner at Maidenhead. The postboys took them to a bustling inn, its yard too busy with ostlers changing teams and loading luggage for anyone to take particular notice of their party.

"I've enough money for a private parlour," Archer said as they paused to let a group of travellers out through the inn door. "But anyone making enquiries would ask about—"

"No parlour," Bella decided. Archer nodded, and led the way indoors. Inside, the taproom seemed as busy and noisy as the yard, but Archer managed to find a table large enough for five. The meal, when it came, was a lukewarm stew swimming with grease. Squashed between Molly and Langton, with Billy on her lap, Bella forced herself to eat a few mouthfuls, but was happy to spend the rest of the time feeding Billy from the bowl of bread and milk provided. The boy was still sleepy, and Bella wondered if Fletcher had given him a little paregoric. Bella couldn't blame her if she had—the prospect of being cooped up in the chaise for the next couple of days with a fractious child was not an attractive one.

"It's another couple of hours, at the most, to Reading," Archer said, when everyone had finished eating. "We'll find an inn there for the night. Best to get a bit further from London?" He looked at Bella as he spoke.

"Yes. I mean, Molly, are you all right—?"

"I'll be fine, m...Mary," the maid said firmly. "I've got a warm coat."

"I'll get the horses put to," Langton said, and hurried off.

The stew seemed to settle in a cold lump in Bella's stomach. She'd prefer to travel through the night, to lessen the chance of someone catching up with them, but that could be dangerous and wasn't fair on the others. If she was taken back now, she wouldn't only have to live at Marstone Park as she had before, she would be locked in her room and supervised at all times.

Luis counted out his coins in the grey light from the window, ignoring the rattle of rain on the glass as he tried to think of all the expenses he might incur on his journey. He'd never taken much notice of the charges in inns at home, secure in the knowledge that he had plenty of money for his needs, and Don Felipe had paid for most of the expenses on his journey to London.

Once he'd pawned his spare clothing, he might have enough money for the packet boat to Lisbon and on to his home in Spain. An outside seat on the coach would be cheaper, and would help to ensure he had enough money left when he reached Portugal. At least it was summer, he thought sourly, even if the weather here was nothing like the glorious blazing skies at home. He might get wet, but hopefully not too cold.

Luis swept the coins back into the leather purse and placed it beneath the mattress, smoothing the counterpane back into place. He'd try a few more pawnbrokers tomorrow, to see if he could find someone to promise better prices, but he couldn't pawn his clothing until he was ready to leave—Mendes would notice if anything was missing.

He didn't know the best places to go, that was the problem. As he'd explored further from the fashionable parts of Town, the pawnbrokers became more ready to accept clothing rather than jewellery, but the sums they offered were only a tiny fraction of the initial cost. The insinuations that he'd stolen the clothes he wore were as insulting as the feeling that he was not being offered a fair price.

Smiling without humour, he thought that he was the last person who should be complaining about cheating others. Lady Milton, when she'd sent him away, had called him a boy who could not think beyond his own pretty face. She was almost correct—all he'd thought about was claiming what he thought should be his, without any consideration of others.

Well, the face hadn't got him far, but perhaps he was beginning to grow up.

Footsteps sounded in the hall, and he hurriedly picked up the book he was pretending to read. Don Felipe burst into the room without ceremony, his face thunderous.

"Lady Brigham says you paid no attention to Lady Sudbury at the ball two nights ago, although she was present, and you have not been seen in public since then. Where have you been?"

Luis set the book down and got to his feet. "It's only two days, Don Felipe. I've been seducing Lady Sudbury, as you instructed me." He allowed some annoyance to show in his voice, as if he was irritated about being questioned.

"No-one has seen you with her." Don Felipe's tone was a little milder this time.

Had Don Felipe had him followed everywhere? Surely he could not have done, or he would now be asking about visits to pawn shops.

"I have been discreet about it," he said. "I assumed you would want that."

"But the Marstone girl—you failed there."

Luis shrugged. "I tried, but Lady Isabella is another woman with honour. I may yet succeed. Should I concentrate on Lady Sudbury?"

Don Felipe did not respond immediately, but stood with narrowed eyes, one finger tapping his lips. "No," he said at last. "In fact, I don't think the Sudbury woman will be worth pursuing at all. No, I have a different task for you." He ran his eyes over Luis's embroidered waistcoat, and the matching coat lying over a chair. "One that will require quite a different wardrobe. Mendes will bring you suitable garments and take those away. I will brief you tomorrow."

Luis swore as Don Felipe left. What now? He needed money from selling his clothes to pay for his journey. He could pack up now and find a pawn shop, but at this hour of the night, and clearly in urgent need of funds, he was likely to get even less than he'd been offered when making his enquires. And who knew when Mendes would return? He could be caught while leaving.

No—he should concentrate on not losing the money he already had. He pulled the leather purse from beneath the mattress again, and assessed its bulk.

CHAPTER 24

$\mathcal{N}$ ick slid off his rented hack outside the inn in Newbury—
it was time to hire a new horse, and to break his fast. Not
for the first time, he wondered if he was making too much of this.
While he was at Marstone House the day before, a note from Isabella
had been delivered to Brooke Street. She had explained that she'd had
no option but to run away, but was suitably escorted by several people
including Archer, so he need not worry.

Archer was a competent man, but Marstone was sure to be issuing
orders to fetch his daughter back if he hadn't succumbed to an
apoplexy after Nick left him. Archer might need help if they were
caught up by someone like Staverton with Marstone's authority to
involve a local magistrate or constable.

That was only an excuse, he admitted to himself as he handed his
mount to an ostler. Even if his help was not needed, he could not
remain in London while Isabella might be in danger—whether from
the hazards of travel or from being back in her father's power.

"Breakfast," he said to a passing waiter, sinking into a chair in the
half-empty taproom. Riding until after dark and then getting up with
the sun might not have been such a good idea—he was lightheaded
with hunger and fatigue.

He felt more human after a plate of ham and eggs and a pot of coffee.

"In a hurry, sir?" the waiter asked, seeing Nick put his money on the table.

"Trying to catch up with some friends," he said. "A young lady, with a maid and a couple of menservants. Have they passed through here?" Newbury was an obvious place for them to stop to change horses, or even to have a meal, and this was the main post-house. He could not be far behind them now, although no-one at the other inns he'd stopped at recalled them passing.

"Funny you should say that, sir. You're the third person to ask."

Third?

"Who else is enquiring?"

"A gent, older than you, a couple of hours ago. Said something about the lady's father being ill, and she needed to go home."

That would be Marstone's man—Nick had expected to be behind him. He'd spent over an hour changing into riding gear and getting directions to Wingrave's place in Devonshire, so Staverton was likely to be ahead of him, and may well have ridden longer into the night.

"The other was a family, about an hour ago. A couple with a baby, and some servants. In a yellow bounder, they were." He scratched his head. "Funny thing is, they was heading west on the Bath road, like the first gent—even asked how far to Marlborough—but they went off towards Andover instead."

Nick gave the man a coin for his information. Coaches to Exeter normally went via Bath, but Wingrave's place was east of Exeter and could also be reached via a more southerly route.

Could the 'family' be the chaise he was after? If so, they had changed their route when they knew Marstone's man was ahead of them. Sensible, as he might backtrack if he could find no trace of them. He had to admire whichever of them had thought to ask the same question a pursuer would—it would not have occurred to him to do so.

But where did Isabella get a baby...?

Billy Fletcher, of course.

Nick shook his head with a smile as he spread a roll with strawberry jam and wrapped it in a napkin to take with him. If that wasn't Isabella's idea, she had a quick-thinking ally.

His anxiety for her safety abated, but he wasn't going to turn back now.

He hired a new mount several more times that day, encouraged by news of a family changing horses at the Star and Garter in Andover less than an hour before him. Even so, he was nearing Salisbury by the time he came up behind a post-chaise with a man and a woman travelling outside. As they turned to look at him, he recognised Langton and Molly, their expressions of alarm changing to relief as he drew closer. Langton faced forwards again, and he heard a faint shout, then the vehicle began to slow. As it came to a stop, a figure in a plain blue round gown scrambled down into the road and Archer appeared from the other side.

"It's only Mr Carterton, my lady," Molly called from her seat at the back.

A feeling of lightness spread through him as Isabella leaned against the carriage and closed her eyes. She was unharmed, and he could make sure she reached Devonshire safely.

"I'm sorry, I didn't mean to frighten you," Nick said as he dismounted beside her.

"I'm fine, thank you. I thought it was someone from my father." She took a deep breath, her expression wary. "Why have you come?"

"Your brother asked me to look out for you. It would have been easier if you'd told me before you set out." Disappointed that she didn't seem to be happy at his arrival, his words came out more sharply than he'd intended. He glanced at her escorts, all looking on with interest—this was not the place to discuss the rest of their journey. "I will accompany you to Devonshire," he went on. "Your father's man will eventually realise he is ahead of you, and if he retraces his route the waiter at the inn in Newbury will probably remember you now that I, too, have asked after a young lady."

Isabella nodded, and this time she smiled. It was only a little curving of the lips, but he was happy to see it.

"We were planning on stopping in Salisbury for a quick meal," Archer said.

"Good. We can compare notes then."

~

"So you have found nothing of use," Don Felipe stated, dragging out a chair and taking a seat at the grimy table. The taproom was loud with the talk and laughter of dock workers, and stank of spilled ale, sweat, and tobacco smoke.

Luis, sitting in his merchant's clothing, suppressed his resentment. "It would help if you told me what I was supposed to be listening for."

"Shipping movements."

"Santa Maria! This is London—there are dozens of ships coming and going on every tide. More! I cannot list every one. And besides, there must be easier ways of finding out when merchantmen are setting out."

"No sign of convoys being assembled?"

"Convoys? The war in America is over—why would there be a convoy?"

"Not to America. To Gibraltar." Don Felipe glared at him. "You have heard of it?"

"Of course I have. In the south."

"That's all it is to you? Something in the south?"

Luis leaned away, taken aback at Don Felipe's sudden fervour. "It belongs to the British, which is inconvenient."

"It is a stain on Spain's honour," Don Felipe spat. "It should never have been surrendered in the first place—"

"Sir!" Luis tilted his head towards the occupants of the next table. "Lower your voice."

Don Felipe's frown deepened, but when he spoke again it was more quietly. "Now we are trying to regain it, with our French allies. We are close, very close."

Luis wasn't sure what any of this had to do with him.

"We could have starved them out by now," Don Felipe said. "But last year a convoy got through. If it had not..." He pressed his lips together and turned his head away. When he looked back, his eyes burned with hatred. "The English blew up one of our magazines last year. If that convoy had not arrived, my son would still be alive."

"I'm sorry," Luis said, knowing the words to be inadequate. But his unease was deepening. The look in Don Felipe's eyes was not grief.

"We will regain it soon," Don Felipe stated, "but the garrison must not be resupplied. I want word sent if a convoy is being gathered."

"Wouldn't a convoy for Gibraltar gather in..." He tried to remember the map of southern England he'd studied on the voyage over. "...Portsmouth, or one of those ports?"

Don Felipe nodded. "I have men there, too. But no matter—I can pay others to listen here, and I have a more important task for you now. Do you have a pistol?"

"A small one," Luis admitted cautiously. Who did not go armed?

"Hmm." Don Felipe stared at the ceiling, his gaze unfocussed. Then he fumbled in a coat pocket and brought out a leather purse. Luis eyed it with interest—if he was about to be given more money, his problems could be over.

Then Don Felipe shook his head and put the purse away. "I will send Mendes to you. You may need more than one pistol."

"What for?" There had been no mention of firearms when Don Felipe's associate had persuaded him to come to England.

"I will tell you when the details are confirmed. This should be soon. In the meantime you will familiarise yourself with the major roads in southern England, in case you need to travel to carry out your task. Be here at the same time tomorrow." Don Felipe left without waiting for Luis' acknowledgement.

Luis ordered another mug of ale, and sat thinking. He didn't like the sound of pistols. Not that he was afraid, but he'd been told he would be gathering information, not killing people. The weapons might be needed for self-defence, but he didn't believe Don Felipe cared for his safety. He had also assumed he would be working for the

Spanish government, even if not officially. But, as with so much else, he hadn't bothered to find out more. He could not undo his stupidity now; all he could do was try not to make things worse.

No. Spying was dishonourable enough; he was not going to make things worse by killing someone, if that was what Don Felipe intended.

He had to find a way of extricating himself from the situation he'd got himself into.

~

Bella drank her tea gratefully. Molly was already tucking into a plate of chicken pie and vegetables at one of the nearby tables, Fletcher beside her with Billy on her knee. Bella still felt too nervous to eat her own meal.

"Archer is arranging for a second post-chaise," Mr Carterton said as he entered the private parlour and threw his coat over the back of a chair. "We'll travel faster that way."

"Thank you. It will allow Molly to ride inside, as well."

It had been a shock to find out at Newbury that someone was already looking for her, and had made such good time that he was ahead of them. Last night's stop in Reading might have been a mistake. She could have volunteered to take Molly's place outside, but neither Molly nor Archer would have agreed to that, however much she might insist.

"May I join you?" Mr Carterton asked. Something in the way he looked at her—as if he really did care about her—made her heart beat faster.

"Of course."

He sat and served himself from the dishes in the centre of the table, the savoury smell making Bella's stomach rumble. Everything would be all right now she had his help—perhaps she *could* eat something, after all.

"Mr Carterton, I am glad you have come," she said, recalling her manner when he had first caught up with them. "I was rather abrupt when you arrived." She had expected to be berated for running away, or told that she should have left matters in his hands, but he hadn't said anything. And she *was* pleased to have him here.

"It is no matter," he said. "But we shouldn't linger here. It is still possible that Staverton—if it is he—will catch up with us, but he cannot force you to return with him."

"Should we travel through the night? I didn't want to before, because of Molly and Langton being outside." The pie was as tasty as it had smelled, and she ate a few mouthfuls.

"Yes, I think that's a good idea. Staverton will eventually track you down, but it would be better if he doesn't catch up with you until you are at your brother's place." He put his cutlery down. "Isabella, why didn't you let me know you were running away? I could have escorted you from London."

"I didn't want to involve you in my difficulties." That was one way of putting it.

"I'm already involved."

"Your promise to Will, yes." She took in the tired lines on his face, the dust on his coat and hat, and warmth filled her. He'd gone to a lot of trouble to keep his word.

"No," he said, rather too loudly. Bella glanced at the other table, but their companions were still talking amongst themselves. "No," he repeated, more quietly. "I did it to make sure you were safe."

Her breath caught at the note of sincerity in his voice.

"I called at Marstone House yesterday morning." He gave a lopsided smile. "To find out if you wanted me to steal you away to Devonshire, would you believe? The butler took me to your father— he seems to have given up on Narwood."

She nodded. She couldn't explain that subterfuge to him, but he didn't ask.

"He insisted that I'd been courting you, but I told him it was no such thing."

She pushed her plate away—she must have misinterpreted his expression before. "He was determined to marry me to anyone I'd been seen with. I... well, you have escorted me several times, because of Will." Having someone else care for her as a brother must be a good thing, mustn't it?

"Isabella." He reached across the table as if he were going to take her hand, but hesitated. "Your father—" The door burst open and he sprang to his feet as two men came in and stood either side of the door. They were grooms, from the look of them, with the signs of hard riding in the mud on their boots and breeches.

"This is a private parlour," Mr Carterton protested. "Take yourselves off."

They ignored him. Another man entered, older and shorter than the grooms, but with a commanding air. The pie settled in a solid lump in Bella's stomach as she saw Langton behind the newcomer, one arm firmly in the grasp of another groom. This invasion of their private parlour wasn't a mistake. Mr Carterton had seen Langton, too; she could tell from the way his body tensed, hands curling into fists.

The short man's eyes swept the room. "You must be Carterton," he said, then turned his gaze on her. "Lady Isabella, your father has sent me to fetch you home."

"Who the devil are you?" Mr Carterton asked. Bella saw him glance at Molly and Fletcher, sitting in silence at their table, then at the strangers. His shoulders slackened as he straightened his fingers— had he been planning to fight? Luis would have done so, she was sure —and that would most likely have resulted in some or all of them being injured.

"The name's Jasperson, from Bow Street. I have a warrant for your arrest on a charge of kidnapping, along with your accomplices."

Kidnapping?

Molly and Fletcher had stopped talking, and even the routine sounds of horses and carriages in the yard seemed to fade. Her escape was over, but worse than that, Molly and Langton would suffer for it. Fletcher, too, probably.

This must be her father's doing.

"I did nothing of the sort, I assure you," Mr Carterton said, his demeanour remarkably calm. "I am merely escorting—"

"You set out after her, didn't you? That's what a footman at your father's house told Lord Marstone's man. And she's run off from her father. The ostlers said you all arrived on the London road. If you ain't kidnapping her now, you should be taking her in the opposite direction."

"Mr Jasperson!" Bella waited until he looked at her. "Mr Carterton has only just met us on the road; he could not possibly have kidnapped me."

As she spoke, Billy began to cry.

"I left London of my own free will," she went on. "The others cannot be accomplices, as no crime has—"

Billy's cries had turned to screams, drowning out her words.

"Better take him outside, Mrs Fletcher," Molly said, raising her voice to be heard above the noise. "*If* that's all right with you, Mr Jasperson?"

The runner shrugged and jerked his head towards the door. Bella caught a wink from Molly, and her spirits lifted a little. Of course— Fletcher and Archer could avoid arrest.

As Fletcher left, the man holding Langton pushed him into the room, and he went to sit next to Molly. Bella waited until Billy's cries were muffled by the parlour door. "As I was saying, Mr Jasperson, I have not been kidnapped, so there is no crime. I do not wish to return to London."

"That don't make no difference to me now," the runner said. "I've got a warrant, and I mean to serve it, as well as return the young lady to her family."

"She doesn't want to go," Mr Carterton put in. "If you return her, *you* will be the one doing the kidnapping."

"She's a minor, sir. The law considers she don't know what's best for her. I'm only doing what his lordship says."

The law—and men made the law. Bella was too disappointed, too weary, to be angry. It was always the same—if she wasn't too young to know or decide something, it would be because she was female.

She looked at Mr Carterton. "I'm sorry." He'd done nothing but try to help her—even the parts she'd resented, such as warning her about Luis, had been justified. And now he was being arrested.

"Do not be," he said, resuming his seat. "This will come to nothing. Marstone will not want to parade his family affairs in a public trial."

There might be no trial, but she would be back under her father's thumb. Mr Carterton knew that; she could tell from his grave expression.

He turned to Jasperson. "Did you find us by chance?"

Bella had been wondering that, too—although how he had found them so easily didn't seem terribly important compared to the fact that he had.

"Aye," the runner said. "His lordship sent his man off on the Bath road, but there's many ways you could have got to Devonshire. Seemed to make sense to get to within a few miles of your destination and arrest you there. When we stopped here to change horses, one of Marstone's men recognised Langton. Can't say I'm sorry; it's saved us all a couple of days."

"An excellent plan," Mr Carterton said. "Unfortunate from our point of view, of course. Now, may we finish our meal before we set off again?"

"Don't see why not," Jasperson said. "We can eat, too." He looked at one of the grooms. "Go and order something; tell them to bring it in here. You two, you can eat yours by the door when it comes."

"Don't worry, Isabella," Mr Carterton said, reaching across the table and squeezing her hand. "I'm sure—"

"Oy, no talking," the runner interrupted. "I'm not having you cook up some plan to escape."

She managed a smile at Mr Carterton as he withdrew the comfort of his touch.

CHAPTER 25

*I*t took less time to return to London than it had taken to get to Salisbury, but only because Jasperson refused to stop overnight. Nick spent most of the journey sitting in silence next to the runner in a second chaise, the memory of Isabella's defeated expression haunting him. In his urge to protect her, he'd come very close to launching himself at Jasperson. But however satisfying it would have been to plant a fist in the man's face, he could not risk the women getting injured in the resulting struggle.

He'd set out to protect her, and he'd failed.

One mistake had been to underestimate how badly Marstone wanted to impose his will on his daughter. To get a runner travelling this far at short notice—and travelling hard—must have taken the offer of a sizeable reward. He should have ridden through the night himself.

But the main thing he hadn't done was to consider Isabella—Bella —as a possible wife soon enough. He'd been so set on his original idea of a calm, mature woman who would be a good political wife, that Isabella's impetuosity and rebelliousness had blinded him to her intelligence, her empathy. And her sense of humour, the way she enjoyed new experiences...

He stared out of the window. It was pointless to list her good qualities. None of that really explained the feeling that he wanted her for his wife, and his 'requirements' could go hang. If he'd started to court her properly, they could have got to know each other. If she had come to feel the same way about him, they might even have married with her father's blessing.

Would it have been a misuse of his position as stand-in brother to attempt to court her? He couldn't suppress a wry smile that had Jasperson regarding him suspiciously—Bella would have told him directly if he'd stepped out of line.

The outskirts of London finally came into view in the early morning light. That damned Portuguese still bothered him—what did she feel for him? He didn't want Bella as a wife if she was in love with someone else.

"Stay here," Jasperson ordered, as the chaise drew up outside Marstone House. "I'll take you to Bow Street as soon as I've handed over Lady Isabella."

Ignoring the runner's order, Nick made to follow him out, but one of the accompanying grooms stood by the door and opened his coat to show a pistol. Nick sat back against the squabs again—it would be foolish to get injured or killed just to tell Bella not to give up, no matter how much he wanted to speak to her.

Bella and Molly crossed the pavement and mounted the steps to the front door. Bella looked towards him, but was hustled into the house by Jasperson before either of them could make any kind of signal.

Damn. Now all he could do was await Jasperson's return, then try to talk his way out of incarceration when they reached Bow Street.

The butler stood to one side as Bella and Molly entered the hall, and a waiting footman shut the door behind Jasperson. The sound of the latch might have been that of a cell door closing.

"I'm not staying," the runner said. "Just making sure Lady Isabella is delivered safely. I'll return to see his lordship later in the day."

"Very well." Mowbray gestured to the footman to show Jasperson out again before turning to Bella. "His lordship instructed that you be taken to him as soon as you arrived, my lady. Follow me."

Bella didn't move. She was about to have her whole life dictated to her by her father, but she was *not* going to be ordered around by a servant. Her father was likely to lock her in her room for running away—what more could he do? "I will have a bath and a rest first. See that hot water is sent to my room." She headed for the stairs, Molly following.

Mowbray stood frozen by the front door for a moment before hurrying after her. "My lady, his lordship was most insistent. He is not well. His physician insists that he not be upset."

Bella stopped and turned, and the butler almost ran into her. "Then do not tell him I have arrived. If you tell him I am here and have refused to see him, then it is *you* who will be upsetting him." She glared at the butler until he nodded. "Hot water?"

"Yes, my lady."

Bella reached her room and flung off her bonnet with relief. The small victory over the butler was pointless—delaying her interview with her father would change nothing.

"You'll feel more the thing after a bath, my lady," Molly said, readying a set of towels. "What do you think happened to Archer and Fletcher?"

"Safely back in London, I hope."

Aunt Aurelia walked in after a perfunctory knock on the door. "Bella, I'm sorry to see you back here. I never thought Marstone would go so far as to set the law on you and Carterton."

Bella wrapped her arms around herself, wishing she was still in the nursery where Nanny might have given her a hug. Aunt Aurelia was now on her side, but she was not a hugging kind of woman.

Her aunt's words triggered something that must have been lurking at the back of her mind. "Aunt, the runner said he had a warrant to arrest Mr Carterton. How did Papa even know Mr Carterton might come after us?"

"He called the morning you left," Aunt Aurelia said, coming into the room and sitting down. "I told him you were heading for Wingrave's place. I can only assume we were overheard—but why Marstone accused him of kidnapping, I've no idea. It was clear you'd run away long before Carterton arrived." She tilted her head to one side. "Isabella, why didn't you tell me Carterton was... interested in you? My brother might have accepted—"

"He's not," Bella said. Unfortunately. "Will asked him to look out for me in his stead, while he was away." She eyed her aunt warily, but Aunt Aurelia only gave a wry smile. "He was trying to find out something he could use to persuade Lord Narwood not to marry me."

"It seems there was even more deception going on than I knew about. A pity that's his reason, though. I think he would have made a good husband."

He would—she knew that now. But he'd denied courting her, and he'd escorted Jemima several times. Although there had been the way he'd looked at her when they talked in Salisbury...

Footsteps on the landing heralded the arrival of several footmen, the first bearing a bath and the others carrying buckets of hot water.

"You could attract Carterton if you tried, I'm sure," Aunt Aurelia said quietly, her words hardly audible above the sounds of pouring water. "I'll leave you for now, but best not to take too long over your bath—if Marstone finds you've been in the house half the day before he sees you, it'll do nothing for his temper."

"D'you want some breakfast, my lady?" Molly asked, once Aunt Aurelia and the footman had left.

"No, but you go and get some as soon as I've finished bathing."

She couldn't eat a thing. Not until she knew what her father was going to do next.

The coffee shop was getting busier, but no-one had asked Luis to move along yet. He ordered another drink that he didn't want and, as it could still be considered the breakfast hour, more rolls. Eating them slowly, he turned a page in the newspaper now and then as if he was reading, wondering if he should be here at all. He was not going to assassinate someone at Don Felipe's order, but he could just go home instead of trying to see Lady Isabella again. Yet he felt he had to make amends for his behaviour somehow, and she was the only person he could think of who might believe what he had to say without having him instantly arrested.

He resisted an impulse to look at the clock on the wall—one of the urchins he was paying would turn up when he had something to report from Grosvenor Square. There had been much coming and going at Marstone House the previous day, but the boys he had paid to watch had not seen anyone resembling Isabella. He wished he could watch himself, but he would be too conspicuous loitering around the square all day.

Half an hour later, one of the brats appeared in the doorway, managing to attract Luis' attention before the waiter manhandled him out of the door again. Luis left enough coins on the table to pay his bill and stepped out into the street.

The child was waiting for him a few yards away.

"Well?"

The boy rubbed a sleeve across a runny nose. "Two chaises come, guv'ner. Two maids went into the house, and a man with them."

"I'm not interested in maids," Luis said.

"They went in the front, and the butler cove bowed to one of 'em."

Luis handed over a sixpence. "Describe them. How tall were they?"

The child shrugged. "Normal size, I dunno. One was shorter than the other. Had dark hair, I reckon."

It could be Isabella, although it seemed an odd time for her to be entering her home, not to mention the brat mistaking her for a maid.

"The second chaise?"

"No-one got out of that. They both drove away."

"Well done." Luis handed over another coin.

"My mates was watching, too," the urchin protested, examining his meagre reward. Luis sighed, and gave him more. Then he held out a silver crown and the boy's eyes widened.

"I need to talk to someone from the house," Luis said. "Secretly. A footman, or a maid."

The boy reached his hand out for the coin. Luis returned it to his pocket.

"It's yours if you find me someone to talk to. They'll get the same. Can you do that?"

The lad nodded so hard his cap slid back on his head.

"I'll be in the Queen's Head. Today. I need to talk to someone today."

Nick settled into a parlour chair with a sigh of relief. Something to sit on that didn't rock and sway, and with a softer seat than the chairs at Bow Street. He badly needed a bath, shave, and change of clothing, but for now he settled on a large mug of ale and some hastily prepared sandwiches.

"Better now?" Lord Carterton asked as he hobbled into the room.

"Much better, thank you."

"I can't believe that fool Marstone tried to have you arrested." Nick's father sat down.

"He *did* have me arrested," Nick pointed out. Thankfully, not half an hour after Jasperson had delivered him to Bow Street, a clerk had appeared with a paper rescinding the arrest warrant. Jasperson had, reluctantly, agreed that he was free to go. "Thank you for sorting that out, but how did you know?"

"Wingrave's man called to tell me this morning, not long after sun-up. He persuaded Hobson to let him see me."

"Sorry about that, Father." He'd seen sunrise himself from the chaise, hours before he or his father would normally be out of bed. Archer must have ridden hard to arrive so far ahead of the two post-chaises.

"No matter, I don't sleep much these days anyway." He chuckled. "I had no compunction in knocking that fool magistrate up and making him sort it out."

"You went—?"

"Oh, don't worry, boy. I took a chair, didn't even have to climb into a carriage. Does me good to get out of the house now and then."

Nick inspected his father anxiously, but he didn't seem to be any the worse for his exertions.

"This won't be the end of it, Nick. I suspect Marstone must have laid out considerable blunt to send a runner after you so quickly, and quite possibly bribed the magistrate, too."

"Yes, I'd worked that out."

"I suspect he'll want some kind of revenge on you for attempting to thwart him."

"What can he do?"

"Not much, probably, but he could cause scandal or gossip." He struggled to his feet. "Not that a bit of scandal should bother either of us, unless it puts off your Miss Roper."

About to correct his father's assumption about Miss Roper, Nick thought better of it. He would explain, but later.

"Best get yourself bathed and have more breakfast," his father went on. "I gather Marstone's on his last legs, and he'll want to force his will on as many people as possible before he pops off."

Father was correct, as he usually was. Nick enjoyed soaking in a hot bath for half an hour, then shaved and donned clean clothes before going to the library. What he really wanted to do was to check that Bella was well, but that was impossible under the circumstances. Instead, he turned to the correspondence that had arrived while he'd been away. He'd only answered a couple of queries when Hobson brought in a sealed letter.

"There's one for his lordship, too," the butler said.

Quickly breaking the seal, Nick turned straight to the signature. Marstone, as expected. "Where's my father?"

"In the parlour, sir."

"Thank you, Hobson. I'll take his letter to him."

Nick handed the letter to his father and then quickly scanned his own. "Marstone demands I take Isabella to wife," he said. The writing was too firm and neat to have been written by Marstone himself, but he could hear the earl making the threats. "Or he'll have me prosecuted for kidnapping or breach of promise."

"This says the same," his father said, dropping the letter onto a side table. "The man's mad—he cannot prosecute you for both."

"He might intend to pursue whichever route seems the more likely to succeed," Nick suggested.

"Do you object to the girl?"

"No."

Lord Carterton looked at Nick over his spectacles. "That's not the impression I got last time we discussed your future wife."

"Things change." His father's expectant gaze made him feel uneasy. "Miss Roper is… is not…"

"Is boring?"

"Er… yes." He would not have put it so bluntly, but he could not deny it. "I don't think I'd ever be bored with Isabella. And she's…" Beautiful, enthusiastic, entrancing. Was this feeling what the poets meant?

"No need to go into detail, my boy." His father had a satisfied smirk. "All's well, then. You get a bride you actually like…"

More than like. Much more.

"No."

"I thought you might say that. Let me guess—you're not going to take a wife at Marstone's bidding, even though she's the one you want. Don't let pride get in your way, Nick."

"It's not that. I don't want to take a wife who has probably been forced into it." And may be in love with someone else. He glanced at his own letter again before screwing it into a ball and throwing it at the fireplace. "I'm not worried about these stupid threats, but if I decline he'll find someone else. There must be no end of men who'd marry her for the dowry Marstone can afford to offer. I don't understand why he's in such a hurry, though."

And he still didn't know why she'd run away when she did, or what she'd been doing in a dim room with da Gama and Lady Jesson at the ball. He would have asked her at Salisbury, if Jasperson hadn't arrived.

"You'll go and see Marstone, then?"

"I must."

CHAPTER 26

*B*ella walked over to the parlour window. The garden was bathed in sunshine, the rose blooms glowing red, gold, and white against dark leaves. The cheeriness of the scene seemed an affront to her mood, and she turned away.

"For heaven's sake, sit down, Isabella," Aunt Aurelia said, not for the first time. "It wouldn't be the end of the world, being married to Carterton—you said so yourself."

"It's not fair on him, Aunt. He was only trying to help." Turning back to the view, she tried to concentrate on a blackbird foraging along the edges of a low box hedge.

"Carterton may not agree," her aunt said. "Then Marstone might find someone worse."

Bella closed her eyes—anyone else would be worse. But she wasn't worried about him refusing—he would agree if Papa told him that *she* wished it. He was too much of a gentleman to do otherwise.

"I suspect you'll soon find out," Aunt Aurelia said, tilting her head towards the door. Bella heard voices, but could not make out any words.

"Mr Carterton, my lady," Mowbray intoned, then closed the door behind their visitor.

Bella tried to make out his expression. He did not look angry—that was something—but nor did he look pleased to be here.

"Marstone's threats worked, then?" Aunt Aurelia asked, a shade of disappointment in her tone.

"Not exactly, my lady," Mr Carterton said, a brief frown creasing his brow. "I have just come from him, and I wish to talk to Lady Isabella. Alone, if possible."

Aunt Aurelia stood. "I will not do that—for your own protection. I wouldn't put it past my brother to have several servants swear to finding you behaving improperly and use that to force your hand."

"Is he so desperate?"

Aunt Aurelia shrugged. "He's always wanted to make others obey him, but lately he's become... well, obsessed is the only word for it. I will sit over there." She pointed to the far corner of the room. "If you do not raise your voices, I will not hear you."

"Thank you, my lady."

He sat down next to Bella as Aunt Aurelia moved away. Bella clasped her hands in her lap—knowing that her future might depend on this interview seemed to be fogging her mind.

"We have as much time as we need, Bella. Why did you run away when you did? I gathered that your father had given up on Narwood."

Bella let out a breath. That was easy to answer. "He had, but he was going to send me back to Marstone Park until he found someone else for me. It would have been much harder to escape from there."

"What went wrong with Narwood? Did he not offer, after all?"

There was no sense in trying to hide the truth. If they were to be made to wed, honesty was the only way they might come to a good understanding. And she wanted that with him—more than that, if she could.

"Narwood wants an heir of his blood, but I could *not* marry him. So I gave Father to understand that I might be... might be carrying another man's child."

His brows drew together.

"I am not; I could not be," she added hurriedly, and the muscles in his face relaxed. "I merely told him so, and threatened that Lady Jesson would spread that gossip if I asked her to."

To her relief, his lips twitched as if he were about to smile, but then he became serious again.

"Your father says you have agreed to a marriage with me. If it is his threat of prosecuting me that made you accept, you may ignore that. I am not afraid that he will win, and any scandal will soon blow over."

"I did worry about that, yes." But she had believed him when he'd told Jasperson that such a charge would not succeed, and her aunt had backed up that view. "You would not be in this position if you had not tried to help me, and it wouldn't be fair to put you through that, even if he did not succeed." She took a deep breath. "But he also threatened to have Molly and Langton arrested for kidnapping. It would not go well for them, I think." Langton was currently locked in a room in the cellars and the rest of the servants were keeping a close eye on Molly. Fletcher might get dragged into it, too, if Father ever found out about her part in things. She had to trust that Archer had made sure Fletcher had the means to return to Maria's house.

"I can pay for good lawyers."

She had guessed he would make that offer. "Thank you, but no. I cannot risk them being found guilty, or even imprisoned before the trial. They were only trying to help, and without any reward, really. I could not benefit from their loyalty and then abandon them to my father's revenge."

"Your decision does you credit," he said. "Is the match distasteful to you?"

She tried to work out what he was thinking, but his face gave no clue. Honesty was best, again. The truth, even if not all the truth.

"It is not distasteful to me, not at all. But any match where the parties are forced into it is… is not a good idea. But I have no choice, in all honour."

He nodded slowly. "If I decline, what will your father do?"

She swallowed hard. "I don't know. He may give up, but he may decide it's my fault for not being able to persuade you, and he could still have Molly and Langton arrested. If Will were here…" But there was no use wishing for that.

"He may be returning soon," Mr Carterton said. "However, your father wants the marriage to happen tomorrow—he must have bribed several of the archbishop's clerks to get a special licence so quickly. But even if Wingrave were to return in time, he might not be able to prevent Marstone carrying out his threat." He ran a finger around the inside of his neckcloth. "I can ask him to give me another day or two."

"He will say that you have been courting me for weeks. That is what my aunt thought, too."

"Very well." He looked at the floor, then into her eyes. "Lady Isabella, will you do me the honour of becoming my wife?"

She closed her eyes—what would it be like to have a man ask that question of his own free will, because he liked her? Loved her. If only *he* could have asked in those circumstances.

"Yes, I will. Thank you, sir."

"Nick. My name is Nick." His smile was so kind, so sympathetic that she felt the prick of tears in her eyes. Perhaps he really wasn't unhappy at the prospect?

"Bella, I will still try to find a way out of this—neither of us wishes to be forced into a match."

Oh. "Thank you… Nick." She was pleased her voice sounded almost normal.

He rewarded her with a fleeting smile as he stood. "I will tell Marstone I accept, although I will attempt to persuade him to allow a few days' delay."

He bowed, and raised her hand to his lips before turning to leave. Bella watched him go, the feeling of that brief contact still warming her.

"It is settled, then?" Aunt Aurelia put one hand on Bella's shoulder, an unexpected gesture of friendliness that nearly broke her composure.

"Yes, Aunt." For good or ill.

. . .

When Nick arrived at Marstone House the next morning, he was shown into the library and asked to wait. After ten minutes of pacing, no-one had appeared to summon him, so he helped himself to a glass of port from a decanter and stood looking at the grey clouds beyond the window. He'd arrived at the specified time of eleven o'clock, and could only suppose that there was some problem with the special licence, or the priest.

Yesterday, Marstone had been adamant that his marriage to Bella should take place today. In one way, Nick hadn't been sorry—if they were married, he would have time to court her properly, and hope that she could come to love him in the way he now realised he loved her. But the logical part of his brain kept reminding him that it would be a road to misery for both of them if she was in love with someone else.

And who would have thought Father could be so devious? Nick had had no idea how he could delay things once Marstone had insisted, but his father had thought of a way. They might only need a day or two. He fingered the note in his pocket—Talbot had summoned him to a meeting with himself and Wingrave on the morrow, at which point Wingrave could resume responsibility for his sister. There was even a chance that Wingrave would arrive in London today, so Nick had written back outlining the situation and asking Talbot to send Wingrave straight to Marstone House if he appeared. Not that he could do much good at this point if Father's plan failed.

At last, after being left to kick his heels for nearly an hour, Nick was taken upstairs to Marstone's bedroom. The bedchamber was not as gloomy as the last time he'd been here. Marstone was propped up on pillows in his bed, his cheeks sunken and dark shadows circling his eyes.

Bella stood next to Lady Cerney, wearing a cream gown with some lacy trimming. She held a little posy of roses in one hand, and met Nick's gaze with a tentative smile. Nick felt a rush of admiration for her spirit—she was making the best of things. He wished he could reassure her, but he could not say anything without Lady Cerney, at least, overhearing.

"Smythe is my physician," Marstone wheezed, "and will witness the marriage along with Lady Cerney."

Nick dragged his eyes away from Bella. A rotund man near the window gave a brief bow. "Hobson will conduct the service," Marstone added. "I take it you have no objection to any of this?"

"None whatsoever, my lord."

Nick avoided meeting Hobson's eyes, aware of the absurdity of the situation. In other circumstances, it would be amusing.

"Dearly beloved," Hobson began, peering at the book in his hands and stumbling a little now and then. "We are gathered here…"

Nick stopped listening, gazing at the man in the bed and wondering how someone came to be such a tyrant. It wasn't as if his daughter's marriage could secure the succession. Wingrave would have ensured that Bella married someone suitable; she would not be friendless when Marstone died.

Hobson coughed, and Nick paid attention—it was time to make his responses. He repeated his words, and Bella made her own vows in a quiet but firm voice.

Bella felt the tension in her relax as the priest started reciting the final prayers. Mr Carterton—Nick—was a decent man. They could make a good life together, and perhaps they would come to love each other in time.

"…pledged their troth either to other, and have declared the same by giving and receiving of a ring, and by joining of hands; I pronounce—"

Loud voices sounded beyond the door, and Hobson's words faltered.

"Carry on, man," her father called impatiently. "Get it over with."

Hobson glanced at Nick, then started reading again. "I pronounce that they be man and wife together, in the name of—"

"Stand aside, Mowbray."

Will?

It *was* Will! The door burst open and her brother stepped into the room, a footman still protesting behind him.

"What on earth are you doing?" Will asked.

"It should be obvious what is happening, Wingrave," their father said, his voice surprisingly strong considering how ill he appeared. "And you are too late to intervene." His laughter turned into a coughing fit, and the physician hurried towards the bed.

"I only asked you to look out for her, Carterton," Will said, looking at Nick. "You didn't have to marry her." He looked around the room, his gaze coming to rest on the priest with a puzzled frown. "What's your father's butler doing reading the marriage service?"

Butler? The guilt on Hobson's face told Bella it was true.

Did that mean she wasn't married to Nick? The sudden emptiness inside revealed how much she'd wanted this match, even though she hadn't fully realised it until now.

Her father's coughing changed to painful gasps, and the physician turned and flapped his hands at them.

"Come away, Bella." Will took her arm and led her out of the room, putting one arm around her shoulders and giving her a quick hug. "Wait for me in the parlour; I'll come as soon as I can."

CHAPTER 27

*B*ella looked at the clock again. It was only ten minutes since Will had sent her to the parlour, but it felt much longer.

A step sounded in the hall, and she rushed across the room as the door opened.

"Oh, Will! I'm so glad you're back."

He caught her, hugging her close. To her dismay she felt tears forming, and suddenly couldn't stop herself from crying. She hadn't seen him for two years, and then it had only been a clandestine midnight meeting in her bedroom.

"I'm sorry, Bella, I should have been here. I might have stopped all this happening." He let her cry on his coat until her sobs eased. "Come, sit down. We need to talk."

Bella reluctantly let go, sniffing. Will handed her a handkerchief, then sat beside her on a sofa as she blew her nose.

"Aunt Aurelia said something about running away. It seems you've been having an adventure."

"It wasn't *fun*, Will," Bella said, irritated by his smile.

"No, I imagine not. I'm not laughing at you, but at poor Carterton, having to deal with you."

"Deal with? I'm not a problem to be dealt with!" Bella took a deep breath as his smile widened. "You're deliberately trying to annoy me," she accused.

"Guilty as charged," he said, raising a hand. "I'd rather you were cross than a watering pot." He touched her shoulder. "Cheer up, Bell. All is not lost."

His childhood name for her made her smile. She blew her nose. "Will, am I married or not?"

"Not. That was an ingenious plan Carterton came up with to fool Father."

To her dismay, her lips started to tremble again.

"I thought that was what you wanted?" Will said, bending his head to look her in the face.

"So did I," she sniffed. "Until it happened. Nick said he'd try to find a way out, but I didn't think he had managed to. What about Papa—is he in another rage?"

"He's not well."

"He wasn't well before."

"No, I mean seriously. The doctor was talking about preparing ourselves for the worst."

"Oh." She couldn't feel sorry. "Is it my fault for defying him?"

"No, it isn't—do not think that, Bella. Carterton arranged to substitute his butler for the priest, and I blurted out the truth without warning. No-one made him get in such a rage just because you didn't want to marry the man he chose."

"Aunt Aurelia upset him first, before we came to Town. She told him that Lady Wingrave wasn't her father's daughter. Oh," she added, a sudden doubt occurring. "You did know that, didn't you?"

"Of course I did. Connie told me herself."

"You don't mind?"

He smiled and shook his head. "No. In fact, I took great delight in the fact, knowing how obsessed with rank and power Father is. But I didn't tell him, in case he found a way to get revenge on Connie. I'm surprised Aunt Aurelia said it in front of you, though."

"She didn't. I was listening at the servants' door."

Will gave a crack of laughter. "A sister after my own heart," he said, giving her another quick hug. "Rest assured, I will make sure he does not force you into another match."

"He threatened to have Molly and Langton tried for kidnapping."

"Don't worry, Bella. He won't. I'll have him declared incompetent, if necessary. You must tell me all the details, but not now. You look as if a stiff brandy would do you good."

"I'd rather have a cup of tea." And something to eat. She hadn't managed to eat any breakfast.

"I'll get some sent in. I need to talk to Carterton, so you have your tea and a rest, and I'll talk to you later."

Nick waited for Wingrave in the library, pacing up and down. He had no inclination for reading, and doubted he'd manage to concentrate if he tried. Waylaying the priest that Marstone's man had arranged had been his father's idea, but he'd readily agreed. The plan would fail if Marstone had already sent notification to the papers, but Father had said he could take care of that, too.

He thought it would be what Bella wanted—she had agreed to marry him, certainly, but only to save her maid and the footman from arrest and trial. Yet she had not looked relieved when Wingrave had inadvertently revealed their subterfuge.

"Is she all right?" he asked, when Wingrave finally appeared.

"She will be," he replied, crossing straight to the tray of decanters and pouring two large brandies.

"Have you come directly here from Paris?" Nick took the offered glass.

Wingrave nodded. "More or less. Talbot sent a copy of your note to the lodgings I use when in Town, so I came straight here. Rather too quickly, as it turned out—it might have been better to let Marstone believe the marriage had taken place."

"You didn't know it wouldn't be valid." He hadn't wanted to put the plan in writing, nor had he been sure the subterfuge would work.

Wingrave took a mouthful of brandy. "What was your intention with that? The deception could not have lasted long."

"Delay," Nick said. "In truth, mainly to gain enough time for you to return, to hand the whole mess over to you."

"Mess?" Wingrave sat down near the window; Nick took a facing chair. "I'll have another talk with Bella later, but won't you tell me what's been happening?"

"I don't know all of it," Nick admitted, but summarised what had happened. Wingrave's expression varied from the thunderous—as he described the St Giles expedition—to amusement as Nick's tale progressed.

"Be fair, Wingrave," Nick finished. "Before you ring a peal over her for going to look for that seamstress, remember that she couldn't be expected to know the dangers she'd face in such a place. Her main mistake was not listening to the advice of her maid and footman."

"And trusting that Portuguese—who is he, do you know?"

"Not who he is pretending to be," Nick said. He related his few encounters with the man, including his suspicion that da Gama had been involved in whatever Bella had been up to at Lady Yelland's ball.

"That's something I need to ask her about." Wingrave swirled the remnants of his brandy, then got up and brought the decanter over. "More?"

Nick shook his head. "No, thank you. As for preventing an unwanted marriage, I'm afraid I didn't do too well. I hadn't got any further than gathering information about Narwood. She was right to avoid him—a deeply unpleasant man, by all accounts, and as dictatorial as Marstone. But there was nothing I could use to bribe or threaten him with. While I was doing that, she extricated herself."

"And look how that turned out," Wingrave said. "No, I'm not blaming you—it seems she had made good preparations for the journey, and you did what you could by going after them. Who could have foreseen the lengths Father would go to in order to get her back?"

Nick looked down at his glass, not wanting to answer the question he suspected would come. "What did you find out in France?" he asked, trying to divert Wingrave's attention. "Talbot will tell me some of it eventually," he added as Wingrave hesitated.

"He will," Wingrave admitted. He put his glass down and steepled his hands—mentally censoring the information, Nick guessed. He didn't mind; he didn't need to know all the details.

"In brief, our original informant is still to be trusted, I think. The new one is, I strongly suspect, working for the French."

"And the similarity in the information?"

"If I'm wrong, then both are bribing the same sources. If the new one *is* a French agent, he has access to the information, and the similarity merely confirms the accuracy of our original informant."

Nick rubbed his forehead. This was a side of working for Talbot that he hated—the questions of loyalty and betrayal, who to trust and who not to.

"Don't worry about it, Carterton," Wingrave said, a laugh in his voice. "That's Talbot's headache." He put his glass down and stood. "If you will excuse me, there's much for me to do here. Perhaps it's time you explained yourself to Bella? She was in the back parlour when I left her."

Luis slipped into the mews behind Grosvenor Square at noon. The urchin had succeeded in bribing one of the parlourmaids, and Luis had spent some time flirting with her on the previous day, but she'd had no further news of Isabella. The maid had been ready enough to talk to him and take his coin, but he wasn't sure how much she would do for him. If she failed to meet him today, he would have to come up with a different plan.

He leaned on a wall, hoping his clothing made him look like a groom whiling away time until his master needed him. He turned his collar up—the damp in the air was turning to drizzle. The noise of traffic in the square was muted here, the only disturbances being when horses or carriages from other houses on this side of the square came and went. The chimes of a nearby church clock sounded the quarter hour, then the half hour, before a figure in dark gown and white apron slipped out of the gate in the back wall of the Marstone House garden.

"Luis!" The parlourmaid hurried towards him, stopping in the meagre shelter of a tree that overhung the wall.

"Hola, querida." Luis went to meet her, wearing his best smile, and she dropped her eyes and giggled. "Have you any news for me?"

"Oh, yes! Ever such a lot. It's like a play."

"What has happened?" Luis tried to mask his impatience.

"Oh, it's ever so exciting." She told a garbled tale of a wedding that hadn't been a wedding, the return of the earl's son, and his lordship being taken ill again. "Even more unwell than before," she finished, lowering her voice. "The doctor says he might be dying."

"Is Lady Isabella still confined to her room?" Luis asked.

"Not any more, not now Lord Wingrave's come. He's taken charge."

"What's he like, this Wingrave?" Don Felipe would be interested in knowing that, too, but Luis wasn't going to tell him.

"I don't really know. I've never seen him before. But she's not watched any more."

"That's wonderful, querida."

She giggled again. "It's lovely when you say that."

"One more thing." He took some coins from his pocket. "I need to speak to Lady Isabella, alone. Can you take a message?"

Her smile vanished. "What are you wanting with her? She's a proper lady, she is."

"I only want to talk to her. Is there somewhere hidden in the garden I can wait? It'll be worth your while," he added, giving her one of the coins.

She folded her arms, her eyes still narrowed. "Just talk?"

"I give you my word of honour."

The maid glared a moment longer, then nodded and took the coin. "There's a little summerhouse in one corner. Everyone's at sixes and sevens in the house, so they ain't likely to look there."

"That is good. Will you let me in?"

241

"Wait." She went back to the gate and opened it. Stepping into the garden, she looked around and then beckoned. "Go along by this wall to the corner. You might have to wait a long time."

Luis dropped the coins into her waiting hand. Mature shrubs lined the edges of the garden, and he crept along between the bushes and the wall until he came to a small octagonal structure, its white paint beginning to peel and its windows sorely in need of cleaning. He slipped inside, moving a chair right to the back where he was less likely to be seen from the house.

No-one was in the parlour when Nick entered, although tea things and a plate of cakes on a table by the window suggested that it had not been unoccupied for long. The single cup had been used, but the teapot was still hot to the touch. Outside, a fine drizzle misted the view—Bella would not have gone out for fresh air in this weather.

About to turn away, he caught a pale flash at the back of the garden, inside a summerhouse half hidden by shrubs. A maid in a dark gown stood outside, sheltering under an umbrella. Inside... Bella, if it was she, appeared to be talking to someone.

Da Gama?

Nick shook his head, ashamed to have jumped to that conclusion, but who else could it be? If someone like Lady Jesson or Miss Roper had called, they would be sitting here in the parlour. Although if their meeting was supposed to be kept secret, she wasn't doing a very good job of it.

It was no use—he'd have to go and see.

Tamping down a sick feeling in his stomach, he made his way along the gravelled paths to the back of the garden. The maid was not much use as a lookout—she appeared to be paying more attention to what was happening inside the summerhouse. He was within a few yards of her by the time she noticed him, and turned to tap on the glass.

He strode forward, pushing open the door as da Gama got to his feet, one hand going to a pocket.

"What are you doing here?" Nick demanded, clenching his fists, his arms going rigid with the wish to punch the man. Only Bella's presence stopped him. "If you've harmed her, I'll—"

"He hasn't harmed me at all," Bella interrupted. "Sally!"

The maid put her head inside the door.

"Thank you, you may return to your duties now. I will be perfectly safe with Mr Carterton here."

The tension in Nick's body eased at those words. Sally bobbed a minimal curtsey and hurried off, looking back once before disappearing into the back entrance to the house.

There was a metallic click. Da Gama was pointing a pistol at him.

"Please, sit down, Nick," Bella said. "You, too, Senhor. And for goodness sake, put that thing away."

"He will have me arrested," da Gama protested, the pistol in his hand not moving. At least he was pointing it at him, Nick thought, not Bella. Why wasn't she worried? Had they come to some arrangement?

"What are you doing here?" he asked again.

"He is trying to talk to me." Her tone was sharp. "Senhor?"

"I have information that someone in your government needs to hear," the Portuguese said. "Lady Isabella is the only person I thought might listen to me." The oily manner Nick had observed in earlier encounters was absent now.

"There is no-one else in the whole of London?" Nick asked. "I find that hard to believe."

"I don't," Bella said. "As Will is here, it would be best to talk to him. *If* you and he will permit the poor man to speak?"

Poor man? Nick bit his lip against the words—he'd already distressed her enough. No, not distressed—angered would be a better description. He nodded.

"And not arrest him?" Bella persisted.

"Why would I want to arrest him?" He'd like to, but attempting to compromise a woman was not actually a crime.

"I think he has not actually done anything wrong," Bella said.

243

"If that is the case, he has nothing to worry about." He was doing his best not to assume a reason for her defence of the man, but it was difficult.

"Do you give your word?"

"Have I not just said so?"

She waited without speaking.

"Very well," he capitulated. "I give my word that I will not have him arrested, *if* he has done nothing wrong."

Bella tilted her head to one side. "And Will?"

"And that I will do my best to prevent Wingrave from doing so. I cannot promise more than that." He hoped for her agreement, but instead she looked to her companion.

"That will have to do," Senhor da Gama said, stepping forward as he uncocked the pistol and slipped it back into his pocket. "Is Wingrave in residence? It will be quicker to tell my story only once, and there may not be much time."

CHAPTER 28

The four of them sat in the library, Mowbray having been instructed that there were to be no interruptions. Nick kept a close eye on the Portuguese as Bella explained that he had something important to tell them.

"So this is the man who nearly compromised your reputation?" Wingrave said.

"Trust me, Will," Bella pleaded. "I can explain that later. Please, listen to what he has to say."

Wingrave looked from her to Nick.

"We may as well hear him, Wingrave," Nick said.

"All right. Bella?"

"He is not Portuguese, but Spanish."

Nick's brows rose—Talbot had been right to be suspicious.

"He is a spy. You promised to listen, Will!" she added, as Wingrave frowned.

"So I did," Wingrave said, then turned to da Gama. "Why are you here? What is so urgent that you must needs risk arrest?"

"I have been instructed to assassinate a Frenchman when he arrives in this country. Either here in London, or at the home of your Prime Minister."

There was a deathly silence in the room. Nick wondered if he'd heard correctly. Sent to kill someone? Bella herself was gazing at da Gama with wide eyes.

"Bella, why do you trust this man?" Nick asked.

"Carterton, this is not helping," Wingrave interjected. "He is here, telling us about it, is he not? And Bella may be able to corroborate parts of the fellow's story. Senhor da Gama, please continue."

Wingrave had a point. Bella knew the man far better than he did, unfortunately. He should concentrate on what the fellow was saying, and not be swayed by his own jealousy.

"I came to London to work for a Spaniard called Don Felipe de Garcia," da Gama said. "I can give you the details later. He wanted me to seduce the wives or lovers of certain men in your government."

Nick stiffened, but a glare from Wingrave stopped him interrupting. This man had dared to court... to *pretend* to court Bella?

"Those seductions failed. Don Felipe then had me trying to gather information around the docks in London. He was particularly interested in possible convoys to supply Gibraltar. Then he said that Rayneval, one of the French—"

"I know who he is," Wingrave interrupted. "Go on."

"He is to meet your Prime Minister. Don Felipe has found out about this meeting and he does not want it to happen."

"The Spanish are allies of the French," Nick pointed out.

"Indeed. And both armies are working together to besiege Gibraltar. Don Felipe..." Da Gama broke off and rubbed his forehead. "He is obsessed with Gibraltar. His son died in the siege and..." He shrugged, spreading his hands wide. "I think he is not quite sane. He thinks Rayneval is meeting Rockingham to confirm that the French will negotiate even if you British do not agree to restore Gibraltar to Spain."

"Why would he need a secret meeting for that?" Nick asked.

"Does it matter?" da Gama asked. "Don Felipe thinks that is the reason."

"Is he working for the Spanish government?" Wingrave asked.

"I don't know. But I do not think I am the only one in England working for him, and I am not sure that he trusts me any longer. I may not be the only person to whom he will entrust this task."

Wingrave kept his gaze on da Gama for several minutes. In spite of his antipathy to the man, Nick felt reluctant admiration. It had taken some nerve to risk arrest in order to tell his tale, whatever his motives were.

Wingrave looked at Bella. "Do you believe him?"

Bella's eyes widened, then she turned to da Gama. "Why did you come here?" she asked him. "To this house, I mean."

That was a good question.

"I do not want to kill anyone," he said simply. "I did not think that would be required of me when I came to England."

He sounded sincere, even though Nick wasn't inclined to give him the benefit of any doubt.

"You could have just gone back to Spain," Bella suggested.

Da Gama's eyes did not leave Bella's face. "I remembered what you said to me at the ball. I was ashamed. If my father hears of this, he will know I also tried to put things right."

"What did she say to you?" Nick asked, his voice sharp.

"I believe him," Bella said to Wingrave, ignoring the interruption.

"Thank you, Bella." Wingrave sat in thought for a few minutes more before addressing da Gama again. "Bella made me promise not to have you arrested, yet you have admitted to attempting to spy on our government."

Da Gama nodded, his face grave. "I hoped that warning you of Don Felipe's plans might counter my original intention—in which I was unsuccessful. I will tell you everything I know. The wish to assassinate one of our allies is... is beneath contempt."

"I cannot guarantee anything yet," Wingrave said. He moved over to the desk in one corner of the room, taking paper from a drawer and picking up a pen. "Carterton, Bella, there is no need for the two of you to sit through the rest of this."

Nick sat close to Bella when they returned to the parlour, and wondered where to start. How could he make her believe he wanted this marriage when he had arranged for it to be invalid?

"I wanted to talk to you about Fletcher, if I may," she said.

Fletcher? After the events of the day, she wanted to talk about a seamstress?

"I didn't realise when I asked her to accompany me to Devonshire that she would be risking arrest," Bella went on. "I want to help her if I can. She has a position with Maria Jesson at the moment, but that cannot be a permanent solution. Is there a way I can help her to set up as a mantua-maker?"

At least he was of some use for advice. "That seems a sudden elevation from a seamstress."

"She is more than that—she has a good eye for colour and design." Bella gestured at her gown. "She gave me confidence, after I head people making remarks about my appearance."

"There is more to a business than an eye for fashion," he said.

"I know. Premises, buying materials, paying seamstresses, finding clients."

"You have given it some thought."

"I had a lot of time to think while that runner was bringing me back."

"Money will help with the first three items you mentioned," he said. "It is unusual for a woman to invest in such an enterprise, though. It might cause gossip."

"I do not care about that." She met his gaze squarely. "Would you?"

"No." Her tentative smile told him that had been the correct answer. "Do you intend to give her money?"

"No. I do not think she would take it."

That tallied with what he had seen of Fletcher—a woman as determined as Bella, although in very different circumstances.

"A loan, then, at low interest? You would need a proper contract drawn up, but I could help you with that, if Wingrave is too busy."

"Or if he disapproves," Bella muttered.

"Is he like to?"

"I don't know; I hope not. Today was the first time I've spoken to him for two years, and before then I only saw him occasionally when he visited Marstone Park."

"You will be able to get to know him now," he said, hating the sadness in her voice. "I gather that Wingrave is intending to take over from Marstone, whether Marstone wishes it or not. He is too ill to protest."

"I know." But she didn't look too happy at the idea.

Being free of her father's rule didn't feel as liberating as Bella had thought it would. It was all very sudden, and although she had never loved her father, now she was beyond his control she didn't actually wish for his death.

She should be happy at the new possibilities—unthinkable only this morning—but she wasn't, and the reason was the man sitting opposite. Would things have worked out differently if she'd realised earlier that he was the one she wanted?

Possibly not, if he wanted someone else. Jemima, perhaps.

"Why did your butler come instead of the priest?" She really wanted to ask why *he* had wanted to prevent their marriage, but she had a sudden fear of what his answer might be.

"Yesterday, I said I would find a way out of it if I could. I hoped it would buy enough time for Wingrave to return."

"And it did." She could not regret that Will was back, but she still had little idea what Nick thought—felt—about her.

"Bella, at the ball... Why were you in a room apart with that Port—that Spaniard?"

"Lady Jesson was there, too," she pointed out. "There was nothing improper."

"He is a spy."

"I know that now, but I didn't when he asked me to..." How much to tell him?

"Asked? What did he ask?" Nick leaned forward, his gaze intent. "And what did you say to him that made him betray his masters?"

"He asked me to marry him," she said, watching with interest as his

249

lips compressed. "I said no, of course. What I said to him after that has nothing to do with his spying."

Nick stood up and walked to the window, then turned to face her. "You would keep confidence about a spy?" Although he hadn't raised his voice, his clipped delivery indicated anger.

Why was he behaving like this? It was almost as if he were...

He was! He was jealous!

A feeling of lightness filled her—this might turn out well after all.

"If Will needs to know, I may tell him."

"I see." He turned to the window, his posture stiff.

"Only because Will seems to be in some sort of spy business," she said to his back. "Are you involved too?"

"No. Yes."

She moved to stand beside him. "That made no sense, Nick."

"I am involved, in a way," he admitted, looking down at her. "But not as much as your brother is. I can claim no right to know on that basis. But I've been acting in Wingrave's place for the last few weeks."

"Is that how you think of me? As a sister?"

"No! Damn it. Bella, I... I—"

"Oh, good."

"—cannot regard... What did you say?" All trace of anger had completely gone now, and he looked puzzled. Adorably so.

"I'm glad you don't think of me as a sister. And I don't want someone like Senhor da Gama." She ran her hands down her skirts— she knew so little of the world, and this was going to be embarrassing if she'd misinterpreted his feelings.

"I want someone honourable," she went on. "Someone who will help me to learn about the world properly, and not order me about as I have been all my life." She met his gaze. "Someone who likes—loves —me for who I am, not for my father's influence or my dowry. Do you know anyone like that?"

Nick stared at her as the meaning of her words sank in. Her shy smile, still uncertain, went straight to his heart.

"Me?"

"Only if you feel the same," she said, her voice wobbling slightly.

He reached out and took her hands, clasping them together between his own. "I do. Bella, did I make a mistake when I prevented our marriage this morning?"

"No." She looked down at their joined hands. "I didn't want to get married at my father's order. I wanted to be free to choose."

"And you choose me?"

She nodded, and he raised her hands to his lips, one at a time, kissing them both. Her blush was delightful—too much so.

"I didn't realise properly until Will told me we were not married."

He wanted nothing more than to pull her into his arms, but she deserved to have this done in style. Releasing her hands, he went down on one knee.

"Bella, will you spend your life with me? Will you do me the honour of accepting my hand in marriage?"

"Of course I will." She was smiling, although tears glistened in her eyes.

He got to his feet, his hands reaching out to her shoulders. "What's wrong? I didn't mean to distress you."

"I'm not distressed." Her voice was unsteady as she said it. "It's just… just…" She swallowed, and dashed an impatient hand across her eyes. "This morning, I was about to be married to someone I thought had been forced into it. Now Will is back and you… I find that you actually wanted it. It is so much to happen so quickly."

"Bella." He pulled her towards him, wanting to kiss the tears away but knowing he'd find it difficult to stop at that. Instead, he pulled her close, wrapping his arms around her. "Cry as much as you like, my love." Her arms snaked around his waist even as her shoulders shook, but gradually she calmed.

"Carterton!"

Nick muttered a curse under his breath at the interruption, but his annoyance subsided as Bella giggled against his chest. Wingrave stood by the parlour door, his thunderous frown gradually clearing.

He loosened his hold, but Bella didn't let go. She raised her head enough to speak. "Will, you may wish us happy."

Wingrave ran one hand through his hair. "You mean you *did* want...?" He shook his head.

"I didn't want Nick to be forced into it, Will." She released him to face her brother.

Wingrave looked into her eyes. "Are you sure, Bella?"

"Very sure."

"In that case, congratulations to you both!"

Nick shook the hand Wingrave held out.

"Welcome to the family, Carterton. Don't judge the rest of us by my father."

"I don't," Nick assured him, pleased at the sincerity in Wingrave's face. "I know it isn't what you expected when you—"

"Not expected, no, but I couldn't have picked a better man. Now, I only came to say we should take da Gama to see Talbot, but I can manage that on my own. When I return, you can let me know if you want me to find a real priest today." He looked at Bella. "The special licence is still valid, but there is no need to hurry into it."

Nick waited until Wingrave left before speaking. "You deserve a proper wedding, Bella, not a rushed ceremony." He took her hands in his again.

"I would like to have my family at my wedding," she said. "But Theresa lives in Scotland, so it will take some time for her to get here."

"I would like my sisters to be present, too."

"I can write to Theresa and Lizzie today. I hope Will's family can come. I've never seen them."

Nick felt anger rise in him at the way Marstone had treated his children, and pressed his lips together against a curse.

"What is wrong, Nick?"

"Your father..."

"He has no power now, Nick. Even if he changes his mind, we are now betrothed, and we have a special licence that *he* applied for. He cannot stop us."

"No, he cannot. But we can discuss this later." There would be time enough for the details. Her earlier tears had gone.

"Oh? What shall we do now?" Her smile, her look, something between shyness and expectation, showed that she had a very good idea.

"We can stop talking," he whispered, and bent his head towards hers.

CHAPTER 29

"Would you turn around slowly, please, my lady?" Sarah Fletcher sat back on her heels as Bella moved, examining the pinned hemline of the petticoat. In the two months since Bella had first encountered her, the seamstress had put on weight, and she now looked healthy and happy. Her salon would be ready soon, with assistants taken on and an order book already filling rapidly, thanks to Maria Jesson and Bella herself.

"That's a lovely gown, Bella," Theresa said. She and Lizzie were lounging on Bella's bed in a most unladylike fashion, as they had done when they were all younger. "Such a pity no-one will see it for some time." She looked down at her own black gown as she spoke, her bottom lip sticking out in distaste.

"We won't wear our blacks tomorrow, Theresa," Lizzie said, eyeing the subtle cream and gold stripes of Bella's wedding dress. "You could have had a much more elaborate gown, Bella; there was time enough. More bows down the front, and more lace."

"This is all I want," Bella said. "Too much ornamentation doesn't suit me." Fletcher cast a quick glance upwards, and Bella smiled. She had learned her fashion lessons well.

"That's all pinned now, my lady," Fletcher said. "Molly and I'll put the final touches if you can take it off."

"Thank you, Sarah." Bella stood as she was unlaced and unpinned, then Fletcher took the gown off to the dressing room. Bella blushed at the memory of other new things stored in there: several items of silk nightwear and an almost sheer dressing robe.

"If only Papa hadn't died, you could have been married at St George's," Lizzie chattered on as Molly helped Bella to don her mourning gown again. "Dozens of people came to my wedding."

"I don't know dozens of people, Lizzie. All I want is my family around me." Including Aunt Aurelia, happy now Will had paid her debts.

"Lizzie didn't know dozens of people either," Theresa said. "They only came because of—"

"Oh, stop it, you two!" The twins had always bickered, but Bella had no patience with it at the moment.

"If you're going to have a private wedding, Bella, why not at Marstone Park? There would have been plenty of room for everyone."

"It feels like a prison," Bella said. Not quite so much now that Will was Lord Marstone, and his wife had planned some redecoration for the main reception rooms and bedrooms. But she'd spent a lonely year there after the twins had married, and wouldn't be sorry if she never saw the place again. "I'm going to arrange the flowers for the parlour now, if they've been delivered. Do you want to help me?"

The flowers had been left on the table in the stillroom, and the three of them spent a happy half hour filling vases and bowls before summoning the assistance of a couple of footmen to carry them to the parlour. Connie, now Lady Marstone, was sitting in a chair over-looking the sunlit garden with her feet up on a stool. Bella wondered how much bigger she could get before the baby was born.

"Will I be in your way?" Connie asked, putting her feet to the floor.

"No, don't move," Bella said hurriedly. "You're not in the way at all." She still felt a little shy around Will's wife, who had arrived a couple of days ago after travelling up from Devonshire in easy stages.

"We haven't had much chance to talk," Connie said. "Will you stay and have tea with me when you have finished your arrangements?"

It didn't take long for the table to be moved to one side of the room and cover it in a white cloth. With the largest flower arrangement on it, it would do nicely as an altar. Lizzie and Theresa departed for the nursery, and Langton brought a tray of tea.

"This is a lovely parlour," Connie said.

"It is now. Will let me have it redecorated to look more cheerful." The pale green walls and patterned curtains made it feel as if the garden extended into the house, even on drizzly days.

"Henrietta is so excited at the prospect of being a maid of honour. I hope she does not get over-tired and make a fuss. Now, who is to attend tomorrow?"

Nick paused in the open door to the parlour, pleased to see Bella talking so animatedly to her sister-in-law. "Ah, Langton said you might be in here."

"Connie was telling me about their home in Devonshire," she said, coming over to him with her hands out. "I hope we can visit—it sounds lovely."

"I'm sure we can." He glanced at Lady Marstone. "If you will excuse us, my lady, I have something to give to Bella."

"Call me Connie," Lady Marstone said firmly, and waved a hand. "By all means, my throat is quite dry from talking." Her smile made it clear she was teasing.

"Shall we go into the garden?"

They strolled between the beds until they reached the little summerhouse, now cleaned and repainted. The sun was warm, so Nick handed Bella the folded paper as they stood by the open door. "Your brother thought you might be interested in this."

Goods delivered safely. Roberts. That was all it said. He shouldn't be worried about her reaction to it, but he had an unreasoning fear that something could still go wrong with their plans.

"Roberts?"

"Your brother asked him to take your Spanish friend home. As a reward for helping to capture Don Felipe and his associates, I suppose." Lady Brigham had faced no charges, but was permanently exiled to her husband's country estate.

"Oh. It's good to know he's safe." She dropped the paper on a nearby chair and poked him gently in the chest. "He wasn't even a friend, Nick, not really. But he had his uses—if you hadn't been jealous about him it might have taken us much longer to admit to each other what we wanted."

He should not have doubted her. "Good. We needn't trouble ourselves about him further, then. Is all ready for tomorrow?"

"Indeed it is. Cook has been busy this past week—there's enough for all the servants to feast as well."

"It's not the wedding breakfast I'm looking forward to," he said, stepping closer. After the ceremony tomorrow, they would journey into Sussex, to his family home, and they would finally be together properly. "It will be good to have you to myself, rather than sharing you with your sisters and their husbands and your brother's family, not to mention my sisters treating this place as a second home..." He shook his head.

"I'm looking forward to being alone together," she said, with a smile and a wicked gleam in her eyes. "I'm sure we'll find some way to pass the time."

"We'll have a few weeks, Bella, but I don't want to leave Father in London too long without my presence. But the doctors say this illness is a temporary thing, so as soon as he is recovered, we can go anywhere you like."

She took the final step that brought them together, winding her hands around his waist. "I would like to visit Will and Connie in Devonshire first. Then see where my sisters live, although that is a long way..."

"We can go to Theresa in Scotland, and stop in Yorkshire to see Lizzie on the way—perhaps next spring."

"Thank you! There are so many things I still don't know, or haven't seen!"

"I can see that you'll keep me busy, but I wouldn't have it any other way. Now, I'm sure you have another ten minutes to spare before you are needed elsewhere."

"Only ten minutes?" she asked, lifting her face to his.

"Until tomorrow night." He hoped no-one was looking out onto the garden, but as he bent his head towards hers, he decided he didn't care. Ten minutes wasn't enough for another foretaste of the joys of their future life together, but it would have to do for now.

EPILOGUE

Oakley Place, Sussex, two years later

Nick finished the letter and sanded it, placing it on top of the notes he'd compiled for Will. Marstone, he should say, but he couldn't help associating that title with Bella's father, so the two of them had switched to using Christian names. Nick still wasn't sure if Will had taken over all of Talbot's roles, but he passed on plenty of information for Nick to analyse.

As long as Will never asked him for more than that, Nick thought, wrapping the package and pressing his signet ring into a blob of wax over the knotted string. He had no taste for deception and intrigue, even though he recognised that what Will did was necessary. Nor was he going to risk his own safety when the happiness of his family depended on it.

Beyond the window, white puffy clouds sailed across a blue sky, making a much-needed change from the cool and wet summer they'd had so far. If he knew Bella, she would be outside somewhere with Robbie, bemoaning the fact that she was becoming too big and awkward—again—to go riding.

He rang the bell and asked the butler to have one of the grooms ride to London and deliver the letter to Marstone House. "Do you know where my wife is?" he asked, as he handed it over.

"In the summerhouse, I believe, sir," Andrews said.

As he approached the structure he heard a murmur of voices and laughter. The summerhouse itself was empty, but Bella and his father sat on chairs in a sheltered alcove in the yew hedge. A table held the remains of afternoon tea.

"Come to Grandpapa," Lord Carterton said, leaning forward in his chair. Robbie staggered towards him, the nurserymaid holding his hands to support him. Bella regarded them both with a fond smile, leaning back in her chair.

Nick stopped to gaze at the scene, once more thankful that he had chosen this woman to be his wife—and that she had chosen him. Robbie reached his target, and grabbed at Lord Carterton's knee with a crow of delight. Father was still frail, but was looking better than he had been for some time. Having his longed-for grandson around, not to mention another daughter, seemed to have given him a new lease of life.

Bella looked up as Nick moved forward, and held a hand out to him. "Nick, Papa says he feels well enough for us to take a trip to the coast tomorrow, if this weather holds." The glance she cast at Lord Carterton showed all the affection she might have had for her own father, had he been a decent man.

Nick gave Bella's hand a quick squeeze before turning to his father. "Are you sure?"

"Don't fuss, boy," Lord Carterton muttered.

He grinned—that was Father's usual response. "Good, I'll warn the coachman."

"Shall we take a picnic?" Bella asked. "We can always find an inn if the weather isn't warm enough to eat out of doors."

"Good idea." He looked at Robbie, now fascinated by a jewelled fob that Father was dangling before him. The pair of them would play happily together for some time.

"Will you take a turn about the gardens with me, Bella?"

She nodded, holding her hand out again, and he pulled her to her feet. They walked slowly, stopping to look at the roses, larkspur and delphiniums in the borders and discussing the details of tomorrow's expedition. Even after two years of marriage, Nick still marvelled at the joy to be had simply walking with the woman he loved beside him, talking of matters of no import to anyone else.

"You look serious, Nick."

He stopped and turned to face her, bending his head close to hers. "I was just thinking how well your father's machinations turned out for us in the end. I might never have met you otherwise, or only known you as another man's wife."

"Well, in a way, he got what he wanted," she said, putting one hand on his arm. "We have made a *very* suitable match!"

HISTORICAL NOTES

GIBRALTAR

The French diplomat Reyneval did come to England in 1782 for a secret meeting with the British Prime Minister, but not until September. By that time the Marquess of Rockingham (referenced by Luis in Chapter 28) had died, and the Earl of Shelburne had taken his place as Prime Minister. There is, however, no indication that Gibraltar was part of these discussions.

Gibraltar has been a bone of contention between Spain and the UK for centuries, and still is. It is a small isthmus of only a few square miles on the southern tip of Spain, in a strategically important position at the entrance to the Mediterranean. It became a British possession in 1713 via the Treaty of Utrecht, which ended the War of the Spanish Succession

In 1779 the French and Spanish signed the Treaty of Aranjuez, in which Spain agreed to support France in its war with Britain, and the French agreed to help the Spanish recover former Spanish territories: Gibraltar, Menorca and Florida. As a result of this treaty, Spain became involved in the American War of Independence. The fact that there were four nations now involved in the war, all with different ambitions for territorial settlements, complicated the peace negotiations enormously.

At the time of this story, Gibraltar had been under siege for nearly 3 years. The British were able to defeat a huge attack by the French and Spanish in September 1782, and Gibraltar was resupplied in October of that year. News of this strengthened the British hand in the formal peace talks. The siege ended with the signing of peace treaties in January 1783.

RELIEF OF THE POOR ACT 1782

Gilbert's act was real, and some of its intentions are described accurately by Nick in the story. The Georgian attitude to the poor was more understanding that that of the Victorians, who tended more towards the idea of 'the undeserving poor'.

FASHION DOLLS AND FASHION PLATES

The fashion dolls referred to in the story were also known as Pandora dolls. This story takes place just before the first fashion magazines became popular, so dolls were still used to give customers an indication of both styles and fabrics. Once fashion magazines were in wider circulation, the fashion plates more commonly referred to in stories of the period took the place of dolls.

AFTERWORD

Thank you for reading *A Suitable Match*; I hope you enjoyed it. If you can spare a few minutes, I'd be very grateful if you could review this book on Amazon or Goodreads.

A Suitable Match is Book 2 in the Marstone Series. Each novel is a complete story with no cliffhangers.

Find out more about the Marstone Series, as well as my other books, on the following pages or on my website.

www.jaynedavisromance.co.uk

If you want news of special offers or new releases, join my mailing list via the contact page on my website. I won't bombard you with emails, I promise! Alternatively, follow me on Facebook - links are on my website.

ABOUT THE AUTHOR

I wanted to be a writer when I was in my teens, hooked on Jane Austen and Georgette Heyer (and lots of other authors). Real life intervened, and I had several careers, including as a non-fiction author under another name. That wasn't *quite* the writing career I had in mind!

Now I am lucky enough to be able to spend most of my time writing, when I'm not out walking, cycling, or enjoying my garden.

THE MARSTONE SERIES

SAUCE FOR THE GANDER

Book 1 in the Marstone Series

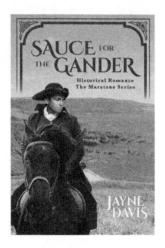

A duel. An ultimatum. An arranged marriage.

England, 1777

Will, Viscount Wingrave, whiles away his time gambling and bedding married women, thwarted in his wish to serve his country by his controlling father.

News that his errant son has fought a duel with a jealous husband is the last straw for the Earl of Marstone. He decrees that Will must marry. The earl's eye lights upon Connie Charters, unpaid housekeeper and drudge for a poor but socially ambitious father who cares only for the advantage her marriage could bring him.

Will and Connie meet for the first time at the altar. But Connie wants a husband who will love and respect her, not a womaniser and a gambler.

Their new home, on the wild coast of Devonshire, conceals dangerous secrets that threaten them and the nation. Can Will and Connie overcome the forces against them and forge a happy life together?

Available from Amazon on Kindle and in paperback. Read free in Kindle Unlimited. Listen via Audible, audiobooks.com, or other retailers.

A WINNING TRICK

A Winning Trick is a short novella, an extended epilogue for *Sauce for the Gander*.

What happens three years later when Will has to confront his father again?

It is available FREE (on Kindle only), exclusively for members of my mailing list. Sign up via the contact page on my website:

www.jaynedavisromance.co.uk

If you don't want to sign up, a paperback is available on Amazon.

A SUITABLE MATCH

Book 2 in the Marstone Series

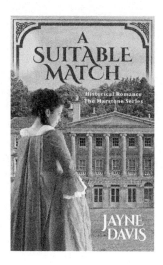

England 1782

Lady Isabella has been kept on a tight rein by Lord Marstone, her overbearing father. She's excited when he packs her off to London to make an advantageous match, confident her brother will preserve her from an unsuitable alliance. But when her brother is called away on vital business, he asks Nick Carterton to stand in for him.

Nick, a scholar who relishes the quiet life, has avoided marriage for years but is finally giving in to his father's request that he seek out a bride. Looking out for a young miss new to society is the last thing he'd choose to do.

Will Nick's attempts to help merely reinforce Isabella's resentment at having her life arranged for her? Can Nick keep the headstrong Isabella out of trouble, put off unsuitable suitors, and still find himself a wife?

Available on Kindle and in paperback.

PLAYING WITH FIRE

Book 3 in the Marstone Series.

France 1793

Phoebe's future holds little more than the prospect of a tedious season of balls and routs, forever in the shadow of her glamorous cousin and under the critical eye of her shrewish aunt. She yearns for a useful life, and a love match like her parents', but could such a thing ever be possible for an unwanted, poor relation?

But first she has to endure the hazards of a return home through revolutionary France. Her aunt's imperious insensitivity arouses a suspicion that quickly develops into mortal danger. Can a stranger encountered on the road prove to be their unlikely salvation?

Alex uses many names, and is used to working alone. A small act of kindness leads him to assist Phoebe and her party, even though it might come at the expense of his own, vital mission in France. Ignoring his own peril, he is willing to risk all in the hope of getting them safely back to England. Unexpectedly, as he and Phoebe face many dangers together, he finds his affections growing towards the resourceful and quick-witted red-head, despite their hopeless social differences.

Even if they escape France alive, many troubles may still lie ahead.

Available on Kindle and in paperback.

THE FOURTH MARCHIONESS

Book 4 in the Marstone Series

Publishing 2021

THE MRS MACKINNONS

England, 1799

Major Matthew Southam returns from India, hoping to put the trauma of war behind him and forget his past. Instead, he finds a derelict estate and a family who wish he'd died abroad.

Charlotte MacKinnon married without love to avoid her father's unpleasant choice of husband. Now a widow with a young son, she lives in a small Cotswold village with only the money she earns by her writing.

Matthew is haunted by his past, and Charlotte is fearful of her father's renewed meddling in her future. After a disastrous first meeting, can they help each other find happiness?

Available on Kindle and in paperback. Listen via Audible or AudioBooks.com.

AN EMBROIDERED SPOON

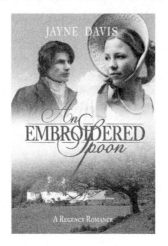

Wales 1817

After refusing every offer of marriage that comes her way, Isolde Farrington is packed off to a spinster aunt in Wales until she comes to her senses.

Rhys Williams, there on business, is turning over his uncle's choice of bride for him, and the last thing he needs is to fall for an impertinent miss like Izzy – who takes Rhys for a yokel.

Izzy's new surroundings make her look at life, and Rhys, afresh. But when her father, Lord Bedley, discovers that the situation in Wales is not what he thought, and that Rhys is in trade, a gulf opens for a pair who've come to love each other. Will a difference in class keep them apart?

Available on Kindle and in paperback. Listen via most retailers of audio books.

CAPTAIN KEMPTON'S CHRISTMAS

A sweet, second-chance novella.

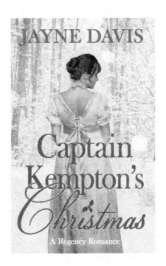

Lieutenant Philip Kempton and Anna Tremayne fall in love during one idyllic summer fortnight. When he's summoned to rejoin his ship, Anna promises to wait for him.

While he's at sea, she marries someone else.

Now she's widowed and he's Captain Kempton. When they meet again, can they put aside betrayal and rekindle their love?

Available on Kindle and in paperback.

Printed in Great Britain
by Amazon

44938573R00155